HARD ROCK SIN

A ROCK STAR ROMANCE

ATHENA WRIGHT

ISBN-13: 978-1546345800

 Created with Vellum

Cameron Thorne has had a starring role in my fantasies for years.

But the sinfully hot rock star, known for his wild parties and lady killer reputation, is the bassist in my brother's band. And I know my brother. He'll kill Cameron if he looks at me twice.

Which means the two of us will never be more than friends.

Only... Cameron keeps staring at me like he wants to throw me on his bed. He keeps licking his lips like he's thinking of tasting me.

Cameron wants me too.

We know there will be hell to pay. I'm his bandmate's little sister. But neither of us can fight it.

This rock star god will do anything to keep me.

Hard Rock Sin is a New Adult Rock Star Romance. It is the third novel in the Darkest Days series, but can be read as a standalone with a HEA.

Author's note:

This book is complete and utter fangirl wish fulfillment. It is not realistic in the slightest. But who reads rock star romances for realism, anyway? ;)

CHAPTER ONE

The press of warm bodies had turned the concert hall stifling hot. I wasn't used to it. It had been years since I'd been at a concert this size. Even then I'd always been backstage with at least one bodyguard watching over me. My big brother Noah made sure of that.

I wasn't that girl anymore. I wasn't the baby sister, the one who needed to be taken care of. I was nineteen now. I was an adult. Of course, I knew Noah would never see me that way. In his eyes, I'd always be his baby sister.

I'd shown up at the venue alone because I'd wanted to surprise my brother by coming home early.

Well. That wasn't quite true. Mostly, I was worried if I didn't come home, he'd change his mind and I'd be stuck overseas forever.

I'd bought a concert ticket to make sure I could get in, but my plan hit a snag when I realized I had no idea how to get backstage.

I saw a couple of event venue staff hanging around the entrance to a side hallway, chatting. That would be my best chance. I casually made my way over, pretending to stare at my phone. I only had to wait about ten minutes before the two of them got distracted by a rowdy concert-goer, who had clearly taken pre-drinking too seriously.

The moment they turned their heads I snuck in behind them and hurried down the corridor, taking turns left and right. The hallway was lined with unmarked doors. I dithered about which one to open. A door at the end said staff only. Success. I pushed open the door, smiling to myself.

My smile froze.

There was a women flat on her back on a sofa. Her legs were spread wide. A man was crouched over her. His head was between her thighs.

I had about three seconds before the situation sunk in.

Any sense of smugness was replaced with shock, which was just as quickly replaced with horror.

"I'm so sorry!" I blurted out. "I didn't mean— I'll just—"

The man lifted his head. His hair fell over one eye.

"You gonna stand in that doorway all day, Angel?" The dark blue eye pinning me down sparkled with humor. "Or are you going to wait for your turn?"

I squeaked as recognition set in.

Cameron Thorne. Bassist in my brother's rock band Darkest Days. He looked the exact same as he had years ago, the last time I'd seen him. Still with that dyed, fire-engine red hair and that familiar carnal grin.

Also still sinfully hot.

"Cam!" The woman on the sofa with her legs splayed wide tugged at a handful of his hair, whining. "Keep going, I was almost there."

"Sorry gorgeous." Even though he was replying to her, he didn't take his eyes off me. "You staying, Angel? Or leaving? I'm cool with either."

"I'm—" *Going to die from embarrassment.*

Cameron slowly looked me up and down. With that single stare, I swore I could feel his tongue licking every inch of my body.

My face felt hot, cheeks burning. I turned on my heel and ran out of the room, slamming the door behind me.

"Cameron!" I heard the woman whine from behind the closed door. The wicked chuckle I heard in response made my insides flip.

I ran away as quickly as I could.

I'd just walked in on Cameron Thorne having sex. I wanted to melt into the floor and die. How was I ever going to face him again? He was in my brother's band. I couldn't avoid him forever.

I got to the end of the hallway and stopped, leaning against the wall. I put my face in my hands and groaned. How embarrassing.

I tried to console myself that Cameron Thorne was probably used to people walking in on him, if this was the sort of thing he did regularly. My sudden appearance clearly hadn't fazed him. He hadn't freaked out or yelled at me to get out.

He'd asked me to join in.

That caused a flush of a whole different kind to warm my cheeks.

I'd always thought Cameron was cute, in the way that fourteen year old girls thought older boys were cute. He was my brother's friend. He played bass guitar in a rock band. He was tall and cool and didn't seem to mind Noah's annoying little sister hanging around.

He turned my insides upside down whenever he flashed one of those familiar, cheeky grins. One nice word from him sent butterflies flapping madly through my stomach.

Of course, he'd always been too busy chasing girls with big boobs and long legs to pay anything more than vague attention to me.

I had wondered if I still looked too young, if everyone I'd known from before would take one look at me and treat me like the baby sister again. I could now rest assured. Cameron Thorne clearly thought I was old enough to hit on.

He must not have recognized me. If he did, he would never have talked to me like that.

Or would he?

That question caused long-forgotten butterflies to take wing again. I fought to push them down, pressing my palms into my eyes, careful not to smudge my makeup.

After several minutes I'd calmed somewhat, my breathing evening out.

Cameron hadn't minded me walking in. If he could play it cool, I could play it cool. The next time I saw him, I'd pretend nothing out of the ordinary had happened. Hopefully he would do the same.

And hopefully my insides would stay where they belonged and not spew out of my mouth like they had threatened to do.

Resolved, I continued down the hallway, looking for an entrance to backstage. Most of the doors led to offices or storerooms. I saw a small flight of stairs winding upward and began climbing.

Finally. I found myself backstage, with event staff rushing around in headsets.

HARD ROCK SIN   5

I'd taken no less than two steps before I was confronted by a tall, beefy bodyguard with a short buzz cut and a dour expression.

I knew it had been too easy.

"Where's your staff pass?" he grunted.

I blinked. "Staff pass?"

"If you don't have a staff pass, you're not allowed backstage."

He moved to take my arm. I jerked back. I hadn't thought about this part. I thought once I'd made it backstage I'd be safe.

"I'm not staff, but I'm allowed back here. I'm Noah Hart's sister, Lily."

"Sure you are. No pass, no access." He did take my arm then, gently at least, and tried to guide me back down the stage.

"I really am Noah's sister." I tried to make myself sound as sincere as possible. "Just ask him. I came here to surprise him, but he'll tell you it's really me."

"You think you're the first to use that story?"

"I'll call Noah. I have his number. He can tell you himself."

"You got your boyfriend on the other end ready to lie for you?"

I really should have thought this through.

"She's with me," a voice said from the top of the stairs.

I turned.

My mouth gaped open.

I was confronted with the full force of Cameron Thorne, rock star god. He must have taken the time to get ready for the stage. Leather pants molded to his hips and thighs. His thin, white cotton t-shirt was tight enough to cling to every deliciously toned ab. His hair was still messy, still falling over one eye, but it sparkled somehow, shining in the dim lighting as if he sprinkled silver glitter over the strands. Black kohl rimmed the one visible deep blue eye, an almost gothic style.

I let out a shaky breath. My heart pumped wildly in my chest. This Cameron Thorne wasn't anything like the cute boy I'd known. This Cameron Thorne went beyond rock star cool and into another stratosphere altogether.

The rock star god in front of me was hot enough to melt my panties.

"Sorry Angel, I forgot to give you your pass."

"What?" I said dumbly.

Cameron gave me a pointed look, then nodded to the bodyguard. "I said she's with me."

I nearly had a nervous breakdown as Cameron hooked his arm around my waist and tugged me against his side. His body heat seared through my thin dress and onto my skin.

"We cool here?" Cameron asked the bodyguard.

The beefy man waved to let us through. Cameron guided me through the crowd of people, his arm still around me.

"What was your grand plan?" he asked, squeezing my waist.

"Grand plan?" I repeated, unable to make my brain work properly.

"How were you planning on getting in? Usually fans sneak backstage. Just walking up to the security guard was pretty bold."

That confirmed it. Cameron had no idea who I was. I was just another girl in a short skirt and high heels.

I was just another girl who had apparently caught Cameron's attention.

"So? Your plan to sneak inside?" he prompted.

Cameron Thorne had his arm around my waist. I fought to make myself speak, forcing down the rising hysteria.

"I— I didn't think that far ahead."

"It's a good thing I came along when I did, then."

If he'd known who I was, he probably wouldn't be talking to me like this. Touching me like this. My insides quivered when his hands tugged me close to his side.

"So which one of us were you planning to score with tonight?" he said playfully.

I stammered, trying to protest. He interrupted.

"How about we boost my ego and pretend it was me, hm?"

"I don't think your ego needs boosting." I snapped my jaw shut, appalled at myself for blurting that out.

Cameron looked shocked for a moment before laughing. He tweaked a long strand of my hair. "You're cute."

I instinctively made a face of disgust. Cameron patted me on the hip, consoling.

"Hey, there's nothing wrong with being cute. Would you prefer I call you hot and sexy?"

I flushed, looking down and murmuring something vaguely affirmative.

"Now who's looking for an ego boost?" he teased.

"Cam! We're on!"

I recognized one of the twins in my brother's band, with tufts of brown hair sticking up from his head and a faded Ramones t-shirt.

He stood near the curtains at the edge of the stage holding his guitar with fingers polished black at the tips.

"Sorry gorgeous, gotta go." Cameron's arm left my waist. I mourned the loss of his body heat. "But why don't you hang around after the concert? Maybe we can get to know each other better."

He flashed me a smirk. I flushed as I realized exactly how Cameron wanted to get to know me.

"Sure," I said after a moment. "I'll be here."

CHAPTER TWO

Cameron took his place on the dark stage, darkness enveloping him. Now that he wasn't by my side I was able to think clearly again.

I'd just walked in on Cameron doing... *that*... with a girl, and there he was, already flirting with someone else.

I couldn't help but be flattered that person was me.

It had been long enough between my awkward adolescence and my now burgeoning adulthood that I was no longer the baby sister. With a hot pink minidress, high heeled pumps, and expertly applied makeup — I'd finally mastered the art of contouring — I was as hot as any of the other girls who'd been waiting in line to see Darkest Days.

A sense of something like accomplishment filled my chest, replacing the nervous excitement that Cameron's proximity had caused.

I found a spot backstage to watch the concert. I made sure to stay out of the way of the busy event staff and band members of the other acts who were still milling around.

My brother was front and center, his low voice growling and crooning into the microphone. His hands stroked the mic stand up and down, a sensual caress. The spotlights reflected in his black hair and eyes, the same features I shared. It turned his gaze into an almost fiery look.

I'd lost count of how many times I'd seen him perform, but every time I couldn't help feel a sense of pride. Maybe it was odd that a little sister felt a sort of maternal pride for her older brother, but Noah had come such a long way. He'd always been reserved. Closed off. He rarely showed a smile, except for the times when we were alone together.

The man he was on stage, the raw passion he exuded as he sang — that was the Noah I knew. Growing up, I'd always hoped Noah would someday open up to people. It seemed being on stage freed Noah to be the man I knew he was inside. In the limelight, he channeled his emotions and offered them freely to his audience.

It remained to be seen whether Noah's off-stage persona had also made progress. I hadn't seen my brother in years. It was difficult to know how much he'd changed without seeing him in person. The last few months I'd sensed a change though. Maybe that had to do with his new girlfriend. I hoped she was a good influence on him. I couldn't deny I was dying to meet the girl who managed to break down my brother's guarded walls.

The other members of the band, the twin guitarists and platinum blond drummer, looked much the same. The twins were both broader in the shoulders and full of frantic energy as they ran around on stage. The drummer's face was more well defined, almost regal with its angular jaw. His ice blue eyes were narrowed and focused, his arms a blur as he pounded away on his drum set.

They were all a handful of years older now and had filled out. They were no longer the young boys I'd remembered, but fully adult and wholly masculine.

With that thought, I let my attention turn to Cameron.

Gorgeous as ever, he stood at the edge of the stage. Hands reached out of the crowd to grab at him. He crouched low over his bass, slapping his hand out to brush a few fingers. A chorus of female voices started a chant.

"Take it off, take it off!"

Cameron put a hand to his ear and cocked his head, as if he couldn't quite hear. They shouted louder in answer. The grin on his face told me he knew exactly what they were asking.

The girls screamed their lungs out over the noise blasting out of the speakers. Cameron played at the hem of his shirt and gave the audience a teasing look.

Anticipation fluttered in my chest. Was he really going to—?

When the voices reached a fever pitch Cameron smirked and tossed his shirt over his head.

Heat flooded my system. My cheeks must have gone bright red. The well defined torso outlined through his thin t-shirt had done nothing to prepare me for the sight of Cameron's bare chest and abs. The man must live at the gym. There was no way playing bass on stage was enough of a workout to produce a body that exquisite.

The girls in the audience, and even a few young men, flipped out, screaming and hooting. They fought each other to rush the stage, reaching their hands out again, nearly causing a riot.

With a satisfied smile on his face, Cameron returned smoothly to his bass guitar, barely missing a note. He sauntered away from the left side of the stage, making his way over to the right, making sure each fan had the chance to gaze upon the glory that was Cameron Thorne.

It was such an egotistical move. If anyone else had done it, I might have felt a tinge of distaste. But there was something about the bassist of Darkest Days. His teasing smiles, his sultry stares. It seemed perhaps he wasn't doing it to boost his own ego, but simply giving the fans exactly what they wanted.

Paying any attention to the rest of the concert was impossible with Cameron shirtless like that. It was all I could do to keep from drooling. I fought to stop myself from melting into a puddle.

By the time the concert wound down, the flush on my cheeks had abated and my breathing was steady. I didn't want to be a frazzled mess when I surprised my brother.

The last song of the encore finished and the audience erupted into cheers. The other band members stayed on stage to throw guitar picks and drum sticks to the crowd. Noah, as always, stalked off first, not basking in the adoration of his fans. The perfect opportunity for me to ambush him alone.

"Noah!" I called out.

He stopped. His brows furrowed as he tried to place the familiar voice. I ran up behind him and threw my arms around him. He stiffened immediately.

"Surprise," I cheered, before he could shrug me off, thinking I was a stranger.

He turned, his face wide open with shock.

"Lily? What are you doing here?"

"Since I got accepted into the summer program I decided to come home early."

"But you're not supposed to—"

"Shut up and give me a hug."

He paused, scowling for a brief moment, before the lines on his face relaxed. He wrapped his arms around me, squeezing tight.

"You're not supposed to be here for another few weeks. I thought you were still at that artists' retreat."

"I couldn't wait that long."

I didn't want to wait and risk him changing his mind.

"I'm still not sure if this is a good idea," he began, like I knew he would.

I smiled to myself. Always so overprotective.

"I'll be fine," I reassured him.

Noah pulled back and took a good look at me. "What the hell are you wearing?"

"There's nothing wrong with what I'm wearing."

So what if the dress was a little short?

"You look like—"

"It's nothing worse than what the other girls at this concert have on," I pointed out, cutting him off.

He grunted, but didn't continue arguing. A small smile graced his lips as he stroked my hair. "I'm really glad you're here. I missed you."

A sting of tears hit the back of my eyes. "I missed you, too."

"I want to hear about everything. The artists' retreat and your summer course."

"The retreat was..." I searched for the right words. "Interesting. The other women there were very much the hippie, Bohemian artist types."

"I hope you didn't feel out of place."

"It was kind of fun actually. Like having a bunch of cool older aunts."

Noah and I both went silent for a moment. We were no doubt both thinking the same thing. We didn't have aunts, or uncles, or any other family that we knew of. It was just the two of us. It had always just been the two of us.

"I'm sure I'll have a lot more in common with the students at college," I continued. "They'll be around my own age, at least."

"And you're absolutely sure you don't want to go to college in London? It's not too late to change your mind."

"I'm sure. It's been long enough. It's well past time for me to come back home."

"It's even worse than last time," Noah warned. "The band is more popular than ever. There's media following our every move, and crazy fans. Not to mention, you're an internet celebrity now. After that stunt you pulled, everyone knows you're here."

Ever since I'd gone on a social media spree, posting selfies and updating the world on my whereabouts, my brother hadn't stopped lecturing me.

"You know why I did that," I told him reasonably. "If I hadn't, you would have kept me locked away like Rapunzel. I've had enough of that already." The all-girls boarding school I'd attended through high school hadn't exactly let me spread my wings.

"After what happened last time..." he began.

A small spike of adrenaline hit me. Anxiety raced through my body. I twisted my hands together to hide the shaking.

"I can handle myself," I said with a surety I didn't feel.

Noah looked doubtful and opened his mouth to argue. Before he could, one of the assistants ran up with a bottle of water and a towel. He eyed me for a moment before taking the towel. While he soaked up the sweat droplets in his hair and chugged down his water, I surveyed the backstage.

The place was even more crowded now that the concert was over. Roadies and crew took down the equipment for my brother's band and set up equipment for the band going on after them. There were a few bands playing at the venue that night, which explained why I'd seen more leather pants and eyeliner than usual.

Across the room my eyes caught Cameron's. His attention immediately switched from the girl in front of him with a water bottle and onto me. Our eyes locked. A wicked grin crossed his face.

My heart thumped loudly in my chest. Those butterflies were starting to become a familiar companion.

Cameron strode over with confident steps.

Now hydrated and dried, my brother turned back to me.

"How did you even get backstage, anyway?" he asked.

"I had help." I nodded to Cameron, who was now steps away from me.

"Hey there, Angel," Cameron said with a teasing glint in his eyes.

"You helped Lily get backstage?" Noah asked him. "Thanks for that."

Cameron stared at me with confusion. He turned his gaze to Noah. Recognition dawned on his face.

He went pale.

"Shit."

CHAPTER THREE

"Now that Lily's back, I want to introduce her to Jen," Noah continued, not seeming to notice Cameron's terrified expression. "You mind watching over my sister? I don't want any of the assholes here hitting on her."

"Ah. Sure," Cameron croaked. "No problem."

Noah gave me a one-armed hug around the shoulders before leaving to find his girlfriend.

"Lily?" Cameron asked, almost cringing.

I hadn't thought he'd be so taken aback. "Yeah, it's me."

"You look..."

I raised an eyebrow. "You better think carefully about the next words that come out of your mouth."

"Different."

"You mean I look like an adult now and not the little girl you remember?"

"I'm so fucking sorry," he blurted. His face was tinted vaguely green. "I never would have talked to you like that—"

"It's okay," I interrupted. "I know you're a flirt. Besides," I flushed, but forced myself to meet his eyes. "I liked it. It was flattering."

His eyes flicked down my body, as if seeing me for the first time. His gaze honed in on my legs. The ill look on his face slowly melted away, replaced by a simmering heat.

"Why didn't you tell me?" he asked.

"I—"

Was too overwhelmed by your gorgeous, sexy, god-like presence to put two words together.

"—didn't think it mattered," I continued.

"The hell it doesn't matter."

"It's fine. You flirted with me. Whatever. It doesn't mean anything."

To my complete and utter shock, Cameron Thorne actually seemed vaguely abashed. "When you walked in on me with that woman..."

Now it was my turn to feel abashed. "I'm so sorry about that. We can never mention it again if you like."

"No. We should talk about it. So I can apologize."

I blinked. "For what? I was the one who walked in on you."

"For all of it. Asking you to join in. Asking to hook up with you after the concert. Putting my arm around you." He ran his hand through his sweat-dampened hair, pushing it back from his forehead, expression pained. "I *really* shouldn't have done that."

"Why?" A pang of hurt hit in my chest. "Because I'm Noah's sister? I don't want to be treated any differently because of who my brother is."

"Unfortunately for you, you don't get to make that decision." Cameron looked disconcerted. "I just thought you were another fan looking to score with a rock star. If I'd known..."

"If you'd known, you would have treated me like everyone else does. Like a little kid."

"How old are you now, anyway?" Cameron closed his eyes and lifted his head upward. "Please for the love of god be legal."

"You don't need to have a crisis of conscience. I'm nineteen."

Cameron cracked an eye open. "With all that makeup, I'd have taken you for twenty-five." His gaze roved over me, from my glossy, raven hair to my high heeled shoes. He kept flicking back to my exposed thighs. I shifted my weight from foot to foot, nerves and anticipation flowing through me.

"So were you telling the truth before?" I asked.

"About what?" he murmured, eyes still locked on my legs.

Twisting the material of my dress between my fingers, I gathered the courage to ask my next question.

"Were you telling the truth when you said I was sexy?" My voice wavered slightly on the last word.

He pinned me down with a look that blazed with an inner fire.

A pulsing heat flared between my thighs at that look. My insides began to tingle, an unfamiliar feeling. A nervous fluttering started up in my stomach.

I'd had such a crush on Cameron growing up. I'd never in a million years thought he might ever feel the same way about me.

Maybe now that I was all grown up...

I took a step toward him.

The heat in his eyes extinguished just as quickly as it flared up.

"Fuck," he cursed, his mouth twisted. "Fuck, he's going to kill me." He shoved a hand in his hair, pushing back the strands that covered one eye. "I can't be here." He turned on his heel and stalked off.

"Cameron!" I called after him. "You don't need to—"

But he was already gone.

Disappointment welled up in my chest. I'd finally found someone who treated me like an adult. Finally found someone who saw me as a grown woman. Someone who might even return my long suppressed feelings.

Even without being present my brother still managed to scare him away.

I was still mourning Cameron's vanishing act when Noah returned with a young women in tow. Her wavy brown hair and light brown eyes both contrasted and complimented my brother's dark features. She was slightly on the short side. I was a bit taller than average for a girl but she wasn't so short I towered over her.

"Lily!" Jen threw her arms around me in an enthusiastic hug. "It's so good to meet you in person." She pulled back and gave me a beaming smile. "This is such a surprise, though. I wanted to throw you a welcome home party."

"I just couldn't wait to finally be home."

"Noah told me all about your summer program." She looked as excited for me as I'd felt when I'd got the acceptance letter. "I want to hear all about it."

"I'm just taking a few courses this summer before college officially starts. I'll get some first year requirements out of the way so I can concentrate on my art classes during the school year."

"No wonder they accepted you. You're incredibly talented. I've seen some of your art." She nodded to the tattoos on my brother's arms. "Using photos of your brother's body for your application was certainly unique."

"It was his idea."

I couldn't stop the yawn that escaped my mouth. My brother immediately looked concerned.

"I'm just tired." I told him. "It was a long flight."

Not to mention the ups and downs my emotions had been wrung through dealing with Cameron.

"Let's get you back to my place," Noah said.

"Your place?" Jen and I said at the same time.

"Lily's staying with us."

The surprise on Jen's face no doubt matched my own.

"I planned on staying at the hotel until school starts," I said carefully. "It'll only be for a few months. Then I'll be in the dorms."

I waited for his reaction. All I got was an eyebrow twitch.

"Why?" he said flatly.

"I just want some privacy."

"You think I won't give you privacy? I'm not going to snoop and read your diary."

"There's no need to be a Mr. Cranky-Pants," Jen laughed.

I shared the laugh. What a perfect nickname.

"I want to give *you* privacy, then," I continued. "Do you really want me to walk in on you and your girlfriend having sex all the time?"

Jen stopped laughing and flushed. "Maybe Lily's right. I mean, she is an adult. She can't live under her brother's thumb forever."

"I want to make sure someone's keeping an eye on you. The last time you were alone—"

"You don't have to keep reminding me." I tried to push down my rising unease. I didn't want to think about what had happened, but my brother seemed determined to bring it up again and again.

"You're tired," he said. "Let's go home for now. We'll talk about it later."

"Okay," I agreed. "Later."

I did want to spend time with my brother. I missed him as much as he missed me. But that didn't mean I wanted to live under his thumb. Staying with him for a while might be nice. But I was resolved. After boarding school dorms and spending the last six months living in a communal artists' retreat, eventually I was going to need my space.

A small trickle of dread ran down my back at the thought. I shoved it away ruthlessly.

I refused to let old fears control my life.

CHAPTER FOUR

I opened the door to Noah's condo and shrieked.

"Oh my god, seriously you guys, on the kitchen counter?!"

Jen's expression was one of pure mortification. Noah looked unperturbed.

The shopping bags in my arms dropped to the floor as I rushed to cover my eyes with my hands. Dramatic, but it got the point across.

"That's it," I declared. "We're having that talk. *Now.*"

"What talk?" I heard Noah ask.

"About where I'm going to live."

I could hear the frown in Noah's voice along with the buckling of his belt. "We'll keep it to the bedroom from now on. You can look now," he added.

Gingerly lowering my hands, I saw Noah was dressed and Jen had fled the room.

"This is not happening again," I told him. "I'm moving out."

"It's just for the summer. You said it yourself, you'll be in the freshmen dorms soon."

"Not soon enough. I'm serious, Noah. I need my own space."

"We'll talk about it later." He turned his back, dismissing me.

"No, we'll talk about it now," I said in my most reasonable voice.

"I've got to leave for Cameron's. We're already late."

"You can't keep putting this off—" I halted. "Wait. Cameron?"

"He's throwing another one of his crazy parties. Jen's friends are going to be there." The distaste in his face was plain enough. Jen was clearly dragging him along.

Something inside me went giddy.

A party.

A party at Cameron's.

A rock star party.

At Cameron's.

"I want to go," I blurted out.

"No." My brother shot me down with a look. "I don't want you anywhere near those things."

"I haven't met the rest of your friends yet. I barely remember them. I want to see everyone again."

"You'll get a chance to meet them."

"I've been stuck at a boarding school for years," I pressed on. "I want to live a little."

He scowled, eyeing me.

"I'll stick close to you and Jen the whole time," I promised.

With a sigh and a grunt, he nodded once.

I threw my arms around his neck with a cheer and kissed him on the cheek. "Thank you. I promise I'll behave."

"It's not your behavior I'm worried about."

I bit my tongue as I picked up my bags from the floor and went to change quickly.

I'd finally gone shopping for more appropriate clothing. All I owned were school uniforms, yoga pants for the weekend, and grungy paint-spilled jeans and t-shirts I'd worn during my time at the artists' retreat. Aside from that one hot number I'd worn at my brother's concert, I had nothing that could be considered mature. Adult. Sexy.

My cheeks flushed, remembering the look on Cameron's face as he scanned me up and down.

I wanted to be mature.

I wanted to be sexy.

I settled on a classy little black dress with a hemline just shy of scandalous. Noah narrowed his eyes at me when I stepped out of the bedroom. I lifted my chin up, challenging him. He frowned and turned away, not saying anything. One point to Lily.

When we were all ready, Jen, Noah and I filed into a taxi. Jen's red face told me she wasn't quite over her embarrassment. I gave her an apologetic smile, knowing the awkwardness would fade after an hour or two, as it always did.

The taxi took us into the fancier part of town, full of mansions owned by celebrities, star athletes, and rich CEOs.

"Why don't you own a place here?" I teased my brother. "Aren't you a rich and famous rock star?"

"There's a difference between being well off and being obscenely wealthy."

As we pulled up to a mansion, I had to agree. The place was massive, with a handful of floors on a vast, expertly landscaped property.

Expertly landscaped, aside from the trash, beer bottles, and cigarette butts tossed haphazardly on the lawn. Loud music blasted from every open window. More than two dozen people mingled in the front yard, dancing, stumbling, and laughing in their drunkenness.

"I see Natalie!" Jen hopped out of the taxi the moment it came to a stop. As I climbed out, I watched a bodyguard at the front gates nod her through. Noah exited the vehicle and tugged me close to his side.

There were even more people milling about in the marble-floored foyer than there had been out on the front lawn. Everyone had one drink or another in their hand, whether it was a beer, a cocktail, or some other concoction in a red plastic cup. A few were even drinking straight out of liquor bottles.

As I took in the high ceilings, crystal chandeliers, and fancy art on the walls, something vaguely skunk-scented wafted through the air. I wrinkled my nose at the smell. Alcohol wasn't the only substance being consumed. Despite the classy decor surrounding us, this was like every frat party I'd seen in the movies.

People eyed me as we made our way through the mansion. Girls with quizzical looks on their faces whispered to each other, before recognition set in. Guys leered and started making their way over to me before their friends pulled them back with a shake of their head and a warning.

Great. Thanks to my social media stunt, everyone knew I was Noah Hart's little sister. Everyone was staying away. Especially the guys.

"Stick close to me," Noah said. "Don't talk to those guys over there. And whatever you do, knock before you enter any bathroom."

"Are you going to tell me not to take candy from strangers, too?"

"I don't want you getting into trouble."

"I'm here to hang out with you and your friends, maybe dance a little. That's all. Speaking of..." I looked around the room, not seeing anyone familiar. "I haven't seen August or the twins in forever. Can we go find them?"

Noah escorted me through the mansion room by room, looking for his bandmates. From what I recalled, the twins had always been mischievous pranksters, always trying to mess with me. August had been more distant, but he looked out for me when Noah couldn't. It had almost been like having a handful of brothers.

Of course, my feelings for Cameron had never been familial in the slightest.

Remembering that this mansion was his home gave me pause. I knew my brother's band was popular, but surely Cameron's royalties couldn't pay for a place like this. Like Noah had said, there was well off, and then there was obscenely wealthy. This mansion was close to being obscene.

"His Royal Highness has made an appearance!"

A blur of bright red hair streaked across the room and threw itself at Noah. Cameron gave my brother a cheeky grin as he wrapped an arm around his neck.

A slow flush creeped up my cheeks at the sight of Cameron dressed in his rock star best.

He wore dark blue skinny jeans, chains hanging from the belt, and a faded white-shirt. I shouldn't have been surprised to see him wearing eyeliner, which was even more on point than mine usually was. Cameron was dramatic — of course he would be dressed for the stage at his raging house party.

The muscles of his inked arms flexed as he clung to my brother. Heat pooled between my legs. I clenched my inner muscles, forcing myself to stay cool in the presence of Cameron Thorne, Rock Star God.

"Get off," Noah grunted, shoving an elbow in Cameron's ribs.

Cameron hung on tight, unperturbed. "And is the lovely Jennifer also in attendance?"

"She's with her friends." Noah gave in and allowed Cameron to cling to him. "I brought Lily, too."

The bassist froze. Cameron slowly turned his head toward me. His dark-rimmed blue eyes met mine before dropping and zeroing in on my legs.

There they were again, those butterflies taking wing in my stomach. Cameron must be a leg man. I was suddenly very glad I'd decided to wear this dress.

"Hey Cameron," I said, feigning a casual tone. "Good to see you again."

"Yeah." He met my eyes and paused, as if looking for words. After a few moments he seemed to give up. "You too."

I didn't know what Cameron was thinking. He could have been thinking any number of things. Remembering our various encounters, maybe. He'd invited me to wait my turn to receive oral from him. He'd caressed the small of my back. He'd asked if I preferred to be called hot and sexy.

Cameron had also run away from me, terrified that Noah would find out and murder him.

I didn't want him to run away again. Cameron was one of the few people who saw me as a grown woman.

But I also knew he was right. Noah would gut him if he thought Cameron was having dirty thoughts about his baby sister.

"Have you seen the others?" Noah asked, not noticing the slight tension between Cameron and I. "It's been a while since Lily's hung out with the gang."

"Aw, you missed us?" Cameron flashed me an almost nervous smile, aiming for normalcy.

I returned it. "Noah's told me stories, but I want to catch up with you guys in person."

"The twins are out back in the pool."

"You have a pool?" I asked excitedly, forgetting about the awkwardness between me and Cameron for moment.

Cameron eyed me with interest. "You like swimming?"

"I love it."

"Didn't get much of a chance in rainy old England? We could all go for a dip, if you like." Cameron spoke to the both of us but his eyes were trained on me.

"That would be awesome, but I don't have a swimsuit," I said.

Cameron and I were holding a normal conversation like two adults. This didn't have to be awkward. Or filled with tension.

I was relieved, until I realized that spark of interest had turned into something else. Cameron's eyes flashed, his gaze sweeping up and down my body with a quick look.

I just knew he was imagining me in a bathing suit.

Or perhaps less.

"Let's go," Noah said. "I don't want Lily out too late."

"I'm not a kid," I protested, embarrassed at how Noah was treating me.

"Noah's right," Cameron said reluctantly. "The later my parties go, the crazier things tend to get. You're probably better off heading home after a few hours."

If even Cameron called it crazy, I couldn't argue.

I followed the two of them through the vast house, trying not to gape, both at the ostentatious decor and the wild, lascivious acts being performed by the drunken party goers.

"Cover your eyes," Noah ordered.

"It's nothing worse than I've seen you and Jen doing," I shot back.

"You've walked in on Noah going at it?" Cameron shook his head with a fake wince. "I'm so sorry. That must have been traumatizing."

"After the third time it just became tedious."

When we reached the pool we found the twins splashing at shrieking people, along with Jen and two other young women I assumed were her friends.

The twins, Damon and Ian, had stripped down to their swim trunks, displaying their wet, tattooed chests. Almost as tempting as Cameron. With their dazzling green eyes and tempting smiles, I could see why all the girls fell at their feet. They were identical, from their faces, to their bodies, to their matching tattoos. I'd never been able to tell them apart. In the few years since I'd last seen them in person, that hadn't changed.

"Whoa, is that little Lily Hart?" one of them called out from the pool. With less makeup and Noah at my side, it must have been easy for them to recognize me.

"You asshole, why didn't you tell us your baby sister was coming home?" the other added.

"We would have given her a warm welcome," the first continued.

Noah glowered. "It'll be a cold day in hell before I let the two of you give her any kind of welcome."

They both laughed and shared a grin.

"Don't worry, she's safe," one of them said. "I'm taken, remember?"

"But I'm not," the other said with a naughty smirk. "Better watch out, little Lily Hart."

They resumed their splashing, causing shrieks and squeals to fill the air.

The look on Noah's face was murderous.

Jen left her friends and came over to us.

"Don't worry," she told Noah. "Damon's just been acting out ever since his brother settled down."

Noah's expression didn't ease.

"We were just thinking about stripping down and going into the pool," Jen continued, turning to face me. "You want to join?"

"I don't have a swimsuit," I said regretfully.

"We've all gone in just in our bras and panties before. It's fine."

Cameron's gaze quickly flicked mine, his eyes glimmering with a hint of heat. They flicked away.

"Not gonna happen," Noah cut in.

"Can you stop with the overprotective big brother thing?" I finally lost my patience. "It's one thing to force me to live with you but you can't dictate my every move."

"Speaking of..." Jen looked hesitant. "Can we talk about Lily's living situation?"

"Sick of me interrupting your sexy times?"

Jen flushed and ducked her head. "I love having you stay with us. Really. But it would be nice to get our privacy back."

I gave Noah a pointed look. "Just what I was thinking. So I'll go stay at a hotel for the summer like I planned."

"I don't want you on your own."

"I can look out for myself," I said stubbornly, even as a small spike of anxiety hit my system. I didn't want my brother to know I was still a little nervous about being on my own.

"What if she stays here?" Jen said suddenly.

"Here where?" Noah asked.

"Cam's."

My heart stuttered in my chest. Cameron's expression froze.

"Are you shitting me?" Noah said flatly.

"Why not?" Jen shrugged. "He's got eighteen bedrooms." She turned to Cameron. "You could practically give Lily an entire floor to herself. You could go days without seeing each other."

"He's a party animal," Noah said as if Cameron wasn't standing there gaping right beside him. "He has a new woman over every night of the week. He lives off pizza and beer. He's the least responsible person I've ever met."

"Cam's got a fancy security system," Jen continued earnestly. "No one can get in or out. Even his parties have bodyguards guarding the front door with a guest list."

"I don't know." Noah looked hesitant.

"Lily couldn't be safer anywhere else," Jen continued. "And it's only going to be for a few months, until she's in the dorms."

Wait. Was this really happening?

Cameron's eyes were wide as he glanced between me and Noah.

My brother frowned at the bassist. "What's wrong with you?"

"N-nothing's wrong," Cameron stumbled over his words.

"Lily's got to stay somewhere," Jen told him. "Noah needs someone to keep an eye on her."

"I suppose it makes sense," Noah said grudgingly. "But Cameron has to agree to keep his dick in his pants." My brother glared at him. "You touch my sister, you die."

An odd expression flickered across Cameron's face in an instant, a combination of hunger and panic.

"I'm serious," Noah growled. "You mess with her, I will end you."

"You've got tons of room," Jen continued, completely glossing over Noah's threat. "Your place is totally secure. There's no reason not to, right?"

"Ah. Sure. No reason not to," Cameron repeated, looking numb.

And that was how I came to live with my rock star crush.

CHAPTER FIVE

I t wasn't as if I'd been railroaded into staying with Cameron. I could have said no. I could have insisted on staying somewhere else. Somewhere I wouldn't have to live with a big brother-by-proxy.

But every time I started to protest, something stopped me.

I wanted my freedom, it was true. Living at Cameron Thorne's mansion wouldn't really afford me that. I'd still have someone watching over me.

But I couldn't deny the real reason I hadn't fought too hard against the idea.

Cameron was one of the few people who treated me like an adult.

I'd grown up as a child under my brother's watchful eye.

I'd spent my teen years at a strict boarding school.

I'd spent the last six months at a secluded artists' retreat, in the middle of rural France. My only company had been eight other women, all in their mid-thirties or older, who treated me like their own daughter.

Up until a few days ago, I couldn't have told you the last time someone looked at me like an adult.

Until I'd walked in on Cameron having sex and he'd invited me to join in. Until he'd put his arm around me and called me hot and sexy. Until his eyes had met mine and glinted with a simmering heat.

Every morning I woke up to thoughts of that look, wondering when I'd see it again. If I would see it again.

But it had been days since I'd moved into Cameron's home and I'd only seen him once, on the day I arrived. Noah and Jen came with me. Cameron greeted us at the door. He had only been wearing jeans and a t-shirt, no eyeliner or leather pants. The sight of him was still enough to make my insides flutter madly.

Cameron took us to the third floor and let me have my pick of bedrooms. After investigating a few rooms, I found one with a comfy padded bench beneath a window, the perfect reading nook. It also had a vanity that could double as a desk. The decor was white and light purple, with throw rugs and a four-poster canopy bed.

"It's like I'm a Disney princess," I joked.

"Cameron's certainly no prince," Noah muttered under his breath.

Jen nudged him in the ribs with her elbow. "Behave."

The two of them left me to unpack.

"Just remember what I told you," Noah hissed to Cameron he left the room.

"What did he tell you?" I asked when Noah and Jen left.

"You know, the usual. I touch you, I die."

But despite Cameron's flippant response, he looked perturbed.

"What else did he say?"

Cameron stopped in the doorway, a strange look on his face. He opened his mouth to say something, but paused, as if he were thinking better of it.

"Nothing. See you around," was all he said before walking out of the bedroom and shutting the door behind him.

That was the last I'd seen of Cameron Thorne.

Half the time I wondered if he was avoiding me. The other half told myself I was being silly. The mansion was huge. I practically did have the entire floor to myself. Cameron stuck to his side of the place, with no reason to come over to my side. He might not even have had a reason to step foot in the same floor as me at all.

That meant I had to learn my way around by myself. I hoped Cameron didn't mind me snooping, but at the very least I had to find the kitchen so I didn't starve.

For all that Noah said Cameron lived off pizza and beer, the kitchen was fully stocked. The fridge was overflowing with fruits and vegetables and the cupboards were filled with non-perishable goods. Cameron also owned every kitchen appliance and cooking utensil known to man. Most were sparkling clean, looking brand new. I had to wonder if he'd ever used even a single one of those fancy gadgets.

I'd been living in Cameron's home for a week when I finally encountered him.

I was in the kitchen putting together a sandwich. One day I would brave the daunting kitchen and try out something more adventurous, but for now I stuck to simple foods and easy recipes.

My back was turned as I sliced thin pieces of cucumbers to wedge between ham and cheese.

"Oh. Hey," came a voice from behind me.

I jumped a foot in the air and shrieked. Whirling around, I clutched the knife in a tight grip, brandishing it.

"Shit, sorry!" Cameron said, holding his hands out as if giving me a peace offering. "I didn't mean to scare you."

My heart thumped rapidly in my chest, adrenaline still flowing through me. I lowered the knife in trembling hands.

"No. I'm sorry," I said through a shaky breath. "I shouldn't have freaked out like that."

My heartbeat was still racing. I inhaled slowly, trying to calm down.

"You okay?" Cameron's brows drew down into a frown as he examined me. It was a different look from the previous ones he'd thrown my way. No signs of heat or lust. There was concern and perhaps a little uncertainty.

"I'm fine," I said, waving my hand dismissively. I realized I still held the knife in my hands. I hastened to put it down on the counter. "I've always been jumpy." That was a good enough excuse.

"Still. I'm sorry."

"Maybe you should wear a bell so I can hear you coming."

"You really want to hear me coming, Angel?"

I flushed, both at the words and at the term of endearment. It was the same pet name he'd called me before. "I didn't mean it that way. I just meant, so you can't sneak up on me again. That's all."

"I believe you." Cameron gave me a teasing grin. "I'll try to make some noise next time."

That tilt of his lips was vaguely familiar. Not smug or cocky. It was almost boyish. Without all that eyeliner and rock star fashion, Cameron Thorne looked just like the young man I'd known as a girl, before his fame and fortune. Although considering this mansion, maybe Cameron always had fortune.

I was about to reply, to tell him again that it wasn't his fault I'd been startled, when my brain finally kicked in.

Cameron's tight t-shirt was nearly soaked through, clinging to every muscled ab. His inked arms gleamed with beads of sweat, tattoos glistening. Damp strands of bright red hair stuck to his cheeks. He'd thrown a towel around his neck and carried a water bottle in his hand.

A distant part of my mind thought this must be why Cameron was so built, if he regularly exercised at home.

Every single other part of my mind was stuck on a single fact.

Good god this man was gorgeous.

My breathing went shallow.

"Lily?"

"Yeah?" I replied weakly.

"My eyes are up here."

I shot my head up, embarrassed at having been caught staring. I met Cameron's gaze. There was that smug look. His boyish grin was nowhere to be found.

"See something you like?" There was a wicked glint in his eyes.

My nipples had peaked under my thin tank top. I'd begun to think of this place as home. I hadn't thought to throw on anything more than a tank and a pair of yoga pants. I hoped to the high heavens he hadn't noticed.

"Sorry." My face felt hot. Other parts of me felt hot, too. "I didn't mean to stare. Maybe I've just been at an all-girls boarding school for too long." That would a good enough excuse for having my tongue hanging out.

"It's cool," he said breezily. "I have that affect on women."

"I know." I tried to play it cool, as if drooling all over yourself was just something one did when confronted by a gorgeous, half-naked rock star. Although, if Cameron's reaction was any indication, it apparently was. "I was sort of surprised, really."

"At what?"

I leaned against the counter, feigning a casual stance. "That Noah let me stay with you, considering your reputation."

"Yeah, this place is pretty much party central."

"No, I meant..." I faltered, but powered on, "your reputation with women. I thought for sure he would have much more to say about his baby sister staying with someone so—"

"Slutty?" Cameron supplied with a raised eyebrow.

"I wasn't going to put it that way."

Cameron shot me a wary glance as he snagged a new bottle of water from the fridge. For the first time since he'd entered the kitchen, Cameron's eyes left my face. He eyed me up and down, taking in my tight tank top and yoga pants slung low on my hips. His heated stare made my stomach clench.

The beginnings of desire made itself known between my legs. I fidgeted with the hem of my shirt. I wondered whether or not to broach the subject, but I had to get it out there.

"You never answered me, you know," I said nervously.

"About what?" He didn't take his eyes off my legs.

"Whether you were telling the truth when you said I was sexy."

Cameron's eyes shot up to mine. "You shouldn't ask me things like that."

"Why not?"

His gaze burned into me. "You really want to know why not?"

I swallowed hard. "Yes."

"'Cause when you say things like that, it makes me want to drag you off and do indecent things to you."

Heat pulsed through me, centering between my legs.

"So you weren't lying?"

"Angel, any man with eyes can see how fucking sexy you are."

A thrill ran up and down my spine.

Cameron Thorne just called me sexy.

"And that's why you flirted with me at the concert?" I asked.

"I told you." He ran a hand through his damp hair, looking chagrinned. "I thought you were just another fan."

I fisted the material of my shirt between my fingers in a nervous gesture. I gathered my courage.

"And now?" I asked.

Cameron gave me a careful look.

"And now, nothing. You're Noah's baby sister. As much as he and I like to give each other shit, I'd never betray his trust." He wandered to the fridge again and leaned over to stick his head inside, avoiding my eyes.

Disappointment welled up inside me. Of course it would be a betrayal of trust. Noah was counting on Cameron to watch out for me, not try to get me into bed.

God, the thought of what Noah would do if he found out Cameron had come on to me that first night at the concert...

The bassist would be lucky to escape with his life.

"Besides, I'd hate to have to find a new band," Cameron added.

"What do you mean?"

Cameron laughed. It wasn't a happy sound. It sounded vaguely sick. "You think your brother would let me stay in Darkest Days if he found out I hit on you?"

I grimaced. "Noah can't unilaterally kick you out."

"I'm not willing to test it."

Cameron cracked open the bottle of water and chugged it down as he walked out of the kitchen.

"Try not to kill yourself with that thing." He nodded to the knife on the counter as he sauntered out.

I continued putting together my forgotten sandwich, thinking over Cameron's words.

Noah wouldn't *really* kick him out, would he?

CHAPTER SIX

When I realized Cameron was never going to stick around long enough to give me the grand tour of his mansion, I made it my mission to find every secret nook and cranny. There were dozens of bedrooms and bathrooms, multiple parlor rooms, a couple of small den-like libraries, a few offices — and that was just the three floors I'd searched already. There was still the finished basement, top floor, and vast yard to explore.

During one exceptionally hot day, I remembered Cameron's pool in the backyard. I hadn't yet gone out to buy a swimsuit. No one else was around so I decided a bra and panties was good enough.

The backyard patio looked even larger than it had when I'd first seen it at that party. There had been dozens of people in the backyard, both in and out of the pool. That had made it seem smaller somehow. Now that I had the entire thing to myself, I had to wonder if this was what an Olympic sized-pool looked like. It was certainly big enough.

I stripped down to my underwear and dipped a toe in the pool. It was heated. Of course it was a heated pool. I gingerly climbed down the steps leading into the shallow end, taking my time, getting used to the temperature. It was heated, yes, but that didn't mean it was warm. The water was just a few degrees shy of being too cold. Cool enough to be refreshing, but not a shock to my system, either. Just right.

Feeling almost like Goldilocks, I jumped the last few steps and immersed myself in the water. I turned onto my back and floated lazily, using my arms and legs to propel myself this way and that.

My thoughts turned to Cameron, as they'd had a tendency to do over these last few days. He'd made himself scarce again. After our run in while I'd been making that sandwich in the kitchen, it really did feel like he was avoiding me. I couldn't help but feel slighted.

I still had my schoolgirl crush on Cameron. That hadn't gone away. But I knew nothing would ever happen. I didn't expect him to flirt with me, or make a move on me. Not now that he knew who I was. My brother's wrath was fearsome. But I'd hoped I could at least hang around someone who didn't treat me like a little kid.

The fact that the *someone* also happened to be devastatingly gorgeous would have just a bonus.

I'd been alternating between floating and swimming for about thirty minutes when I heard the patio door slide open. There was only one person it could have been.

I swam to the shallow end of the pool to greet Cameron, wondering why he'd decided to make an appearance.

"Oh. Hey, Lily. I didn't realize—" Cameron cut himself off, going silent.

He wore swim trunks and a tight t-shirt. His long red hair was wild as the wind blew it around his face, falling over his deep blue eyes. I wanted to run my fingers through that tangled mess. I wanted to smooth it back and reveal his handsome features. I chided myself for thinking like that.

"Did you need something?" I asked.

"Ah. No. Nothing." His stare could have burned a hole straight through me.

I realized then that I was only wearing a wet bra and panties. A now see-through wet bra and panties. I ducked down into the water, covering my chest with my arms.

"I still don't have a swimsuit," was the only explanation I could give as my face grew warm.

"Right."

Cameron fought to lift his eyes to mine in what seemed to be an epic struggle. He opened his mouth to speak and paused for a second.

"It's pretty hot out here today," he said eventually.

I had a feeling that wasn't what he was originally planning on saying.

"It's been boiling for days," I pointed out.

"I wouldn't know. I go from an air conditioned house to an air conditioned car to an air conditioned recording studio."

"You need to get out more."

"I get out plenty."

"You need to get *outside* more," I clarified.

"That's why I was planning on taking a dip."

The thought of Cameron taking off his shirt, the thought of a gleaming wet chest covered in tattoos, sent flutters throughout my insides.

"You can join me," I offered, against my better judgment. "It's a big pool."

He played with the hem of his t-shirt for a few moments. He looked oddly hesitant. Maybe he didn't want to undress in front of me. That was unexpected.

"Are you shy?" I asked, trying to sound teasing. "You take your shirt off on stage all the time."

"It's not the same."

"Why?"

He looked me straight in the eye. "You know why."

So Cameron was acknowledging the sexual tension that had sprung up between us.

We were both silent for a few moments.

"I don't want things to be awkward between us," I finally said. "If I'm going to be living here for a few months..."

"Angel, just a few weeks ago I asked if you wanted me to eat you out."

My face felt hot again. "You didn't know who I was at the time."

"And just a few days ago I told you I wanted to do indecent things to you."

I flushed. "If you're worried about my brother, you should know I didn't say anything to him about it."

"I know. If you had, I'd be six feet in the ground already."

"He's not that bad."

Cameron gave me an incredulous look.

"Fine, he is that bad," I conceded. "But since I moved in, you've been a perfect gentleman."

Which was almost disappointing, really. It had been nice to have someone pay that kind of attention to me. Thrilling, almost.

Cameron snorted. "Gentleman? That's a word I haven't been called in a while."

"Maybe we can start over and just be friends?"

"I don't know if that's possible. I might not be able to hold off with the innuendo." He gave me a forced smile. "It just comes naturally."

"You flirt with everyone. I know you don't mean anything by it."

My heart clenched at those words, no matter how true I knew they were.

He gave me a careful look before nodding. "Okay. Friends it is."

Relief mixed with regret inside my chest. I didn't want Cameron ignoring me all summer. It was a good thing for us to be friends. But a small part of me had hoped he'd continue showing me the same attention he had at that concert. Before he found out who I was. Before he found out who my brother was.

I supposed that was too much to ask for.

Cameron pulled his shirt over his head and dived straight into the pool with barely a splash. To my great disappointment, I didn't have time to ogle his naked chest.

He did a few laps, front stroke first, then back stroke. Swimming must have been part of his exercise regimen.

I let myself float on my back, trying to stay out of his way. I got too close to him a few times and ended up getting splashed. After the third time it happened I stopped floating, intending to move to the other side of the pool.

I turned to find Cameron treading water in place, not swimming. I pushed my wet bangs out of my face.

"If I'm getting in your way, just tell me to—"

I sputtered as another splash of water hit me. I wiped the water from my eyes, blinking them open only to find Cameron grinning at me.

"You jerk!" I complained. "You were splashing me on purpose."

"Not the first time," he said. "But I love seeing that disgruntled look. It's the same as Noah's."

I felt my eyebrows draw down, mouth pinching and nose wrinkling. It was probably the exact expression he'd just pointed out. I fought to smooth my face.

"You like to piss people off, don't you?"

He flashed me a cheeky grin. "It's my sole purpose in life."

"No wonder my brother always complains about you."

Cameron raised an eyebrow. "His Royal Highness mentioned a lowly subject such as myself?"

I gave Cameron a curious look. "Why do you call Noah His Royal Highness?"

"Such a great nickname, isn't it? He's so aloof and stiff. Like some stuffy, stuck up prince. I came up with it myself," Cameron added with a smug tilt of his chin.

"My brother talks about you a lot. Always complaining about your latest antics."

"Aw, I'm touched."

"You should be, you know. Noah doesn't like very many people. The fact that he's always talking about you means something."

"It means he wants to murder me half the time."

"Noah's always been the big brother. But he never got to experience having a brother himself. I think it's good he has someone who, as you said, gives him shit."

"I never thought about it that way," Cameron said thoughtfully. "I never had a brother. It was always just me and my parents."

"That sounds lonely."

Cameron stilled. He glanced at me carefully. "Not really," he shrugged eventually.

I noticed the pause. "Would you have liked a brother?"

He snorted. "I'm sure my parents would have."

"What do you mean?"

He avoided my eyes. "Nothing."

Cameron swam to the shallow end and began climbing the stairs.

"I'm going to get dried off."

He grabbed a towel hanging from one of the poolside deck chairs and padded his way inside, leaving me alone in the pool.

Somehow, without meaning to, I'd struck a nerve.

CHAPTER SEVEN

W hen my summer classes finally started, I was too busy with schoolwork to keep track of how often I saw Cameron.

The study schedule was rigorous. We were given our readings and assignments to complete on our own, and attended day-long seminars once a week. The arrangement allowed students to continue working summer jobs while also getting ahead on first year credits.

My goal was to take English 101, Philosophy 101, and Psychology 101 so I could fit in more art classes in my freshman year. That meant I had three full days of seminars every week. It kept me busy.

On the days I didn't have class, I spent my time reading Shakespeare and Descartes, taking copious amounts of notes, and highlighting what seemed like every other sentence in my textbooks. I also tried to fit in as much work on my art as I could. I didn't want to get rusty.

If my brother wondered whether I spent all my time having fun at Cameron's crazy parties, he had nothing to worry about.

In fact, Cameron hadn't thrown any parties since I'd moved in. I'd thought perhaps he was doing it for my benefit. I hadn't been able to ask him though. I'd been too busy studying to track him down. We hadn't seen each other since that afternoon in the pool.

I'd said something that had made him run off. I didn't know what it was. Something to do with his parents. It must have been a sore point. I had made a mental note to not bring the subject up again, but it didn't matter. I'd hardly seen Cameron at all over the last week.

That was why I jumped and squeaked when I heard a knock on my bedroom door. I hadn't expected anyone to interrupt my study time — I looked down at the doodles I'd been sketching instead of working — what was supposed to be my study time, that is. Cameron was the only other person in this place.

My heart was still racing when the bedroom door swung open.

"Shit, did I scare you again?" Cameron gave me an apologetic smile. "I heard you yelp."

"It's okay," I said, still breathless. "I told you, I'm easily startled. I didn't think anyone was home."

I had been sprawled on my bed, lying on my stomach, surrounded by books, papers, and pens. No tablet for me. I was old school that way.

I'd nearly rolled off the bed in my surprise and found myself sitting on the edge, facing Cameron.

"Do you need me for something?" I asked him.

Cameron's eyes narrowed for a brief second as the beginnings of a smirk crossed his face. His lips twitched as he seemed to force it down. My insides fluttered as I wondered what thoughts he might have had to cause that smirk.

"I'm ordering Indian take out," was all he said. "Just wondered if you want some."

I wondered why he'd finally broken his silence and asked me to eat with him after acting like a ghost for days. I decided not to question it, and just be grateful he wasn't ignoring me.

"You're ordering spicy food in this heat?"

"I like to live dangerously."

I laughed. "I'll pass."

"Something else, then? Pizza?"

That was more like it. "I can always go for pizza."

"Hawaiian okay with you?"

I grimaced. "Fruit doesn't belong on pizza."

"A purist, are you? I can do plain cheese and pepperoni."

"I like broccoli and spinach."

Now it was Cameron's time to blanch. "You're one of *those* people?"

"Let's do half and half."

"I can live with that." Cameron pulled out his phone. He didn't make a call, just tapped a few buttons. "It'll be here in twenty minutes."

"Only twenty? That's fast."

"Time it and you'll see." He shoved his phone back in his pocket. He nodded towards the papers on my bed. "I thought you weren't taking art classes this summer."

He noticed my sketches. Some of the papers were covered with small lilies, a design I'd been drawing since I was old enough to hold a pencil.

I flushed when I realized what else I'd been absentmindedly doodling.

Cameron on stage. Sketches of his eyes shining, his hair flying everywhere as he played his heart out. Sketches of his fingers against the strings of his bass guitar. Sketches of his mouth tilted in that familiar smirk that sent my stomach fluttering.

I quickly gathered the papers and shuffled them, not wanting him to see.

"I was just taking a study break. I felt like my eyeballs were bleeding from all my readings."

He eyed my drawings with interest. "Can I see?"

I pulled out the one sheet of paper that was just lilies, no Cameron. I handed it to him.

He whistled appreciatively. "This is really good."

"I've been working on that design forever. It's gotten more and more intricate throughout the years."

"This is awesome. What else have you got?"

I panicked. "I don't like people looking at my unfinished work." It was a lie, but a reasonable one.

"When you're done, I'd love to see some more of it."

I flushed, imagining the look on Cameron's face when he realized what I'd been working on instead of studying.

"You've seen my other stuff already."

He nodded. "Right, Noah's tattoos. Those are some amazing pieces. But you do other art, right? Paintings and stuff?"

"I like to try a bit of everything but drawing and painting are my first loves."

"When you finish something new, I want to see it."

My heart began pounding. I didn't know why.

"Sure. I'll show you something."

Something that didn't reveal my obsession with him.

"Can I keep this?" Cameron gestured to the paper.

I looked to him surprised. "Why?"

He smirked. "I want to put it on the fridge."

I made a face. "I'm not a little kid."

"Don't I fucking know it," he murmured, eyeing me. He averted his eyes and looked around the room. "You've made yourself at home."

I cringed as I took in the pile of dirty laundry in one corner and empty cans of diet soda stacked on the nightstand. "I'm sorry. I'll clean."

"Don't bother. The maids will do it, if you leave your door open."

"You have housekeepers? I haven't seen any."

"They come in every Wednesday. Keep the place from turning into a filthy pigsty." Cameron's eyes stopped roving over my room and came to settle on mine. "Of course, if you have anything you don't want the maids to see, I suggest you hide it."

I frowned, confused. "Why would I care what the maids see?" All I had were clothes and books, mostly.

That smirk returned. "Are you telling me you don't have any fun toys laying around?"

"Toys?"

The smirk on his face grew wider as he took in my confusion. Understanding dawned on me. My face turned red.

"Oh," was I all said.

"You don't have to worry too much. The maids have seen anything and everything. I doubt anything *you* would own could shock them at this point."

A small fit of pique rose in my chest. Did he still think I was just an inexperienced kid?

Well, the inexperienced part was right, but...

"How do you know?" I folded my arms over my chest. "Maybe I'm into something really weird and kinky."

Cameron raised an eyebrow. "And what exactly might that weird and kinky something be?"

I wracked my brain. I couldn't come up with anything racier than handcuffs, and maybe a paddle for spanking.

"Don't strain yourself," he said, his eyes twinkling with humor. "I don't expect you to be well versed in the perverted arts like I am."

I suspected he was just making fun of me. "And what weird kinks *are* you into?" I challenged.

"Ever heard of Daddy Dom?"

I made a face instinctively. "You're really into girls calling you *Daddy?*"

"Is that judgment I hear in your voice?" he teased.

I fought to smooth out my expression. "Well. I mean. I guess if that's what does it for you..."

Cameron laughed in my face. "I'm just fucking with you. There's nothing weird about my tastes."

"What do you consider *not weird*?" I had a feeling Cameron Thorne and I had very different standards for *weird*.

He shrugged casually. "I like sex."

"That's it?"

"I didn't clarify *how* I like to have sex."

There were several ways I could imagine Cameron having sex. And I was vividly imaging it happening with me.

I swallowed hard as Cameron's eyes flashed, half full of wicked amusement, half full of simmering heat. As if he knew exactly what I was thinking. As if my thoughts were written across my face.

"Maybe little Lily Hart does have perverted thoughts after all?"

"Don't call me that," I said automatically. "It's bad enough when the twins do it."

"You have some sort of complex about that, don't you?" he asked curiously. "You hate it when people remind you how young you are."

"I'm not young," I retorted. "I'm older than you were when your band first hit it big."

"That's different."

"How is it different?"

"I'm not anyone's baby sibling."

"Just because Noah—"

"It's not just Noah," he interrupted. "I still remember when you were in knee high socks and pigtails."

"I never wore pigtails."

"It's a metaphor." Cameron gave me a rueful smile. "It's hard to look at you now and not remember the little girl you used to be."

I looked down at the papers and books on my bed, avoiding his eyes. "Is that really how you see me? Just a little girl? A little sister?"

He went silent.

"No," he said eventually. He didn't elaborate.

I met his eyes. "I've always been treated like a kid. First Noah acting like the protective older brother my whole life, then being stuck at boarding school. I hoped that by coming home I'd finally be able to live the kind of life I want."

Cameron cocked his head at me. "And what kind of life is that?"

I opened my mouth to speak, but paused.

"I... don't know," I said slowly. "All I ever cared about was coming home, going to art school. I didn't think much past that."

"You really have a problem with thinking ahead, don't you?" Cameron teased, referring to my failed plan to show up backstage and surprise Noah.

"I hate feeling like I've missed out on half my life," I blurted out. "I feel like I'm years behind everyone else."

Cameron looked at me thoughtfully. He strode across to room and sat next to me on the bed.

"Listen." His tone was earnest. "I know you're insistent on everyone treating you like an adult, but you're only nineteen. You have the rest of your life ahead of you. Whatever you think you missed out on, you've got time."

"I've never been drunk," I blurted out.

Cameron looked astonished. "Never?"

"The other women and I at my artists' retreat would have wine with supper. That's it. Anyone caught sneaking in alcohol at my boarding school got expelled, so few risked it." I took in a deep breath. "I've never gone to a rock show that wasn't my brother's. I've never gotten high. I've never snuck out of my bedroom window at midnight."

The appalled expression on Cameron's face would have been amusing, if I hadn't been so disgruntled. I gave him a helpless look and gestured wildly with my hands.

"I've missed out on so much. I want to finally experience life, and I don't want it to be under someone else's rules. Is it really that hard to understand?"

"No. I get it. I guess we had the opposite problem." Cameron ran a hand through his bangs, revealing both blue eyes. "As someone who had to grow up too fast, I can tell you there's nothing wrong with taking your time."

"I think my brother would have a word or two to say about you applying the word *grown up* to yourself."

"I haven't set fire to the place yet. That counts for something, doesn't it?" He flashed me a grin before going serious. "I promise, I don't see you as a little girl."

My heart thumped in my chest as I met Cameron's eyes.

"How do you see me?"

I knew what answer I wanted.

I wondered what answer Cameron was going to give me.

"Lily..." His face was pained.

Cameron's phone buzzed, saving him from having to respond. He gave it a quick glance.

"Pizza's almost here," he murmured. "Let's head down to pick it up."

I followed Cameron silently through the mansion. We didn't speak. Our footsteps echoed against the walls. This place was so empty. It wasn't creepy-empty.

Just lonely-empty.

I was beginning to understand why Cameron threw so many parties.

He met the pizza guy at the front door and pushed a wad of cash into his hand. From the look on the guy's face, the tip must have been over the top.

"Thanks, man!" he said with a wide grin.

"All the delivery guys fight over who gets to bring me my food." Cameron kicked the door closed with one foot, holding the box of pizza in his hands. "That's why it never takes more than twenty minutes for it to get here. They speed the whole way. They all want the big tip."

Cameron threw me a look, close to a leer, and wriggled his eyebrows.

Big tip.

I groaned. "That's awful." But secretly I was pleased. Cameron was back to his usual self, flirting and using innuendo around me.

"Lots more where that came from, Angel."

That pet name made me flush. It was the same thing he'd called me before. It reminded me of that night at the concert. Reminded me of his offer.

I had to stop thinking of that. Had to stop remembering those words on his tongue, and the look in his eyes as he said it.

We were just friends.

That's all we were ever going to be.

CHAPTER EIGHT

I followed as Cameron took the pizza to the kitchen. He pulled out two plates from the cupboard. I was half surprised he didn't just eat off paper napkins. I told him as much.

"I know I have a bachelor reputation to uphold, but I do know how to behave like a civilized human being."

"Do civilized human beings casually talk about their kinks and love of sex?"

"I said I know *how* to act civilized. I didn't say I always did it."

As we spoke, Cameron placed slices of pizza on the plates. He handed me mine with three slices. Just the right amount of broccoli and spinach, perfectly proportioned.

"You sure you want to eat that?" The look of distaste on Cameron's face made me laugh. "There are more vegetables than pizza on that plate."

I nodded to his slices. "So fruit on a pizza is fine, but vegetables are gross?"

"Point taken." His eyes met mine, as if debating something internally. "You want to watch a movie while we eat?" he finally asked.

I was surprised he wasn't planning on just running away again.

"Sure. I could use a break from studying."

I thought Cameron would show me to one of his living rooms, probably with a big screen TV and comfy sofas.

Instead, he took me to the fourth floor and opened up a set of double doors. Inside was essentially a small movie theater. A dozen soft leather armchairs faced the screen, which took up most of the far wall. From what I'd seen of the house so far, I should have expected it. I was still taken aback.

"Have you got a bowling alley tucked away somewhere, too?" I asked. "A helicopter pad on the roof, maybe?"

Cameron looked around, as if seeing the place for the first time.

"It is a bit much," he agreed.

"If it's too much, why did you buy the place?"

"You thought I bought this mansion?" He shook his head ruefully. "Rock stars make a lot of money but I wouldn't blow all of it on a place as crazy as this." He gave the room another look, not meeting my eyes. "This is my parent's house."

I stifled a giggle. "You live with your parents?"

Cameron threw me a dirty look. "No. They've got another place of their own. This one's mine now."

"I can't believe the famous rock star Cameron Thorne still lives at home."

The disgruntled look hadn't left his face. "Laugh it up. You're just jealous you don't have a swanky pad like this."

"It is pretty swanky," I agreed. "What in the world do your parents do, that they can afford a place like this?"

His face fell for a brief instant before he flashed me a smile, covering up the downcast expression.

"Dad's in banking. Some sort of high powered CEO. I dunno. I never paid much attention to it. They've got more money than they know what to do with."

"So they just gave you a mansion?"

"It was my sixteenth birthday present."

I frowned, reading between the lines. "Is that when they stopped living here?"

He took note of my frown. "Yeah, well, they were always off traveling together for business or whatever. Turning sixteen didn't make much of a difference."

I couldn't believe Cameron's parents had moved out and left him alone at the age of sixteen. "I'm sorry."

"You kidding? Being given free rein was like a dream. I could do whatever I wanted, whenever I wanted." Cameron threw me a forced grin. "Best birthday present ever."

I smiled back, but my heart wasn't in it. The whole story just sounded sad. He'd been left all alone while he was still just a teenager.

I understood what it was like to be abandoned. My mom had taken off when I was young. My brother had gotten me out of foster care the moment he could, but then...

My mind quickly skimmed over the *but then*.

Afterwards, I'd been sent to boarding school overseas. I knew Noah had done it for my own benefit, but still. I would have much preferred to stay at home with him.

"So if you're worried about anyone walking in on you swimming in your bra and panties, you don't need to be. I'm the only one around."

Cameron was back to his usual self. Using innuendo to deflect.

"Jen promised to take me shopping soon," I told him. "I'll pick up some swimsuits then."

"Don't put yourself out on my account. I don't mind the bra and panties thing."

I flushed and crossed my arms over my chest.

"Just teasing," he said with a laugh. "I promise I'll be on my best behavior."

What if I don't want you to be on your best behavior?

The thought came to me, but I didn't say it out loud. I liked how Cameron had flirted with me at first, but I knew he'd never follow through now.

Cameron flopped down on the armchair closest to the screen. It was the perfect distance away. Not too close so as to hurt your neck while craning up.

"So which movie do you want to watch?" he asked.

"What have you got?"

"Everything."

"Are you telling me you own every DVD in existence, too?"

"I've got this cool little box. You hook it up to your TV and it gives you anything you could ever want. Even movies still playing in theaters."

I gave him a skeptical look. "Is that legal?"

"I'm sure it's not *il*legal." He stressed the first syllable.

"Between the weed I smelled at your party, the speed at which your food delivery guys drive, and now this, I'm beginning to think you're a bad influence."

"Only *beginning* to think? Damn, I'll have to try harder." He threw me a remote with a slow underhand toss. I fumbled to catch it with both hands. "Scroll through and pick something. I'm easy."

"So I've heard," I replied without thinking.

"Ouch," he said, deadpan. "I'm wounded."

"Sorry."

"You're going to keep throwing my reputation in my face?"

I opened my mouth to throw out a snappy comeback. His expression made me pause. He did look vaguely wounded. Was he really that sensitive about it, or was he just playing me?

"I won't bring up your sex life if you don't bring up mine," I said instead.

He arched an eyebrow and sat up straight. "So there is a sex life to speak of?"

"Didn't I just say we weren't going to talk about it?"

"No. You said you won't talk about mine if I don't talk about yours. I'm more than willing to let you speculate on my sexual escapades if that means I can tease you about yours."

"You really do like pissing people off, don't you?"

"Not my fault you and your brother are such easy marks."

"Remind me why I agreed to move in here again?"

"My incredible wit? My not-inconsiderable charm? No, wait." He faked a thoughtful pose. "It was my astounding good looks, wasn't it?"

I couldn't disagree with that, so I kept quiet.

Cameron got serious. "If you really don't want me talking about this kind of stuff with you, I can try to keep a lid on it." He gave me a sly look. "But that might mean I won't have much else to say."

"I'm sure you have more to add to a conversation than just sexual innuendo."

The quickest of expressions crossed his face. Something almost like surprise. Then he smirked and it was gone. "Thank you for thinking so highly of me. Not many would."

I knew Cameron could hold a regular conversation. He'd talked about his parents, and how they moved out and left him alone. He hadn't put it quite that way, of course. But it was the most real I'd seen Cameron since I'd first run into him.

I wanted to drag more of that man out into the light. I wanted to get to know the *real* Cameron. The man behind the wild, crazy parties and playboy ways.

"So you gonna choose a movie or what?"

I looked down at the remote in my hand.

"There's a million buttons on this." I tossed it back to him. "You choose."

He caught it in one hand easily. "Any preferences?"

"Nothing scary. Or sad and tragic. Or too serious and dramatic. And nothing too action-y with exploding cars."

"You want to watch G-rated kid's cartoons, then?"

"Hey, some of those Disney-Pixar movies are emotionally devastating."

"Why don't we watch a classic?" he suggested.

"What do you consider a classic?"

Cameron didn't seem the type to enjoy *Breakfast at Tiffany's* or *Gone With The Wind*.

"Come sit down," he said, ignoring my question.

I took a tentative seat in the armchair next to his. He flipped through various options, finally settling on one. The title came on the screen. I laughed.

"*Back To The Future?* That's your idea of a classic?"

"Of course. It's the quintessential eighties movie."

"I thought that was *The Breakfast Club*."

"Technically it's *Ferris Buller's Day Off*, but I'm in the mood for a trilogy. Now, you want to watch a movie or you want to debate the definition of *classic*?"

I sat back in my seat and nibbled on a piece of now-cool pizza. We'd taken our sweet time deciding what to watch.

As the movie began, I noticed Cameron's expression relaxing. There had been slight tension in his forehead I hadn't even noticed was there until it was gone. His lips were soft and slightly parted. The one deep blue eye not covered by long bangs reflected the light of the screen, making it shine. He looked as boyish as he ever had. No defenses.

"This part here is my favorite," he said suddenly.

I blinked, my attention taken away from the movie. "Oh," was all I said. I wondered why he'd bothered to tell me.

Cameron continued to talk through the movie. He recited some of the lines along with the characters and imitated some of the sound effects. He laughed out loud at the funny parts and cursed at the dramatic parts.

Was he going to be like this through the whole thing?

An hour in he turned to me and found me staring.

"Something wrong?" He tilted his head, questioning.

I gave him a weak smile and shook my head. I returned my attention to the screen.

Maybe that explained it. Why Cameron had come to my room and asked me to eat with him. Asked me to watch a movie with him.

How long had it been since Cameron had last done this? Sat and talked through a movie with a friend, making jokes and laughing together?

He always had tons of people over. Always had a house full of friends drinking and partying.

But how many of them stayed the next morning when the weed and alcohol had run dry? How many would sit and watch stupid eighties movies with him?

"This part right here." He turned to me. "It's so cool, right?"

"It's definitely cool," I agreed.

As the movie continued to play and Cameron continued his commentary I couldn't help remembering one thing.

How lonely this place had felt as I walked through its halls.

CHAPTER NINE

I hadn't meant to take that long of a break. I still needed to finish the readings for my seminar the next day. But when Cameron put in the sequel, and then the threequel — which was a real word, according to him — I hadn't been able to say no.

It was past midnight by the time we finished our impromptu movie marathon. I hadn't realized it was so late.

The hallway was dark when we finally stepped out of the movie theater room. The tall windows which had let in so much light during the daytime now showed only the dark night sky. The curtains were all wide open. I saw my own reflection in the blackness. I shivered.

"Shit, it's pretty late, isn't it?" Cameron pulled out his phone to check the time. The glow lit up his face in the darkness, making it ghostly, eerie. "You've got class tomorrow, right?"

"At nine in the morning. I should get to bed."

"Sorry for keeping you up."

"That's okay. I had fun. Can't study all the time, right?"

I glanced out the window again. The shiver returned.

"Thanks for humoring me." Cameron opened his mouth to say something, then stopped, staring at me. He cracked a small rueful smile. "Anyway. See you later." He turned to walk off.

"Wait!" I called out anxiously.

"Yeah?" he asked, turning back.

I cringed inwardly. This was so embarrassing, but...

"Can you..." I mumbled the last few words.

"What was that?"

"Can you walk me to my room?" I said in a rush.

He looked shocked for a second before a devious smile crossed his face.

"Are you afraid of the dark?"

"No!"

"I think you are."

"I just don't know my way around this place well enough yet. I don't want to get lost."

"Want me to hold your hand?" he teased.

I made a face. "Just point the way. I'll find my way around myself."

That devious smile softened into something more understanding. "It's cool. I'll take you there."

"Thanks," I murmured.

"Don't be embarrassed. I was afraid of the dark too when I was a kid."

"I'm not a kid. And I'm not afraid of the dark."

"Maybe I should make you a map," he continued teasing as I followed him. "Don't want you to get lost and end up in Narnia."

"I highly doubt I'd get so lost as to find myself in a wardrobe."

He led me through the mansion, making fun of me the whole way. I scowled behind his back.

Before I knew it we were at my bedroom door. Behind me, every light in the hallway was turned on. I hadn't noticed at the time, but Cameron had been switching on every light as we made our way through the house. Our path was now well lit.

"We've arrived safe and sound," he said. "Want me to check the closet for monsters, too?"

I hesitated for the slightest of moments. Cameron's face turned puzzled. I straightened my back, throwing off the tension in my shoulders.

"Thanks for showing me the way," I said, aiming for a breezy tone. I pretended like I didn't notice the slight frown on his face. "I've got to get an early start."

I put my hand on my bedroom door. I couldn't make myself turn the knob. My hand trembled. My grip on the doorknob made it rattle.

"Are you actually worried someone might be in there?" Cameron asked, concerned.

My heart jumped in my chest at the mere thought. "No. Why would I be?"

"Shit." Cameron's face fell. "Now I remember. You had that break in, didn't you?"

A shot of adrenaline hit my system. All my senses went on high alert.

"What do you mean?" I fought to speak through a tight throat and dry mouth.

"A while back, before you went to London. Some guys broke into yours and Noah's place, didn't they?" Cameron cursed and ran his hand through his bangs, revealing both eyes. His eyebrows were drawn down, looking chagrinned. "I totally forgot."

I took in slow, shaky breaths, trying to keep my racing pulse from going into overdrive.

"I didn't mean to tease you." Cameron seemed sincerely remorseful.

"It's okay." I tried to keep my voice steady. It didn't work.

Cameron looked upset with himself. "I'm such an asshole."

"It was a long time ago."

A thoughtful expression crossed Cameron's face. He pulled out his phone.

"If you're worried about crazy fans or paparazzi trying to get in, you don't have to be." He looked down at the screen and tapped a few buttons. "I've got a state of the art security system."

"Jen mentioned something like that."

"Look."

He turned the screen to show me. It looked like a night-vision view of his front yard, showing the driveway leading to the gates. He tapped again and this time the screen showed a video of the backyard pool.

"I've got cameras hooked up covering every inch of the place," he told me. "It's totally safe here."

The thought of cameras watching my every move should have been creepy. Who knew what kind of perverted things someone like Cameron could get up to with that kind of access?

But instead it made my lingering anxiety ease up some. The vise squeezing my chest loosened.

"You really have cameras everywhere?" I asked.

"Not inside the house, if that's what you're worried about. Just the perimeter."

I took the phone from his hand and tapped around myself, finding different views. The coverage looked thorough.

"There are sensors on the doors and windows," he added. "They trip if anyone tries to break in."

"This is pretty cool." I didn't take my eyes off the screen. I had to admit, knowing that Cameron had the ability to watch every inch of his grounds made me feel a lot safer.

"Give me your phone," he said.

"Why?"

"Just do it."

I pulled my phone from my pocket and handed it over. He tapped and swiped.

"Put in your password." He passed my phone back to me.

"What are you doing?" I asked, but I did it anyway.

"Giving you access to the live feeds."

I stared at him as he entered in a long string of numbers into a brand new app on my phone. "Are you serious?"

He finished and handed it back. "You can watch every inch of this place through that app."

I took my phone back with numb hands. "Are you sure? Isn't that... I don't know, an invasion of your privacy?"

"If you want to watch me swim naked in the pool, you don't need to do it through your phone." He grinned and winked.

I felt myself flush. I held the phone to my chest. "Thank you."

"No problem. I'm sorry I teased you about something that's still bothering you."

"It was a while ago. I should be over it by now."

"Coming home to find your place has been broken into is scary. You shouldn't feel bad about still being bothered by it."

I stared down at the app, avoiding his eyes. Cameron didn't know the whole story.

"Thanks for this," I told him. "I feel a lot better now." I turned the doorknob and opened the door, immediately flipping the light-switch on the wall, illuminating the room.

"There's still one more thing I need to do." Cameron breezed past me, striding into the bedroom.

"What are you doing?"

He crossed the plush carpet to the walk-in closet in the far corner of the room. "I'm checking for monsters."

I groaned. "Cameron..."

"I'm just being thorough. Need to make sure my houseguest feels comfortable." He opened the closet door and poked his head inside.

"I'd feel a lot more comfortable if you weren't rooting around in my personal things."

"Afraid of what I might find? I thought you didn't have anything embarrassing laying around."

"Just because I don't have some Hitachi Magic Wand hidden in there doesn't mean I want you looking at my underwear."

"I've already seen your underwear." He met my eyes. His own were twinkling with amusement. "Have I mentioned how cute that matching bra and panty set was? Cartoon kittens? Adorable."

"They were on sale," I muttered. I didn't want Cameron to go back to thinking I was just some kid.

Of course, I had just asked him to escort me to my room because I was afraid of what could be hiding in the dark. Couldn't get any more childish than that.

"And what is this?" Cameron pulled out a pair of panties with cute cartoon smiley faces on it. "I think I like this one even better than the kittens."

I marched over and snatched my underwear back.

"You can go now," I said pointedly.

"I haven't checked under the bed yet."

"Leave."

I marched him out of my room, shoving at his back with both hands. His firm, muscular back.

Damn, but this guy worked out.

I needed to distance myself from those thoughts. I pushed him through the doorframe.

"Thank you for walking me back, but I'm going to bed now."

I swung the door closed, but he stuck a foot inside the door jam.

"Cameron, I'm serious."

"You sure you're going to be okay?"

He was no longer grinning, his eyes no longer sparkling. His fore-head was lined, a slight worried frown on his face.

My irritation faded. He really had been looking out for me. Joking with me, distracting me from my fears.

Just like a big brother would.

That thought made my heart sink. The last thing I wanted was for Cameron to think of me as his little sister. I thought maybe we'd gotten past that.

"I'll be fine," I told him.

He placed a hand on my shoulder, squeezing reassuringly. His thumb brushed the curve of my neck. My lungs squeezed. I nearly choked on my next breath.

"I programmed my number in there, too." He nodded to my phone. "If you need anything, just text. Or call. Or yell. This place carries sound pretty well. I'm on the second floor."

I nodded silently. I was afraid if I tried to speak, all that would come out was a whimper.

Our eyes locked. I had to tilt my head back. We were so close. He was so tall.

One dark blue eye stared into mine, the other covered by strands of fire-engine hair.

His thumb rubbed back and forth, a slow, sensual caress.

"I really am sorry for teasing you," he said honestly.

"I forgive you," I said with a forced smile.

Cameron continued staring at me for a few long moments.

His eyes dropped to my lips.

Nerves fluttered in my stomach. I played with the hem of my shirt, twisting the material between my fingers. He was so close. He was looking at me so intently. Was he going to...? My heart thumped wildly in my chest. I found myself leaning in unconsciously.

Cameron cleared his throat and backed away.

"Anyway. I'm here if you need me. See you around."

He made his way down the hallway, walking at a brisk pace, almost fleeing.

Disappointment hit my gut like a wrecking ball. Secretly, I kept on thinking maybe something would happen between the two of us. Kept on thinking maybe he felt something for me.

We'd had our fair share of awkward, tension filled moments, it was true, but those had all been about attraction. Lust.

But the more I got to know Cameron, the more I liked the man he was inside. It wasn't simply my old schoolgirl crush resurfacing. It wasn't just because he was hot.

With a sudden spark of insight, I realized my feelings for Cameron were changing.

"Yeah," I said. "See you."

I followed him with my eyes, waiting until he was out of sight before closing the door.

I chided myself as I got ready for bed. I had to rein these feelings in. I couldn't go mooning after my brother's friend for the rest of my life.

Still, I couldn't help but wonder what Cameron saw when he looked at me. *Who* he saw.

A sister to watch out for and take care of?

Just another hot girl, like all the rest who fawned after him?

Or something more?

CHAPTER TEN

It had been about a week after our first movie night. I'd just finished my reading for class the next day and was getting ready for bed.

I paused in the middle of washing my face in my private en suite bathroom. A sharp, tinkling sound caught my attention. Then another. I followed the sound, wandering out into the hallway, wondering what could be making such a weird noise. It almost sounded like...

A loud, blaring alarm blasted over the speakers.

... breaking glass.

My heart immediately ran into overdrive. My lungs shut down, unable to take in a single breath.

Someone was breaking in.

I began trembling, frozen in place. My feet were glued to the floor. I knew I should run into my bedroom and lock the door, but I couldn't make myself move. The alarms continued blaring, sounding harsh to my panicked ears.

My phone began ringing from its place on my nightstand. The thought of answering it didn't even cross my mind.

But the sound did jolt me into action. With a gasping breath I fled the hallway, running into my room and slamming the door behind me. I was so panicked I didn't even think to lock it as I flung open the bathroom door.

I slid down the wall, huddled in the corner, knees to my chest, arms wrapped around my shins. My heartbeat thumped loudly in my chest. The white noise of blood pumping through my veins rushed through my ears. My eyes were wide open, but I didn't see anything.

My fingers were icy cold. My lungs were frozen. I gasped for air, but my throat was tight. I couldn't breathe.

I felt all of this distantly as I stared blankly at the opposite wall, limbs shaking.

The blaring stopped abruptly. My phone continued to ring. I curled up even tighter into myself. My lungs burned. I struggled to take in a single breath. My vision began to go dark.

"Lily?"

A small part of me registered a familiar voice calling my name. The fear had taken such hold inside me I couldn't force myself to answer.

Shuffling sounds and a quiet curse came from outside the bathroom door. The door creaked open. I jolted awake, shooting my head up with my heart in my throat.

Cameron stood in the doorframe, the bright light of my bedroom lighting up the red of his bed-mussed hair, causing a halo to surround his head.

My lungs kickstarted. I let out a whoosh of breath. My vision began to clear, darkness eroding. I was no long in danger of passing out.

"Thank god." Cameron looked around the bathroom. "Isn't this a bit of an overreaction?" He gave me a wry smile.

"C-Cameron," I spoke with a shuddering, choked breath.

Worried immediately flooded his face. He crouched down in front of me. He cupped my face with one hand. My cheeks were wet with tears. I hadn't even noticed.

"I was worried when you didn't answer your phone."

I couldn't do anything but shake and clutch my knees tighter to my chest.

Understanding dawned on his face.

"It's okay," he said in a soft voice. "It was a false alarm. No one broke in."

I exhaled loudly, relief blossoming in my chest.

"Come on." He wrapped an arm around my waist and helped me stand on shaky legs.

He held me close to his chest. He stroked my hair, from the top of my head to the ends down my back.

"I'm sorry." My voice was raspy. My throat hurt, sore and raw from my gasping, struggling breaths. I clung to his t-shirt.

"For what?"

"For freaking out. For making you worry."

"You don't need to apologize."

"I shouldn't still be so..." I trailed off.

"It's okay to be scared."

"I couldn't do anything except cower in a corner."

"If it had been a real break in, I would have wanted you to do just that. Find a safe place and hide."

Those words sent another spike of fear through my chest.

"Has anyone ever broken in before, for real?" I asked, hoping he would say no.

"A few have tried," he admitted. "Mostly crazy fans."

The fear didn't ease.

"You should get some sleep."

Cameron rubbed small circles across my back. The touch would normally have sent a pulse of arousal straight between my thighs, but there wasn't enough room in my overworked brain for thoughts like that.

"I'm sure you have more early classes tomorrow, right?" Cameron guided me to the bed, pulling back the covers and setting me down to sit on the edge.

One dark blue eye examined mine, concern on his face.

"Are you going to be okay?"

I nodded silently.

"I'm just a text away if you need me."

I couldn't stop staring at him. At the worried lines of his brow.

He turned to leave.

"Wait." I reached out and grabbed his hand, my own fingers still trembling.

Cameron looked back at me, surprised. He quickly glanced down to where his hand was gripped in mine. He glanced back up.

"I don't..." My other hand fisted in the material of my shirt. "I don't want to be alone."

Cameron ran a hand through his bangs, revealing both eyes. He flicked his gaze to my bed, then back to mine.

"Lily, I don't think—"

"Please. Will you sleep with me?"

I didn't even blush at the connotation. I was too exhausted, too overwrought, for thoughts of attraction and lust and other, more serious, feelings. All I knew was that I didn't want to go back to that bed alone.

Cameron seemed to exhale a deep breath. He stared at me. I stared back. I don't know what he saw on my face, in my eyes, but he eventually nodded.

"Okay. Just for tonight."

CHAPTER ELEVEN

I awoke with a gasp, launching myself upright in bed. I panted for breath, my heart racing in my chest.

"What? What is it?"

I turned to find Cameron lurching out of bed to sit next to me. His red hair was bedraggled, falling over his face.

I was befuddled for a brief moment before it came back to me. Cameron had agreed to stay the night with me. I'd been too scared to be alone. There hadn't been a real intruder, but that didn't stop my imagination from going into overdrive.

"Was it a nightmare?" His eyes were heavy lidded with sleep, but I could still detect the concern in them.

"I don't remember." My voice was still shaky and weak.

"Why don't you lie back and try to get some sleep?" Cameron suggested.

I nodded silently and settled back into bed, but I was now wide awake. I couldn't remember all of my dreams, but I still felt the effects. Adrenaline spiking through my veins, breathing sped up. I began to tremble.

A small touch on my shoulder made me jump.

"Hey, it's just me," Cameron was still hovering over me. "You sure you're okay?"

"I'm fine."

"I don't think I believe you." His voice held a hint of teasing. That hand drifted from my shoulder to stroke my hair, the same way he had earlier when he pulled me from the bathroom.

God that was embarrassing. I pulled the covers up to my nose and tried not to groan.

But the soft touch of his fingers sifting through my hair was enough of a distraction.

Cameron stilled. He pulled his hand back and shifted away from me, as if suddenly realizing what he was doing.

I began to notice things I hadn't noticed earlier. Cameron was wearing a thin white t-shirt, tight enough that I could see the outline of his abs. The exposed skin of his chest and arms were covered in ink. The shifting of his muscles beneath his skin as he pushed his hair out of his eyes made my mouth go dry.

I averted my eyes quickly. I didn't want Cameron to catch me looking. Didn't want him to see me staring at him as if I were dying of thirst and had just found an oasis.

"Do you want to talk?" he asked. "Sometimes it helps to get things off your chest."

Those words made my thoughts drift back to my dream. That spike of fear returned. My whole body tensed. Cameron must have sensed it.

"There's nothing to be afraid of," he continued. "It was just a false alarm. There was nothing on the security cameras. It was probably just a trash panda."

I couldn't help but let out a small giggle.

"Trash panda?"

"A raccoon," he clarified.

"Is that what you call them?"

"Why not? They look like small pandas. They eat trash."

I snorted out a laugh.

"Do you get many trash pandas around here?"

"Oh yeah. My trash is high quality. All the little rodent creatures fight over who gets to root around in my garbage."

I laughed harder. Cameron returned my laugh with a grin of his own. I nestled down into the mattress.

"Thanks, Cameron."

He continued to hover over me. His eyes glinted, pale moonlight reflected off the dark blue.

"If you want to talk, I'll listen."

I burrowed down into the covers. The bed depressed next to me as Cameron reclined, leaning on one arm so he could look at me. The worry and concern in his face made my heart clench. I closed my eyes.

"Only Noah knows the whole story."

"About the break in?" Cameron's brow furrowed in confusion.

"It wasn't just that our place got broken into." I paused. "I was home that night."

Cameron stilled for a moment before his hand returned to my hair, stroking softly.

"You saw the break in?"

"I didn't just see it. I— I walked in on it. I was in my bedroom. I heard a noise. I stepped out into the living room, expecting to see Noah coming in late from rehearsals. There were two of them. And..."

"Tell me," he said in a gentle voice.

"I knew them," I confessed quietly. "They had been in foster care with me and Noah. My brother got famous. They came around again. Acted like we were family. We trusted them."

"Fuck," Cameron cursed. "That's messed up."

I huffed out a laugh.

"I don't think Noah ever forgave himself for letting it happen. For leaving me alone all night. For trusting the wrong people."

"No wonder he's such a cranky, overprotective, hard ass. Being betrayed like that would really fuck a person up."

"He was always overprotective. And always kind of a hard ass," I admitted. "But this sent him over the edge."

"I had no idea," Cameron said quietly. "I thought you and Noah walked in and found your apartment torn up. I never knew."

He looked almost as distraught as I felt.

"No one knew. I lied to the police. I said Noah and I had walked in together. Noah wanted me to tell, but I refused. I was too afraid." I took in a deep breath. "That wasn't the worst part, though."

Cameron held my gaze. "You can tell me."

"At first, when I walked in on them, they didn't know what to do. I thought they might run. But instead—"

My voice faltered.

Cameron shifted down until we were eye to eye. While one hand pet my hair, the other rested softly on my shoulder. The heat of his fingers was like a fiery brand on my skin.

"You don't have to talk about it if you don't want to."

"I screamed. I think they were afraid the neighbors would hear. One of them took out a switchblade." Unconsciously, I brought my hand to my neck, tracing the faint scar under my chin with my fingertips. "He said he would slit my throat if I didn't shut up."

Cameron wrapped both arms around my shoulders and tugged me closer. "Fuck. Lily. I'm so sorry."

I snuggled down into his warmth, ducking my head into his chest.

"They tied me up." My voice was hoarse. "Put my hands behind my back. Duct taped my mouth shut. Tied my feet together so I couldn't run. I squirmed and struggled but they were too big. Too strong."

Cameron's arms squeezed me tight. He returned to petting my hair.

"They kept on looking at me. Whispering to each other. They must have thought no one was home. They hadn't even bothered to hide their faces."

My eyes burned as tears gathered in the corners.

"I honestly thought they were going to kill me to keep me from telling anyone."

Cameron cupped my cheeks with both hands. He lifted my head from where I had burrowed down into him, bringing us face to face.

"And... that's how Noah found you?"

"He didn't come home until late the next morning. All night I sat there, tied up and terrified they would change their minds and come back."

A pained expression crossed his face. "Fuck. I can't even imagine how scared you must have been."

All the terror I'd felt back then came back in full force. Hot tears fell down my face, wetting Cameron's fingers as he stroked my cheeks.

"I thought I was going to die that night. I thought I'd never see my brother again. See my friends again." My breath hitched. "And then tonight. I heard the alarm. I thought—" My voice broke. I couldn't stop a sob from leaving my throat.

Cameron hugged me tight, wrapping his arms around my waist and burying his face in my hair.

"It's okay," he said in hushed tones. "You're safe. I promise."

His lips brushed the top of my ear as he spoke. Shivers went through me at that slight touch.

"I'll never let anyone hurt you. You can always come to me. Okay?"

Our legs were tangled together, our chests pressed close. I was sure he could feel the rapid beating of my heart through my thin tank top.

I took in a deep breath, trying to calm myself. I only succeed in breathing in his scent, warm and masculine. That smell sent a streak of heat straight to the apex of my thighs. I shuddered in his arms.

"You're safe," he promised again, taking my shaking for fear.

But in his arms, the fear had subsided. A wave of arousal was taking its place.

I was acutely aware of every inch of his bare skin pressed to mine. The soft strands of his hair tickled my cheeks. The tips of my bare toes brushed his legs. And our hips—

I inhaled sharply.

Our hips were flush together, my own fitting neatly against his. So close I could feel him.

So close I could feel his rapidly hardening length against the hollow of my hip.

I shifted unconsciously, tilting my hips, wanting to feel more of him.

Cameron let out a small sound, halfway between a pained hiss and a pleasurable groan. His fingers clenched, gathering fistfuls of my shirt in his hands. I thought he might flex his hips, press himself against me.

Nervous excitement flowed through me.

Was Cameron really...?

He lifted his head from where it was buried in my hair. His cheeks brushed mine. He stared at me, our lips inches away from each other. The expression on his face was heated. Fiery. His eyes dropped to my mouth.

Arousal and anxiety hit me at the same time.

Did I really want to...?

I knew I liked Cameron. But was I ready for this?

I closed my eyes and parted my lips.

In a flurry of motion Cameron launched himself away from me, scrambling to the other side of the bed.

"Fuck," he said roughly. He sat upright, back against the headboard. He ran a hand over his face. "This can't happen."

I played with the hem of my tank top. I nodded slowly, a mix of disappointment and relief welling up in my chest.

"I'm serious, Lily." His voice was hoarse.

"I know."

He moved to get up, sliding off the bed. I grabbed his hand.

"Please stay," I begged.

"I can't—"

"Just to sleep."

I crawled back and nestled under the covers, leaving room for him to settle back down beside me.

He examined me quietly, as if seeking something in my eyes. He sat back down on the mattress with a thump.

His tall frame made a deep indentation in the bed. I felt myself tilt closer to him. It was like a planet gravitating toward the sun. I was drawn in by his presence.

I turned on my side, facing him.

Cameron lay on his back, arms straight at his sides. I could see a gleam of light reflecting in his eyes, telling me they were still open, staring at the ceiling.

"You're a really good guy," I told him.

He laughed, a harsh, deprecating sound. "No. I'm not."

I reached out for him. His hand was balled in a fist. I placed mine over his. I scooted closer, curling in on myself until my head rested on his shoulder.

I closed my eyes and fell asleep to the sound of his heartbeat.

CHAPTER TWELVE

The next morning Cameron was gone, leaving me to wake up alone after we'd spend the night together.

I flushed at the thought. It had so many connotations.

I almost regretted asking him to spend the night with me. I might have sent us back to square one, sent him back to hiding from me.

But when I remembered how scared I'd been, how terrified, I had to admit that without Cameron's presence I probably would have spent the entire night huddled in that bathroom.

It was a couple days later, when I was knee deep in my studies, that Cameron knocked at my door again.

The moment I heard the tap of his knuckles on the doorframe, I cringed. My hair was tied up in a messy bun on the top of my head, wisps flying all over my forehead. My hooded sweatshirt hadn't seen a laundry machine in weeks. The only clean pants I owned were a pair of yoga shorts.

I heaved myself from my bed and cracked the door open an inch.

Cameron's eyebrows were drawn down with something almost like worry.

I began to get nervous. Why was he here, after so many days of ignoring me? Was he going to bring up that night?

"I'm going to ask you to do something you're not going to like," were the first words out of his mouth.

Now it was my turn to frown.

"Do I even want to know?"

"Can I come in?"

I opened the door reluctantly. My room was still messy. I hadn't felt comfortable letting housekeepers clean up after me. Maybe it was my stubborn independent streak, but I wanted to feel like I could take care of myself, even in some small way.

Cameron's eyes scanned my room as he stepped through the door. His eyes fell on a lacy black bra sitting on one of the armchairs in a corner. His eyebrow twitched. I felt my face go red.

"So what am I not going to like?" I asked, blushing.

He forced his eyes away from my bra reluctantly. "I'm throwing a party."

I frowned, failing to see why I wouldn't like that. Understanding dawned on me. I suppressed a sigh.

"Let me guess. My brother wants me to stay in my room the entire time?"

Cameron had the decency to look chagrinned. "I know he's a dick, but I promised I'd keep you safe."

I raised an eyebrow. "And your parties are *un*safe?"

"I promised I'd keep you away from the debauchery," he clarified.

"Sex, drugs, and rock 'n roll?"

"Something like that."

"You are aware I'm an adult, right?"

Cameron slowly eyed me up and down. That heated look, a look I hadn't seen in days, returned as he honed in on my bare legs.

My heartbeat sped up at that look. Warmth began to flow between my thighs.

Cameron looked away. I exhaled a deep breath.

"Promise me you'll stay in your room?" he asked.

"I don't want to be kept locked away like some princess in a tower."

"You're not locked away. You go to class every day."

"Only because I begged my brother to let me borrow one of his cars. You know he offered to pay for a chauffeur to drive me to campus every day?"

"Sounds like His Royal Highness." Cameron gave me a concerned look. "I know you hate being treated like a kid. I'm sorry."

I knew it wasn't Cameron's fault. It wasn't really my brother's fault either. They were both just overprotective.

When it was my brother doing the protecting, it chafed me to no end. When it came from Cameron, I didn't feel upset. Instead, my body felt lighter, like I'd been filled with helium.

The idea that Cameron wanted to protect me — that he cared enough to worry about me — made a happy, fuzzy feelings grow inside me.

"So when is this party?" I asked, ignoring the glow spreading throughout my chest.

"Tonight. People should begin filing in around ten."

"I'll probably be ready for bed by then, anyway."

"I thought that might be the case." Cameron held out his hand. "Here."

I took the two small pieces of orange foam from his palm. "Ear plugs?"

"You're gonna need them."

My heart thudded in my chest.

"Thanks for looking out for me." I waved my hand, indicating I meant the earplugs, not the over-protectiveness.

He just threw me a thumbs up and sauntered away.

I closed the door behind me and made my way back to the bed. I placed the ear plugs on the nightstand. I stood there and stared at them for a few minutes.

It really was a thoughtful gesture. I wouldn't have expected that from someone like Cameron Thorne.

Or maybe I should have expected it. I'd come to see a different side to Cameron since coming to live with him.

A side that made me long for him.

At first, all I'd been able to think about was how Cameron saw me as an adult. It was an intoxicating feeling, knowing that an older man found me attractive.

But this... my pounding heartbeat, my flushed cheeks, the lightness in my chest...

This was getting dangerous.

CHAPTER THIRTEEN

I t did bother me a bit that I was expected to stay stuck in my room while a party raged on around me. Truth be told, I was exhausted from all my studying and had been going to bed not long after ten every night anyway.

I was already in my pajamas when I heard the music start up, a pounding, heavy noise that seemed to vibrate the very walls.

Soon after, loud chattering voices and laughter could be heard from outside my bedroom door. If I'd thought the party would be contained to the first floor, I would have been sorely mistaken.

I put Cameron's earplugs into my ears and pulled the covers over my head, but it didn't block out the music and voices. I buried my head in a pillow, squeezing it to the sides of my head. No luck.

A loud bang rang out. I jumped up with a startled shriek.

"Sorry, sorry!" A young couple stumbled over themselves, lurching and hanging onto the doorframe to keep upright.

"Thought this was empty," said the girl.

"It's not."

They giggled and clung to each other as they exited my bedroom. The door had been flung open, the door knob firmly wedged into the now-dented wall.

With a groan, I heaved myself up to close it. The music was louder and the voices more distinct now that the door was open. Curiosity took hold. I peeked out the doorframe.

At least half a dozen people with drinks in their hands were mingling in the third floor hallway. Two of them were making out in the corner, a different couple than the one who had unceremoniously barged into my bedroom.

Music blasted from speakers in the walls. It had a catchy electronic beat. It made me want to move my body instinctively.

A burst of laughter and cheering caught my attention. A trio of girls were lifting their cups in salute. All three wore pink princess tiaras on their heads.

A sense of envy hit me. Everyone was having so much fun. Dancing, and drinking, and hanging out with their friends. I'd been stuck studying and going to class and doing not much else for weeks.

The hell with it. I didn't care what my brother thought.

I was going to have fun at a rock star party.

I closed my door and ran to my closet, pulling out the cutest skirt and top I could find that wasn't in need of laundering — a purple shimmering tank top and a short black skirt that flared over my thighs.

I quickly threw my hair into a high ponytail and applied a bit of makeup, no more than a quick coat of gloss, mascara, and a hint of eyeliner. I surveyed myself in the full length mirror that hung from my closet door. I nodded, satisfied. I left my bedroom and firmly closed the door behind me.

With a toss of my ponytail I approached the trio of tiara-wearing girls.

"Hey, where'd you guys get those drinks?" I asked.

One of them squealed, a high pitched breathy sound. "Oh my god, I love your top!"

"It's so cute," the second one gasped. "Where'd you get it?"

Would they be repulsed if I said I got it at Forever 21? Was I supposed to make up some fancy brand?

Before I could answer, the third girl tugged on her friends' arms. "She looks like someone." The girl turned to me. "You look like someone. Are you an actress?"

As flattering as that was, I didn't want the girls to figure out I was the infamous Lily Hart, Noah Hart's little sister who had plastered her face all over the Internet.

"I'm not an actress," was all I told them. "I guess I just have one of those faces."

The trio nodded, as if that made complete sense.

"There's drinks in almost every room," the first girl said, "but you should head for the first floor kitchen. That's where Cam usually puts the good stuff."

The other two girls giggled and made fake swooning noises.

"Mm, Cameron. Speaking of *the good stuff...*" the first one spoke up again.

"My god that man is talented," the second said. "Those fingers... that tongue."

"Cameron likes to please the ladies," the other agreed.

The moaning sound all three of them made was embarrassing.

A flush washed over me. It wasn't just the second-hand embarrassment of watching these girls practically moan with lust in the middle of the hallway. It was the thought that all three of them had obviously been on the receiving end of Cameron's aforementioned *talented fingers and tongue.*

I chided myself inwardly for getting upset. I knew Cameron had a reputation. Hell, the very first time I'd seen him, he'd had his head between a girl's legs.

And that was why these burgeoning feelings were dangerous. I couldn't let myself fall for someone like Cameron Thorne.

Ignoring the clenching tightness in my chest, I made my way to the first floor. The girls had been right. There was alcohol on every available surface.

A large metal bucket filled with ice sat on the dining room table. A small ring of water had collected around the bottom rim. That was going to cause a stain on what looked like expensive hardwood. I doubted Cameron would care.

I was at a loss as for what to do with myself. The music I'd heard outside my bedroom door had made me want to dance. Most of the people I'd passed were mingling, playing loud drinking games, or making out with each other. There didn't seem to be much dancing going on.

I supposed I could have found myself a drink, but I hadn't had much experience with alcohol before. I was worried I'd get drunk and make a fool out of myself.

I decided to make my way over to the pool in the backyard. That was where I'd seen the twins the last time. The other band members were the only ones I knew at this party. Maybe they could introduce me to some people, and let me know where the place to be was when it came to dancing. It wouldn't have surprised me if Cameron had a real dance floor complete with DJ and strobe lights hidden somewhere.

The place became more crowded and rowdy the further I got. I had to squeeze my way through groups of drunken party-goers. I knew my way around well enough by this point that I didn't get lost. I was able to make my way straight to the back patio.

When I stepped out of the sliding glass patio doors, I found Cameron surrounded by a huge pack of hangers-on. Mostly girls but there were a few guys as well.

Cameron's smile was ear to ear as he talked, gesturing wildly with his arms, a beer in hand. The group laughed uproariously, no doubt at some joke he had made or some story he had embellished. One guy punched him in the shoulder. Two girls kissed either side of his grinning cheeks. He put his arms around their waists and tugged them to his chest.

A tinge of jealousy flared up inside me, but I forced myself to ignore it. I wasn't going to examine these new-found feelings tonight. Right now I just wanted to have fun.

I made my way to the edge of the group, trying to elbow through. I received a couple of interested looks and not a few lecherous grins for my efforts, before that now familiar knowing look crossed their faces and they immediately moved out of my way.

I hadn't faced anything like this during my classes. I supposed it made sense that everyone at this party had some knowledge of the band, and of my brother's fearsome wrath. The studious, driven college students who got early acceptance probably didn't pay that much attention to celebrity gossip.

"Cameron!" I called out, waving to get his attention.

He cocked his head in my direction, attention successfully diverted from the women in his arms. He met my eyes. A bright smile crossed his face, as if he was happy to see me, before it was replaced by a narrowed gaze. His gaze swept me up and down. The heat of it, the intensity of it, made my heart thump madly.

Cameron whispered something to the two girls. They pouted, but left the circle of his arms, albeit reluctantly.

With a nod of his chin the rest of the crowd dispersed and I made my way over, a faint flush on my cheeks.

"You promised you'd stay in your tower, princess."

"Your ear plugs suck," I shot back. "I figured if I wasn't going to get any sleep I might as well get dolled up and join the party."

I thought he would make a quip about my short skirt, something overly protective and admonishing.

"Nice outfit," he said instead, a small smirk on his face. "Of course, the yoga pants and tank tops were cute, too."

That heat was still in his eyes. I wanted to address it. I wanted to let him know that I knew he thought I was hot. That I liked how he thought I was hot.

"Everyone's always scared of me at these parties," was all that came out of my mouth. "The guys won't approach me."

"They're scared of Noah," Cameron countered. "He made it very clear his baby sister is off limits. To everyone," he added, sounding oddly chagrinned.

"Sometimes I wish I hadn't plastered my face all over the internet."

"Why did you?"

"I didn't want Noah to keep me hidden away."

"And now you're regretting it."

"I should have known my brother would act like this. I should have known he'd never treat me like an adult."

"Then you better hope he doesn't catch you."

"He's here?" My heart sank for a brief moment before I threw it off with a toss of my ponytail. "I'm not scared of him."

"Maybe you should be."

Cameron nodded over to the sliding doors. My brother stood just inside them, a frown on his face.

"And that's my cue to get the fuck out of town." Cameron winced. "I don't want him blaming me for this one. I did my part in warning you off. The rest is on you."

"You don't have to keep running away from me."

"It's not you I'm running from," he said with a nod to my brother. "If you were any other girl..." He met my gaze, giving me an almost sad smile.

"Why?" I asked nervously. "What would you do if I wasn't Noah's sister?"

Cameron leaned forward. His lips brushed my ear. I suppressed a whimper.

"You remember those indecent things I mentioned before?"

I flushed, a tingle forming between my legs.

He pulled back with a mad grin. "Better not throw me under the bus, Angel." He turned and ran towards the pool. "Cannonball!" he shouted as he jumped in, clothes, shoes and all.

Indecent things.

I could vividly imagine all sorts of indecent things Cameron could do with me. Could do *to* me.

I wished I could throw myself into the pool as well to cool down.

The heat of arousal flowing through me was enough to scorch me from the inside out.

CHAPTER FOURTEEN

There was no point hiding from my brother. He'd already seen me. He was no doubt gearing up for a lecture. I made my way over to the patio doors. I'd rather face my executioner sooner rather than later.

"Cameron was supposed to keep you away from all this," he began the moment I stepped through the sliding doors. "I don't want you hanging out with the kind of people who go to these parties."

I raised an eyebrow. "You mean people like you and Jen and her friends?"

Noah opened his mouth to speak again, but I cut him off with a wave of my arm, gesturing.

"I'm not getting into any trouble," I continued. "The party was too loud. I couldn't sleep. I decided I'd mingle, maybe dance, and go to sleep when it starts quieting down."

"These things never quiet down."

"Then I guess I'll pull an all nighter and be exhausted in class tomorrow, like every other student who goes out partying."

The furrow between his brows didn't disappear. I straightened my back. We were going to resolve this, one way or another. I couldn't keep letting my brother control my life.

"Noah. Listen to me." I took his hands in mine and squeezed them. "I know you're looking out for me. I know you want to protect me. But have I given you any reason to worry?"

He scrutinized me carefully before giving in. "No."

"You can't keep me in a cage forever."

"The last time—"

"What happened last time had nothing to do with drugs and parties and boys. We trusted the wrong people. That's all."

"*I* trusted the wrong people," he stressed, that furrow deepening with guilt. "It was my fault."

"We can't live in fear forever." Maybe the more I told myself that, the more I'd believe it. "You need to let me live my own life."

He opened his mouth to speak.

"No." I cut him off. "I'm serious, Noah. You need to back off. Can you do that?"

"It's my job to take care of you," he insisted.

"And you have. You made sure I grew up in a safe environment. But I'm not a kid anymore." I gave him a small smile. "All baby birds need to leave the nest sometime."

"And sometimes those baby birds plummet to the ground and die when they hit the pavement."

"Why are we talking about dead birds?" Jen wrapped her arms around Noah's neck as she came up behind him.

"We were just talking about how Noah is going to let up a little on his overprotectiveness."

Jen's face lit up. "I'm glad you talked some sense into him. He's been grumbling non-stop ever since you moved out."

"I never agreed to—" Noah started.

"I'm so glad that my brother has matured past his stubborn teenaged ways," I interjected. "It's so refreshing to see him act reasonable for once. Isn't it nice to know he can be rational and level-headed?" I turned to Jen. "How about we plan that spa date?"

I ignored the disgruntled look Noah threw my way. Jen and I chatted excitedly about our plans to get matching mani-pedis. It was almost unimaginable that my brother could end up with someone so sweet. She must have the patience of a saint.

"So how are your classes going?" Jen asked after we set a date and time.

"Pretty well. There's a lot of work," I admitted. "It feels like I'm up to my ears in reading and essays and assignments. In fact," I eyed my brother, "this is the first night of fun I've had since moving in."

"Why don't we try to find the gang?" Jen suggested. "You can finally meet the twins and August properly."

Jen linked arms with me and led me through the mansion, leaving Noah to follow behind us.

The party had gotten even crazier in the time I'd spent reasoning with my brother. The chatting had given way to shouting and hollering, the laughter turning into a hysterical uproar.

"I thought that only happened in movies?" I pointed to a young skinny guy with dreadlocks swinging from a chandelier.

"You're lucky if that's the craziest thing you see all night," Jen said.

The music echoing from the speakers embedded in every wall stopped abruptly. A booming voice replaced it, ringing throughout the house.

"Listen up, ladies and gents!" The rabid glee in that voice was unmistakable. Cameron. "It's scavenger hunt time!"

A chorus of cheers swelled up as drinks were raised in a toast.

"Task number one: Find me a drinking straw in the shape of a dick."

Noah grunted. "Fucking typical."

"I thought those things were only for bachelorette parties," I mused.

"You know the rules," Cameron continued. "First person to bring one to the bouncer waiting at the front door gets a point. The person with the most points at the end of the night wins."

The cheers amplified to a fever pitch as dozens of people ran off in a mad dash to either find the item in question, or give it over if they already had one in their hand.

"What do they win?" I asked.

"Whatever they want," Jen explained. "Cameron likes to grant wishes."

"Like he's a goddamn fairy godmother." Noah's voice held a tinge of long-suffering.

"What if they wish for something crazy?" I asked. "Like their own private jet or whatever?"

"Someone once asked for a helicopter. Cameron delivered."

How much money did this guy have, that he could afford to throw it all away?

"Most people ask for reasonable stuff," Jen said. "VIP backstage pass tickets for them and their friends. Or for him to pass along their demo tape to our record label. Maybe a private performance at their house."

"And the guys go along with it?"

"August says to let Cameron have his fun, as long as it doesn't inconvenience us." The sour expression on my brother's face told me what he thought about that.

"Cameron likes to make people happy." Jen rubbed a consoling path up and down my brother's arm. "His methods are just... unorthodox."

"Like when he put his hands all over you to make me jealous?" Noah grumbled.

"It worked, didn't it?" Jen raised an arched eyebrow. "You finally got over yourself and realized your feelings for me."

"Cameron likes to please the ladies," I mused. "That's what everyone says. I always thought it just meant—" I cut myself off with a blush.

"Well. That, too." The flush on Jen's face rivaled my own.

We were distracted from the topic of Cameron's sex life by a noisy commotion. A loud crash and curses sounded from the next room.

"Sounds like one of the twins." A worried frown line appeared between Jen's brows.

"I'll give you one guess which one it is." My brother's lips pressed together in a firm line.

When we crossed the threshold we were greeted with broken glass, splintered wood, and cracked dishes scattered across the floor. Someone had knocked over a china cabinet.

"What the fuck," Noah said flatly.

The twins stood in the middle of the debris. One had an exasperated look on his face. The other's arms were folded over his chest, his expression twisted in a petulant scowl. Both wore matching black and white band t-shirts, some group called The Last Ones To Know.

"I told you not to climb on it," the exasperated twin told his brother.

"I thought there might be one of those dick straws up there. It's not my fault you wouldn't help give me a boost."

"What do you even care? It's just a stupid game Cameron plays."

"A stupid game you used to want to win," the second twin said stubbornly. "If you weren't so busy—"

"Busy with *what?*" the other asked. "Busy hanging out with my girlfriend? Am I supposed to ignore her and go off to play these stupid games with you?"

"Yes!"

The upset twin growled and ran a hand through his hair, pushing it back from his forehead. A small rivet of blood ran down his palm, most likely having cut it on the broken glass.

"Whatever," he grumbled. "Go have fun playing house." He stalked off.

The twin left behind stared down blankly at the mess on the floor. A young woman came up behind him, putting a tentative hand on his shoulder. He placed his hand over hers and squeezed.

"Damon's been acting out more and more," Jen said with sadness in her voice.

The three of us retreated, making sure to avoid the direction Damon had stomped off in.

"He'll get over it," Noah said.

"Don't you remember what it felt like when your guy friends abandoned you after they got girlfriends?" Jen asked.

"No."

I held back a smile. Noah hadn't exactly been the most social of teenagers.

"Well it sucks," Jen explained patiently. "Damon and Ian were always so close. It must be ten times harder on him to see his brother going off, being happy, with someone who isn't him."

"Maybe he needs a girlfriend of his own," I suggested.

Jen burst out in a giggle. Noah snorted.

"I'd love to see the day Mr. Playboy Twin settles down," Jen said.

"Ian found a girl," I pointed out.

"It turns out Ian wasn't the heartbreaker among the two."

"And we have our first winner!" Cameron's voice boomed out from the speakers again. "Congrats to Cheryl! She's really got her eyes on the prize."

I winced. "Man, that's loud."

"You can always ask Cameron to turn off the speakers in the third floor," Noah suggested. "The party is going to last all night. You should at least get some sleep before class tomorrow."

I scrunched up my face in distaste. Noah poked me in the forehead, right where my brow was furrowed.

"That was a suggestion," he added. "Not a command."

I smiled and stood on my tiptoes, pressing a kiss to his cheek. "See? That wasn't so hard, was it?"

Noah grumbled, but a small smile graced his lips.

"I am getting a little sleepy," I admitted. "I'm going to go find Cameron and do just that."

I gave Jen and Noah hugs goodnight and wandered through the mansion trying to pinpoint the host of this crazy party.

But Cameron was nowhere to be seen. I checked the pool, the kitchen, the front yard, everywhere. His voice kept booming through the speakers as the game continued on.

I was beginning to think I'd just have to learn to sleep through the noise when a thought occurred to me.

I headed for the fourth floor movie room. Sure enough, when I pushed open the door, Cameron was there.

I was completely taken aback to find that he was alone. No hangers on. Just him and *The Terminator* playing on the screen.

"We're close to the end, you guys."

Cameron was speaking into his phone, using it like a microphone. There must have been an app connecting it to the speakers in the walls.

"Last item on the list: A pair of superhero themed underwear. Panties, boxers, either one. This one's worth triple the points. It's anyone's game. May the odds be ever in your favor."

"Did you just quote The Hunger Games?"

The top of Cameron's bright red head turned around in his seat. He peeked over the high backed leather chair to find me in the doorway. His hair was still slightly damp from his dip in the pool, strands sticking to his cheeks. Surprise registered on his face.

"What are you doing here?"

"Looking for you."

"I thought Noah would have wrapped you in bubble wrap and locked you in your room already."

"We came to an understanding." I took a seat next to Cameron and nodded at the screen. "Terminator?"

"Not strictly a classic, but one of my favorites."

"I haven't seen it yet." I eyed him carefully. "Can I ask why you're hiding in here by yourself?"

He paused, lips pressing together. A bright grin appeared on his face.

"Hiding? I'm not hiding. The game is more fun if I'm not around."

Cameron had a house full of people and here he was sitting in the dark watching movies alone. I had to wonder what the point of throwing all those parties was for, anyway.

"Is that really all it is?"

"Of course." He appeared puzzled at my question. "No one can pester me about the game or bribe me. Makes it more fair."

"Do I even want to know what you get bribed with?"

"Usually sex," he said matter of factly.

"Gross."

"It's fine. Half the times the winners ask for sex as their prize."

"Double gross." I debated asking my next question. "So... do you ever grant those wishes?"

"If they're hot." Cameron laughed at the look on my face. "You are just like your brother. So easy to rile up." Cameron lifted his eyes to the ceiling and shook his head. "No, I don't offer *my body* as a prize to the winner."

"Good."

"Why?" His eyes sparkled. "You jealous?"

"No! Just... I don't like the idea of people using you like that."

"That's funny," he mused.

"What is?"

"Most people assume that because I'm a rock star, *I'm* the one taking advantage. Like I'm using my fame to plow through truckloads of fans."

"I don't think you're that type of person."

Cameron gave me a wry smile. "Maybe you just don't know me well enough."

"Maybe I know you better than you know yourself."

He laughed. "You've lived here a month or so and you think you know me?"

"Has anyone ever lived with you as long as I have since you turned sixteen?" I challenged.

He paused, as if honestly thinking and doing the math. "No. I suppose not." He gave me a mad grin. "This roommate thing is the longest relationship I've ever had with someone, aside from the guys."

That was... pretty sad actually.

A beep sounded from his phone. He checked it.

"Richard says we've got a winner." He stood from the leather chair, stretching his arms above his head. His t-shirt lifted from the hem of his jeans, exposing a strip of toned stomach. I nearly let out a whimper as a pulse of heat spiked through me.

I knew I shouldn't go there. We'd made a promise to just be friends. But some naughty part inside of me couldn't help but wonder. Couldn't help but hope.

"Better go grant a wish," he said.

"Wait."

I fidgeted with the hem of my skirt. A flush creeped across my cheeks.

"What is it?" Cameron asked patiently.

Taking a deep breath, I reached under my skirt. I hooked my fingers under the elastic of my thong.

Cameron's eyes grew wide, his mouth popping open.

I bent over to peel the thong down my legs, stepping out of it. With a carelessness I didn't feel inside, I twirled them around my index finger.

"I believe this gets me triple the points?"

The wide eyed look on Cameron's face had slowly faded, replaced with a wide smirk and a heated, narrow look.

"Where the hell did you get those?"

"The internet."

I tossed him the pair of Wonder Woman panties. He caught them easily.

"Does this mean you're going to grant me a wish?" I asked, trying not to sound nervous.

Cameron looked at the thong in his hand before flashing me a smirk. "Sure does. What do you want? Fancy new car? Want me to pay off your professors to give you straight A's?"

"Sit with me and finish watching *The Terminator*?"

He blinked. "Are you serious?"

"I told you, I haven't seen it before."

Cameron stared at me, a curious look on his face. A soft smile crossed his lips.

"Anything my Angel wishes."

As we settled down into the leather armchairs I reflected on one thing.

Cameron hadn't given me back my panties.

CHAPTER FIFTEEN

After finishing the movie, Cameron went back to the party, saying he had to entertain his guests. He flashed me a wide grin, but something in his eyes, an almost rueful look, told me his heart wasn't into it.

I'd asked him to turn off the third floor speakers, which he did with a few taps on an app. He must run everything in his house through his phone.

With the music silenced, the party goers who had been mingling outside my bedroom left and presumably made their way to other floors.

I didn't have to pull an all-nighter, but I hadn't gone to sleep until hours after midnight and was up early the next day. I was a zombie throughout most of my classes.

When I remembered the surprised look in his eyes when I found him in the movie room by himself, when I remembered his smile after I asked him to sit and watch *The Terminator* with me...

I couldn't make myself regret it.

As I sat through a seminar, chin in hand and trying not to fall asleep, my mind began to drift. My gaze wandered around the classroom, taking in my fellow students.

Half them looked like their hair hadn't seen a comb in weeks, or had been tossed in a messy bun. They wore paint-spattered jeans and sneakers or hoodies covered in clay dust. A few of the girls wore subtle makeup, but for the most part they were the epitome of the absent-minded artist type.

I supposed I was the same. My own skirt had splotches of paint and my hair was kept in that same messy bun while I was on campus.

The difference between the people at Cameron's parties and the people I sat next to in class everyday was intriguing. His party guests were all movie-star attractive, no doubt the majority of them models, actors, and other peers. Perfect makeup, coiffed hair, and fashionable clothing had been the norm.

One other difference was striking, in that no one in class seemed to know who I was. Or if they did, they didn't care or remark on it. My fellow students and I had been chosen out of thousands who applied to attend this early summer session. We were the best of the best. And to be the best, one had to dedicate their lives to their art. No time for rock star parties.

"Ms. Hart?"

I jolted upright, my hand sliding off my chin. "Yes?"

"Do you know the answer?"

"Um."

I had no idea what the question had been. My mind was clouded with fatigue.

The T.A. cocked his head, an impatient look on his face.

I looked down at my notes. Pure scribbles. Mostly my lily designs, but also some quick character studies that looked suspiciously like Cameron.

"Anyone else?" he asked.

A young woman in a peasant skirt spoke up, answering with ease. The T.A. nodded and moved on.

I stared down at my papers again. This was one of the reasons my brother didn't want me involved in the rock star lifestyle. I was supposed to be concentrating on school, not partying.

But I hadn't spent most of the night partying.

I had spent it watching movies with Cameron.

That thought made shivery butterflies take wing in my stomach, just like a lovestruck fourteen year old girl. It would have been embarrassing if I didn't enjoy the feeling so much.

Whenever I remembered that I'd also pulled off my panties in front of him and handed them over, those butterflies were replaced with an aching between my legs.

One half of me wondered why the hell I'd done that.

The other half scoffed and told me I knew *exactly* why I'd done that.

And I also knew it could never happen.

I continued going to my classes, doing my readings, and writing essays. I was beginning to get exhausted from all the schoolwork. I looked forward to coming home at the end of every day.

Home. I'd begun to think of Cameron's place as home. It was certainly more of a home than the room in the dorms had been at my boarding school. I'd shared it with a roommate. It hadn't exactly been a private space.

At Cameron's I had an entire floor to myself. No sharing bedrooms, or bathrooms, or common rooms. I could hide away in one of the libraries, snuggle up in a comfy armchair, and do my readings in peace. No risk of any students coming in to distract me.

I'd begun to wonder if my brother might agree to let me live with Cameron even when school started. I knew he liked the idea of my living in college dorms. There was round the clock security. Every building needed its own keycard to get in. I could use one of the campus volunteers to walk me home when it got dark. The entire thing was practically a commune unto itself.

But I'd come to enjoy the freedom I had living with Cameron. Coming and going as I pleased, not needing to account for my whereabouts every time I left the house... Living at Cameron's gave me more freedom than I'd ever thought possible.

And as much as I tried to ignore it, there was one more reason why living at the mansion appealed to me.

Every night before I went to bed, I opened the app Cameron installed on my phone and surveyed the grounds. I made sure all the alarms were on, that every door and window was secured. I made sure there was no way someone could be hiding in the house. There was no one lying in wait.

It was stupid. I should have been over it by now. But I couldn't deny the sense of safety and security I felt living in that mansion.

And Cameron. Even when he wasn't home, it still felt like he was there for me. He'd leave me extra slices of pizza in the fridge with a note to help myself. He'd turned the heat up on the pool one degree because I'd mentioned off-hand that the pool was a bit cooler than I had expected.

Cameron Thorne was turning out to be a much different person than I'd originally thought he was.

One evening when I was at home, studying as usual, I heard voices coming from the first floor. Cameron had been right that sound carried well in his mansion.

I wondered if it was Jen and Noah coming to visit. I headed downstairs, intending to greet them.

I stopped and darted back up a few steps when I found an older man and woman in the foyer. The man had salt and pepper hair and wore a business suit. The woman was a light brunette and wore a fashionable shift dress, high heeled pumps, and a casual yet chic updo.

Cameron was there, standing in front of the two of them. His expression was one of shock.

I wondered whether or not to interrupt. For a moment I wondered if these people were Cameron's lawyers — god knows what kind of trouble he could have gotten into — until the woman pulled him into a careful hug. She pressed a kiss to both his cheeks and stood back.

The man took Cameron's hand and gave it a firm handshake. Cameron returned it robotically.

"What are you guys doing here?" He sounded befuddled. "You're supposed to be in Tokyo or Milan or something."

"Plans changed," the man replied in a firm, but not unfriendly, tone. "I hope we're not interrupting anything?"

"No," Cameron murmured. "Just wasn't expecting you." He seemed to recover from his shock and gave them a bright smile. "It's good to see you. Really good, actually. Are you going to be here for long?"

"For the foreseeable future, yes." The woman gave him a bright smile. I could see traces of Cameron's mad grin in that expression.

These must have been Cameron's parents.

The ones who left him the moment he turned sixteen.

I had imagined them as cold, distant people. Without quite realizing it, I had mentally filed them away into my "bad people" category, reserved for strict, sour teachers and the mean rich girls at boarding school who looked down on me because I'd grown up in foster care.

But these people looked warm and friendly, or at least not unwelcoming. And Cameron seemed happy to see them, if not a little taken aback.

Cameron's mom looked around the place, taking in the details.

"You haven't changed the decor," she noted.

"No. It's fine the way it is. I mean, I like it the way it is," he said, almost stumbling over his words. "You did a really great job with the interior designer in the first place."

I found the exchange odd. Cameron didn't seem like the type to have any opinion on the decor in the first place. Precious rugs and antiques were regularly smashed during his parties, and he never seemed to notice, or care.

"What are you doing here?" Cameron asked. He seemed to realize how tactless that sounded and tried again. "I mean, why didn't you guys call?"

"We tried, but your cell phone number was disconnected," Sharon said.

"Right," Cameron winced. "It got leaked on the net and I had to change it. I left a message with your assistant to tell you."

"I recently had to fire my assistant," Grant explained. "He couldn't take the stress. That could be why the message never made its way to us."

"So we decided to drop in and hoped you would be home." His mother's eyes fell on me, still hiding around the corner on the stairs. "Cameron, you didn't tell me you had company."

I flushed and came out from hiding. I twisted the hem of my shirt in my hands unconsciously.

"Hello," I said with a weak wave.

"Mom, Dad, this is Lily." Cameron made proper introductions, gesturing to me. "Lily, these are my parents, Sharon and Grant."

"Very nice to meet you," I said politely.

The both of them scrutinized me carefully.

"Good to meet you, too," Cameron's father said eventually.

I stepped into the foyer, feeling oddly uncomfortable. I hadn't felt out of place at all since coming to live here. With Cameron's parents in front of me, with their shiny polished shoes and perfectly pressed attire, I couldn't help but scratch at a paint splotch on the sleeve of my shirt.

"I didn't mean to disturb you," I told them. "I just thought my brother might have been coming to visit me."

"Visit... you?" Sharon asked as she gave Cameron a forced smile.

"Lily's staying with me for a while," Cameron said.

"I see," was all his mother said.

Cameron shot me a look, almost pleading.

"It's like a roommate thing," I said, hoping that was the right thing to say. "I'm just staying with Cameron temporarily."

"How did the two of you meet?" Sharon practically jumped on me with the question. "Are you in the music industry, Lily? Oh, but you're so beautiful dear, you must be an actress. You did meet Cameron through work, yes? What exactly do you do?"

She shot the questions at me so fast I didn't have time to respond. I glanced at Cameron, confused and wondering why my choice in career was so important to her.

"She's Noah's sister," Cameron said quickly, as if to reassure her. "She's not a fan."

"Oh!" Cameron's mother let out a small pleased sound, looking relieved. "Well then, it's a pleasure to meet you."

To my complete surprise she took me in her arms and gave me a squeeze. I looked at Cameron quizzically over her shoulder. This was overly friendly. He seemed pleasantly surprised at his mother's gesture.

She held me for a few moments longer than was necessary. Her perfume was flowery, but not overly sweet. She held me gently. Just like a mother would.

My breath caught in a small hitch as she let me go.

Aside from my brother, I couldn't remember the last time I'd been held like that, with such a warm, loving, embrace.

I blinked my eyes, forcing away the faint sting of tears, mad at myself for getting so emotional over something as simple as a hug.

"How nice for Cameron to have someone around who's not—" Grant paused in the middle of the sentence and cleared his throat.

Cameron's expression turned pained, the kind of look one got when being stabbed in the chest.

I wondered what exactly his parents thought about the kind of company Cameron normally kept.

"Cam, honey, why haven't you said a single word about your lady friend?" she scolded him gently.

"It's not like we talk much to begin with," he replied. He seemed to regret the words the moment they left his mouth.

Awkward silence fell over the room. Sharon and Grant shared a look.

"Our schedules are so different, I mean." Cameron hurried to say. "Time zones and traveling and all that." He let out an almost nervous laugh. "I should probably make more of an effort to keep in touch."

"Cam, honey, we were hoping to take you out to dinner sometime this week, if you're free," Sharon said. "We'd like to talk to you about something."

Cameron blinked. "Dinner?"

"We're thinking that new French place, La Côte Basque Winehouse."

"Sure, I'd love to," he said with enthusiasm after recovering from his surprise. "I've heard really good things about the restaurant. I've been planning on going there myself. I love French cuisine."

I almost snorted, thinking he was joking, but held it back. Cameron had sounded genuine. I side-eyed him.

This whole thing was weird. It was if he'd had a personality transplant the moment his parents arrived.

His mother turned her attention to me. "You must come out to dinner with us this week, Lily."

"Oh. Um." I glanced at Cameron.

Cameron shot me a look of disbelief as if he couldn't believe his parents had asked me out to dinner with them. I had to assume this was the first time his parents had ever extended an invitation to one of his *friends*. He seemed taken aback, but not unhappy.

"I have some exams to study for," I told her.

Sharon frowned, confused. "It's the summer, dear."

"I'm taking summer classes to get extra credits at college."

Cameron's mother beamed. "How wonderful. You must be a very driven young lady."

"I want to be able to focus on my art during the school year."

"An artist!" Sharon looked delighted. "I'd love to hear more. You must have dinner with us," she pressed. "I insist."

"If Cameron doesn't mind," I said hesitantly. "I'm sure you'd like to catch up with your parents alone."

"No, it's fine," Cameron said, a pleased look appearing on his face. "We'd love to have you."

"Any friend of Cameron's is a friend of ours," Sharon said.

And with that, the plan was set in stone.

CHAPTER SIXTEEN

I hadn't been able to stop worrying about dinner with Cameron's parents.

I had no idea why they'd invited me. It was obvious they hadn't talked to their son in months, or seen him in person for much longer than that. Wouldn't they want to have a private family dinner?

But there had been something about the way Sharon had kept throwing pleased, almost ecstatic glances my way. It was disconcerting.

Cameron hadn't mentioned anything to me about the dinner after his parents left. I would have thought he was upset that I'd accepted, but then I remembered he'd looked almost happy when I'd said yes.

I also remembered how odd he'd acted around them.

I replayed their conversation in my head for days.

Cameron had rushed to tell his parents who I was. To explain that I wasn't a fan.

His father had been about to say how nice it was for Cameron to be around someone other than his usual company. He had cut himself off before he could finish his sentence.

His mother had been overly friendly. Hugging me. Wanting to know more about me. Inviting me to dinner.

And the way Cameron had acted, effusive and enthusiastic. He hadn't been his normal self.

I knew I was missing something, missing some connection. But Cameron hadn't brought up his parents to me again.

All I could do was wait.

I came home from class one day to find DVDs of part two and three of *The Terminator* propped up on the door to my bedroom. I assumed that meant he wanted to continue our movie night. I tracked Cameron down, DVDs in hand.

He was in his gym, working out on the weight machine. I paused in the doorway. Without meaning to, I found myself drinking in the sight of his firm, toned arms, the shifting muscles in his chest, the beads of sweat that ran down his abs in rivulets.

He wasn't bulky. His physique was still lean and trim. But those well defined muscles gave him a toned look that set my heart pounding.

I didn't know how long I stood there, mesmerized, but it was long enough for Cameron to notice. He set down the weights with a loud clank.

"I'd tell you to take a picture, but I'm sure there are more than enough on the internet if you really want to ogle my body."

I started, gripping the DVDs tight in my hand.

"Sorry. I don't mean to stare. It's just... you're just..." My tongue felt glued to the roof of my mouth.

"Really hot?" Cameron smirked.

"Yeah," I said dumbly. I flushed when I realized what I'd said.

"Surely your all-girls school didn't keep you *that* sheltered." Cameron grabbed a towel from a rack and wiped his face. The bright red hair was darker from sweat. "You keep on acting like you haven't seen a half-naked man before."

The flush on my cheeks burned even brighter.

Cameron noticed. "Wait. Are you serious?" A look of shock crossed his face. "Are you telling me you've never.... That you're a..."

Virgin.

It was too embarrassing to say out loud. I nodded silently instead.

"Fuck." Cameron's gaze narrowed, sweeping up and down my body. He opened his mouth to speak, before closing it with a snap. His towel hung limply in his hands.

"Is it that shocking?" I folded my arms over my chest defensively. "So I'm a little sheltered. If you're going to make fun of me—"

"No." He cut me off sharply. The look in his eyes had changed. The surprise had trickled away. Instead, that simmering heat had returned. It was a look I hadn't seen in weeks, ever since that party when I'd shown up in that short black skirt.

Cameron had talked about doing *indecent things* to me.

A warmth began to flow throughout my body, centering between my legs. I squirmed, pressed my thighs together. That look in his eyes, combined with the memory of his words sent my heart beating faster.

"Is it bad?" I asked.

"Is what bad?" He sounded as if he could barely force the words past his lips.

"Being a virgin. Is it that bad?"

"Fuck no." His eyes burned into mine. "You've really never had sex before? So when we were talking about our kinks and you couldn't come up with anything..." He ran a hand over his face. "Fuck, I'm such an asshole."

"No you're not."

"I am." He met my eyes again. "I shouldn't have been flirting with you. I shouldn't have been teasing you. And I sure as fuck shouldn't—"

I twisted the hem of my shirt in my hand, nervous, but wanting to know. "Shouldn't what?"

His eyes blazed. "Shouldn't be thinking of teaching you."

My mind exploded at those words. A pulsing ache throbbed between my thighs. My legs went shaky, my breathing shallow. I slowly approached him.

"What if I want you to teach me?"

"Fuck." He threw his towel to the ground. "Lily, you can't just say things like that."

"I'm sorry," I said automatically.

"No. I'm sorry. I shouldn't have been encouraging this."

I was steps away from him. I closed the distance. I placed a hand on his chest.

"I like it when you flirt with me," I confessed. "I like it when you tease me. I like it when you call me your Angel."

"Lily..." His voice was pained. "You don't know how much I..." His eyes fell to my mouth. "...how much I wish you were just a normal girl."

All the air left the room.

"But this?" he continued. "This can't happen."

My heart sunk. I looked down, not meeting his eyes.

"I get it. I'm Noah's baby sister. You can't betray his trust."

"It's not just that," he muttered. "I can't fucking do this to you."

"Do *what* to me, exactly?"

"You go speechless whenever you see me without a shirt," he said with utter patience.

I flushed, understanding his meaning. "Oh. You mean, because I've never...?"

He gave me an almost wry smile. "Don't you know your first time is supposed to be special?"

"Are you saying it wouldn't be special with you?" I gave him my best teasing smile, trying not to waver. "And here I thought you prided yourself on pleasing the ladies."

He shot me a look. "That's different."

I shifted closer, until I was practically pressed against him. "How is it different?"

"I've never—" He snapped his jaw closed, looking frustrated.

Understanding dawned on me. "Have you never been someone's first before?"

"No." He ran a hand through his sweat-dampened hair, looking exhausted. "At least, I don't think I have." He glanced down at where my hand rested on his chest. He traced the back of my hand with the tip of his finger. Heat radiated from that single point of contact, sending nervous excitement flooding through me. "And I've never..."

I leaned closer, bringing our faces closer together. "Never what?"

His eyes dropped to my lips again. I wet them unconsciously. He shut his eyes with a groan. When he opened them, they were full of fire.

"I've never *wanted* to be someone's first before." His eyes were still focused on my mouth.

"I want you to be mine," I said softly. "I don't want anyone else. I want it to be you."

I mustered all the bravery I could. I wrapped my arms around his neck, until my breasts were pressed to his chest.

"I want you to teach me. I want you to teach me everything."

"Fuck." His eyes blazed. "I told you. Don't say shit like that to me."

"Or what?" I challenged. "What are you going to do?"

He placed his hands on my hips, thumbs rubbing the sensitive skin exposed between my tank top and skirt. A spike of heat hit my gut like a blow, nearly taking my breath away.

"This is such a bad fucking idea," he murmured.

Pushing his hair away from his face with both hands, I met his blue eyes. They were burning with need. I stood on my tiptoes until we were face to face. I leaned forward, until we were inches away.

"I want you, Cameron."

I could practically sense the moment he snapped. The pupils of his eyes dilated, blowing wide open. Cameron let out a low grunt.

"Fuck it," he growled.

He closed the gap and pressed his lips to mine.

Fireworks exploded over my vision.

I dug my fingernails into his shoulders reflexively.

It was a soft kiss, light and sweet. I never would have expected sweetness from Cameron Thorne.

But he kissed me slowly, mouth moving over mine, fingertips brushing my cheek gently.

I stood still, unable to breathe, unable to think.

His tongue swiped at the seam of my lips. I parted them, letting his tongue brush with mine. The heat of it, the taste of him, sent me reeling. I did whimper then, heat surging through my body, filling me to my very core. The beginnings of wetness made itself known between my legs.

He was only kissing me and I was already wet for him. Was that my inexperience showing? Should I have been that turned on from something so simple and innocent? It wasn't my first kiss. There had been teenaged fumblings. But it was my first kiss with someone I cared so much about.

Cameron bit down on my lower bit lightly, before pushing his tongue back into my mouth. Our lips tangled, hot and fervent. He brought a hand to the back of my neck, tugging me closer. Kissing me harder.

There was nothing innocent about this kiss.

His other arm pulled me close, until our hips were pressed together. I gasped when I felt the evidence of his arousal. I clung closer to him kissing him desperately.

The sound of a cell phone ringing made the both of us freeze. We met each other's eyes.

"That's your phone," he said hoarsely.

I contemplated ignoring it. But I recognized the ringtone.

We slowly pulled apart, reluctantly. I took a step back, eyes still locked on Cameron, and pulled my phone out to answer it.

"Hey Noah," I said, trying to fake a casual tone and not sound breathless.

Cameron went pale. He mouthed a curse.

"What's wrong?" My brother asked immediately.

"Nothing. Just doing some school work."

I could sense Noah's skeptical frown.

"What do you need?" I asked before he could continue questioning me.

"Jen's planning a small get together with the guys and her friends. A belated welcome home party."

"That's nice of her."

"She wants to know what weekend you're free."

"I'm free every weekend."

"Don't you go out and do stuff? Haven't you made any friends in your classes?"

"I'm always studying."

I was swamped with readings and essays, it was true, but I couldn't deny that I kept my nights and weekends free in case Cameron wanted to hang out.

I snuck a glance at him.

Cameron had walked to the other side of the room, his back to me. One hand was tangled in his hair. I could sense a freak out was imminent.

"Tell Jen thank you," I said hurriedly. "I'm free whichever weekend she wants to throw it. I'll talk to you later. Love you."

I hung up before he could reply.

"Cameron..." I said hesitantly.

"Fuck fuck fuck," he cursed quietly.

"It's okay."

"No, it's fucking not."

He turned to me, forehead lined with pain.

"That shouldn't have happened," he said.

A pain of hurt shot through my chest. "I wanted it to happen."

"It was still wrong. Maybe—" he paused, avoiding my eyes. "Maybe it's better if you moved out."

"What?" I blurted out. "No! I want to stay here."

With you, went the unspoken words.

"I don't think it's a good idea any more. This — this thing between us — there's no way it can end well."

Cameron picked the towel up from the floor and made his way over to the door where I was standing.

"You're Noah's baby sister. He trusts me to watch out for you. If I betray him like this..."

His eyes were guarded, but I still caught a hint of that heat I'd seen before.

"I'll talk to your brother. We'll figure something out. Find you a place to live."

Cameron gave me one last look, almost mournful, before turning away and walking out the door.

"But I don't want to go."

I should have been embarrassed at the plaintive, almost pathetic, words that left my mouth.

He was already gone.

CHAPTER SEVENTEEN

Cameron wanted me to leave.

That thought kept running around in circles in my head for the rest of the day. I'd holed myself up in my room, trying to do my reading through blurry eyes as I fought off tears.

I couldn't concentrate on my studies. Not after what he said. Instead, I lay on my stomach in bed, clutching a pillow to my chest.

I tried to console myself with the thought that he didn't *really* want me to leave. He was just trying to...

Trying to what?

Avoid temptation?

Cameron was attracted to me. He had been from the beginning. He'd told me as much at the concert. It had only been after he'd found out I was Noah's sister that he had backed off. He'd told me it would never happen again.

Despite the heated looks, the teasing and flirting, along with the moments between us, rife with unspoken tension, he'd stayed true to his word.

Until he'd kissed me.

I rolled on my back, and put the pillow over my face, flushed and hot as I remembered the kiss.

I was just as attracted to Cameron as he was to me. And it wasn't just because he was *really really hot*, as he'd so modestly put it.

Cameron was thoughtful. Sweet. He did everything he could to make me feel comfortable in his home. He ate pizza with me and watched movies with me.

He said he didn't think of me as a young girl. That he didn't think of me as a little sister.

And that was why he was kicking me out of his house.

It wasn't because he didn't want me here.

It was because he wanted me here *too much*.

Cameron said he would never betray my brother's trust. If I wasn't Noah's sister... if I was any other girl...

But I wasn't. I was Lily Hart. Nothing could change that.

I groaned and rolled over to sit up in bed, dangling my legs over the edge. I stared at the floor, wondering if there was any way to change Cameron's mind.

When nothing came to me, I gave up and started getting ready for bed. When I opened the closet doors, I remembered when Cameron had checked it for monsters in jest. When I pulled on a pair of yoga shorts and a tank top, I remembered what he'd said about me looking cute in them.

Maybe Cameron was right. If there could never be anything

between us, maybe it was better if I left. Wouldn't it just hurt more to be near him every day and not be able to be with him?

I'd probably have to move back in with Noah and Jen, at least until school officially started and I could move into the dorms.

That wasn't so bad, I tried to tell myself. I would get to see more of my brother. And I liked his girlfriend. We got along well.

Not as well as I got along with Cameron.

Because we did get along well. We made each other laugh just as much as we pushed each other's buttons. He did thoughtful, sweet things for me, like leaving me ear plugs for his party. I liked to think I did nice things for him, like keeping him company during his movie nights.

We were friends.

We were becoming more than friends.

And despite knowing my brother would disapprove, I couldn't help thinking maybe Cameron and I would be good for each other. We'd gotten to know each other. And we'd come to like each other.

More than like each other.

Cameron was the first boy I'd ever had real feelings for.

The more I thought about it, the more upset I became. It was unfair I couldn't be with someone just because my brother wouldn't approve.

My brother didn't approve of a lot of things when it came to me and how I lived my life.

I knew I'd never get him to see straight when it came to this, when it came to me and Cameron. I was his baby sister, the one he was supposed to take care of and protect. Cameron was irresponsible, a party animal who slept around and never took anything seriously.

If that was all Cameron was, I might have been able to understand. But Cameron was so much more than that. Noah couldn't see past it. But I could.

Even after everything that had happened, Cameron and I were still friends. I didn't want to throw that away.

I decided I wasn't going to let Cameron hide from me any longer. We had to talk about what happened, talk about his reasons for kicking me out.

I had to convince him to change his mind.

I came home from classes late one evening, having stayed at the library late, resolved and with a purpose. I'd find Cameron and force him to listen to me.

Another party was in full swing when I arrived. Music blasted from every window and drunk partygoers spilled out from every entryway.

Cameron hadn't mentioned throwing another party. Then again, he hadn't mentioned anything to me at all over the last few days.

It had been days since I'd last seen him. He went back to hiding from me. That was how he dealt with me with whenever something happened between us. Running away.

I'd lived in dread that every day would be the day Noah showed up to bring me home. So far that hadn't happened. Maybe Cameron was putting it off. Maybe he was just as reluctant as I was.

And maybe he just couldn't figure out a way to explain to Noah why he wanted me to leave without incriminating himself.

It was going to be hard to find Cameron in this noisy, boisterous crowd. The mansion was large enough it might have taken more than an hour to explore every floor trying to track him down.

I shoved and squeezed my way through the mass of people, searching the mansion room by room. I couldn't find Cameron anywhere. He wasn't in the kitchen. He wasn't out by the pool. He wasn't even in the movie theater room. Those were the places I always looked for him first.

I texted him, asking if we could talk, but as I expected I didn't receive an answer.

Dejected, I contemplated whether to just head to my bedroom and try to sleep through the noise, or whether to shake it off and join the party. Without Cameron to shut off the speakers in the third floor, it was going to be a long night.

On my way to my bedroom, I caught the sound of a familiar voice. It was definitely Cameron. The party was too loud and the tones were too low for me to place the other.

I followed the voices to one of the living rooms. I assumed Cameron was going to be surrounded by another entourage. Maybe I could still corner him and make him agree to talk to me later when he had time. Maybe I could convince him to put off speaking with my brother until we had a chance to talk.

I needed to convince him to let me stay.

"Cameron?"

I heard him swear out loud.

I peeked my head into the room.

My heart stuttered in my chest.

It was an almost familiar scene. Cameron, on a sofa. A gorgeous woman beside him. Her hands were wrapped in his hair, about to pull him down for a kiss.

A distant part of me was thankful they at least still had their clothes on.

The rest of me couldn't believe what I was seeing.

Cameron. With another girl.

He jumped off the sofa. "Shit."

"What's wrong?" The woman on the sofa frowned, looking between the two of us.

"Lily, it's not what you think." His voice was desperate. His fingers twitched, as if he were going to reach out for me, but thought better of it.

"Sorry to interrupt," I murmured, blinking back tears, and slowly backing out of the room. "I should have realized you were busy when you didn't answer my text."

Busy sucking face with some other girl.

The tightness in my chest was like a vise grip. I couldn't breathe around it.

"I'll leave you to it," I bit out.

I fled. I heard Cameron call out my name. I didn't stop.

Tears stung my eyes as I ran, pushing people out of the way. I almost tripped over myself climbing the stairs. The hallways were a blur of carousing bodies.

I slammed my door behind me. Slumping against the wall, I stared blankly at the floor.

Some part of me tried to deny what I'd seen. Maybe it had been perfectly innocent.

But when were the words *Cameron* and *a hot woman* in the same sentence ever innocent?

My breath hitched. The two of them had sat close, practically wrapped in each other's arms. The longer I thought about it, the more painful that grip on my heart became.

There was no mistaking what had been going on.

I wiped my wet cheeks with the back of my hand and went to my closet. I took out my suitcase and began tossing my clothes into it haphazardly.

I'd been hoping to convince Cameron to let me stay. I believed that even if we couldn't be together, we could still be friends.

But the clenching of my chest told me that was going to be impossible.

It had been bad enough knowing about Cameron's reputation with women when all I had was a silly crush.

Seeing him with that woman just solidified it.

I couldn't stay here. I couldn't stay in this place as Cameron brought home a parade of women one after another. The thought of it almost killed me.

He had been right. It was better if I left.

Because now I knew.

I loved Cameron.

I couldn't stand to see him with anyone else.

I wanted to be with him.

And I knew, now, that was the one thing that would never happen.

CHAPTER EIGHTEEN

I was still throwing clothes into my suitcase when the door to my bedroom flew open. It hit the opposite wall with a thud.

I half expected to see another drunken couple invading my personal space.

Cameron stood in the doorway, wild red hair haloed by the light streaming in from the hallway.

"It wasn't what you think," he blurted out. That desperation was back in his voice.

"It doesn't matter." I avoided his eyes by concentrating on folding my clothes. "It's none of my business what you do."

"I wasn't going to kiss her."

"It's fine," I dismissed.

"She's a model," he pressed on. "I thought she wanted to talk about starring in our next music video. I didn't know what she was planning on doing. I wouldn't have...." he trailed off. "I didn't mean to hurt you."

I could hear the honesty in his voice. But it didn't matter, did it? Because even though I hadn't caught him kissing another girl *this* time, I knew it would happen eventually. And I didn't think I'd be able to take that without my heart smashing into pieces.

I continued putting my clothes in my suitcase, my back to him. I heard him close the bedroom door behind him.

"What are you doing?" he asked.

"Packing."

Cameron sat on the edge of my bed, next to my suitcase, so I had to face him. "Why?"

I folded another shirt, trying to keep my voice from shaking. "You were right. It's better this way."

"You don't need to go."

"You're the one who said I should. And I agree. This is what's best."

"Is it?"

The dejection in his voice made me stop. He looked lost, his dark blue eyes wide and forlorn.

"You said it yourself," I told him. "Whatever this thing is between us, it won't end well."

Cameron tugged on my shirt, drawing me close. I almost lost my balance in my surprise. I ended up pressed against him, standing between his spread legs as he sat on my bed. The heat of his hands on my hips seared me, even through my clothes.

He leaned forward and planted his forehead on my stomach. "I missed you this last week," he murmured.

My heart thumped in my chest. My fingers clenched into his muscles of his shoulders as I stared at the top of his head.

"You're the one who keeps running and hiding."

"I know. I'm sorry. I thought if I stayed away from you, I could make myself forget about you. I thought if I spent all my time at the studio, if I spent my time partying and drinking, I could forget how much I missed you." He leaned back and looked up to meet my eyes. "I thought I could forget how much I want you. But I can't."

My heart leaped into my throat at the confession.

"I want you so fucking much, Lily." His voice was rough, his eyes dark and piercing.

I swallowed hard. That was what I'd been hoping to hear for weeks. For months.

"I want you, too," I said softly.

He cupped my cheeks with both hands and pulled me down. I sat on the bed. Our legs pressed together. The firm muscles of his thighs sent my stomach quivering.

"I really am sorry you had to see that," he said. "I promise you, I honestly did think she just wanted to talk."

"I told you, it's fine. I believe you."

"I haven't been with anyone since you moved in," he said. "I mean, I could have. There were lots of women who..." He shrugged, looking almost embarrassed. "But I just couldn't stop thinking about you. Wanting you."

My heart gave a little flutter. I wrapped my arms around his neck and pressed myself against him.

"Good. Because I don't know if I can take seeing you with another woman like that again."

Cameron looked pained for a minute, before his expression turned fervent. Both blue eyes pinned me down.

"And I can't stand the thought of some other guy touching you."

Elation welled up in my chest. I opened my mouth to speak, to tell him everything I was feeling inside.

He brushed his thumb against my bottom lip, preventing me from speaking. Preventing me from breathing. That slightest touch sent my head spinning. The room swirled around me as I went lightheaded.

"I know how fucking wrong this is," he said hoarsely. "I know things will go to shit if I let this happen."

He brought his mouth close to mine, until our lips were a mere hairsbreadth apart.

"But I don't care anymore," he murmured. "I don't want you to leave. I want you to stay. With me."

He touched his lips to mine, soft and sweet. Just like our first kiss. Almost tentative, hesitant. It was the lightest touches, barely more than a brief brush of lips.

Cameron pulled back an inch. I whimpered at the loss. That smallest of space between us felt like a gaping void.

"Is this okay?" he asked.

I inhaled a shaky breath. The scent of him was warm and masculine, with a hint of something fresh, like a sunny, summer day. It made my head swim. I lost the ability to use words. I nodded instead.

He cracked a smile. "I want to hear you say it."

"Kiss me," I demanded breathlessly.

His lips returned to mine, firmer this time. He wound his fingers through my hair and tugged me closer. I clung to him, wrapping my arms around his neck.

He ran the tip of his tongue along the inside of my upper lip. A throbbing arousal centered between my legs.

He delved his tongue into my mouth, exploring and searching, taking my breath away. I kissed him back with abandon. The heat inside me rose with every touch of his tongue against mine. That warmth spread from my mouth, to my chest, to my belly, and lower.

His hands went to my hips to steady me, his fingertips exploring the exposed bare skin between my shirt and my skirt.

Shivers coursed through my body. My breath came in short bursts, gasping into his mouth. The sounds of the party raging outside my bedroom door were long forgotten. I was unable to care about anything except this man's lips, this man's touch.

I wanted more.

I scrambled to climb on top of him, knocking him back against the bed. He caught himself on his elbows with a laugh. I hovered over him, straddling his hips.

"So eager," he teased, taking note of my enthusiasm.

With Cameron lying back, I could feel the press of his hardening length against the zipper of his jeans. Could feel his length pressed against my core.

My face was flushed, my breathing rapid. The wetness between my legs was becoming a distraction. I wanted him. I wanted everything he had to give me.

But this was completely new to me. As excited as I was, as eager as I was, slight waves of apprehension started to tingle inside me. The tips of my fingers went cold as my nerves began to get the best of me.

"Hey." Cameron sat up and took my face in both hands.

I looked down, avoiding his eyes, ashamed. I wanted to do this. I'd practically jumped on him. I didn't know why I was so nervous.

"Lily, look at me."

I lifted my head to meet his eyes. Cameron examined me closely. I dug my fingers into the bedsheets.

He smiled and pressed a kiss to my forehead.

"Let's go back to the party," he said.

I blinked at the non sequitur. "What?"

"We can go jump in the pool." He gave me a crooked smile. "To cool off."

My breath hitched. Tears stung the back of my eyes. I threw my arms around his neck. He caught me by the waist.

"Thank you."

He cocked his head. "For what?"

"For understanding. For not pushing things."

He took my hands in his. He pressed kisses to my fingertips. "I will never push you into something you're not ready for."

"I thought I was ready. I don't know why I'm so nervous."

"It's okay to be nervous your first time." He gave me a quick peck on the lips. "Want to go back and enjoy the party?"

I looked down at our joined hands. I was still straddling his lap.

He was still hard.

I was still wet.

I gathered my courage.

"Can we go slow?"

CHAPTER NINETEEN

Cameron's blue eyes darkened with heat at my request.

"You sure?" He cradled my face in his hands and gave me a probing look. "I don't ever want you to feel pressured."

"I'm not." I leaned forward and kissed him once, softly. "I want to be with you."

"You have no fucking idea how much I want you," he murmured against my lips.

I gave an experimental roll of my hips, pressing down against him. "I have some idea."

His hardness was like a fiery brand between my thighs. The rub of his rough jeans against my core sent tingles shooting through me.

Cameron let out a grunted curse, his eyes squeezing shut. He placed his hands on my hips, stilling them.

"Stop squirming. You asked for slow, remember?"

I bucked my hips again.

He cracked his eyes open. "Temptress."

Cameron returned his lips to mine. I sighed into his mouth, enjoying the taste of him, the smell of him. Kissing Cameron was like drinking in pure sunshine.

I ran my hands over the muscles of his shoulders and chest, enjoying the firm, well defined shape of him. My questing fingers went low enough to find the hem of his shirt. I gave it a tug.

He answered the unspoken question, breaking our kiss to toss the shirt over his head.

Although I'd seen Cameron shirtless a handful of times already, the sight of him never failed to surprise me. Lean and toned, the peaks and valleys of his abs called out for me to touch them.

I placed my hands on his bare skin, like silk over steel. I ran my hands up and down his chest, feeling those shifting muscles under my fingertips.

I slid my hands around his sides. His stomach muscles tensed and he inhaled a sharp breath. I pulled back quickly.

"Did I—?" I began to ask, unsure if I'd done something wrong.

"No, it's fine." He squeezed my hips. "Feel free to keep going."

I moved to continue my exploration, but he tensed again. He let out a short, huffing sound.

I paused. That almost sounded like a laugh. Experimentally, I touched his sides with a feather touch. He squirmed away and snorted out a quick laugh that time.

"Are you ticklish?" I asked, astonished.

"Just a little," he admitted.

That was so adorable I almost swooned. The hotter than hell rock star sex god Cameron Thorne... was ticklish.

"I trust you not to take advantage," he continued.

"I would never." I did file the knowledge away for later, however.

As our lips and tongues slid together, I resumed my inspection of his chest and shoulders, keeping away from his sensitive areas.

Cameron moved his hands from my hips to my waist, caressing the skin under my shirt. My hairs stood on end as he began sliding higher, until his hands were inches away from my breasts. I held my breath as he moved to cup them.

"Is this okay?" he asked.

I let out a sound of affirmation into his mouth.

His large hands covered my breasts through my bra. Two thumbs traced my nipples through the thin cotton. I inhaled sharply as that touch went straight to the apex of my thighs.

With a surety I didn't quite feel inside, I grabbed the hem of my shirt and pulled it over my head.

Cameron's eyes zeroed in on my bra.

His lips twitched.

"Cartoon rainbows?"

"Shut up," I said, flustered both by his words and by his touch.

"It's cute."

"It was on sale."

"I didn't say I didn't like it." He stroked the bare skin of my back, skimming over the elastic of my bra, up and down. "But I think I'd like it better if it was off."

He traced a circle around the clasps with a questioning noise. I nodded. With deft fingers he unsnapped the bra.

I shrugged out of the straps and let it fall to the floor. I fought to ignore the reason why he was so experienced at undoing bras with one hand.

With my breasts exposed, I felt even more nervous than I had before. Cameron didn't give me time for the anxiety to kick in full force. He leaned forward and pressed a kiss to the exposed skin of my cleavage. Shivers ran through me.

He kissed my left nipple, then my right. They tightened and peaked under his lips. He sucked one into his mouth and I gasped from the unfamiliar pleasure. Eyes squeezed shut, I buried my hands in his hair and tugged him closer.

Moving from one to the other, he sucked and licked with his lips and tongue. My hips began to rock unconsciously as the sensations went straight to my core.

His hands moved from my hips to my thighs, brushing the bare skin below the hem of my skirt. I trembled, anticipating.

But he didn't move his hands further up. He returned his attention to my breasts, using his thumbs to stroke the soft skin of my inner thighs.

The combined onslaught was enough to have me squirming and panting. My panties were becoming even more soaked. He had barely done anything yet.

Cameron was as affected as I was. His hardness pressed firmly against the zipper on his jeans. I rolled my hips, grinding down against him.

Cameron groaned.

"What did I tell you about taking it slow?" he murmured against my skin.

My only answer was to take his hand and press it between my legs, under my skirt.

He inhaled a sharp breath as he found my wet panties. He bit out a muffled cursed.

"You're killing me," he said.

"Touch me. Please."

He traced the valley between my legs with the knuckles on the back of his hand. I squeaked, an embarrassing sound.

"Have you ever—?" he began to ask.

"No. Not even this. I mean, by myself, yeah..." I flushed but continued on. "But not with anyone else."

"I'll go slow."

With the speed of a melting glacier, Cameron slipped a hand under the elastic of my panties. The tips of his fingers found the small bud between my thighs. I gasped loudly as he pressed down with a thumb. I nearly orgasmed from that touch alone.

"Oh fuck," I choked.

Cameron hummed a pleased sound and repeated the motion. I rocked back and forth unconsciously.

As his thumb played with me, his fingers continued their search. They slipped between my lower lips and found what they were looking for. I nearly flew apart when one finger traced my entrance.

"Is this okay?" he asked.

The bucking of my hips urging him on was the only answer I could give. I was incapable of words.

Slowly, ever so slowly, he slid that finger inside me. I moaned. The rasp of his rough skin against my inner walls was a revelation. I felt myself throbbing around him, muscles contracting in waves.

He pulled out and pushed in again, slightly faster this time. My fingers dug into his shoulders as I squeezed my eyes shut. Sparks of pleasure shot across my closed eyes.

"More," I begged.

He obliged, pressing two fingers against my entrance this time. He returned to the slower pace, pumping in and out, my wetness easing the way.

The ache inside me was getting almost painful. I could feel his length against my thigh, straining to burst out of his jeans.

I placed my hand on him and pressed down. He cursed and fell forward, his forehead resting on my shoulder. I rubbed him slowly, feeling him grow even harder under my fingers.

"Lily, if you don't stop..."

I tugged on his hair, pulling him up to meet my eyes. "I don't want to stop."

His eyes blazed with an inner fire. "You sure?"

"Yes."

With one arm around my waist, he shifted us until I was lying down on the bed. He knelt at my feet. The sight of Cameron shirtless, wearing only dark jeans with wild, messy red hair, sent more tingles shooting through me.

"You're so hot," I blurted out.

Cameron laughed. My cheeks burst into flames.

"I mean, there are other things I like about you, too," I stammered. "You're funny and thoughtful and an amazing musician and—"

He pressed a kiss on my calf. "And you're cute."

I shivered.

He slid higher and kissed my knee. "And an amazing artist."

With two hands he spread my legs and pressed a kiss to my inner thigh. "And kind."

My legs tried to clamp together unconsciously. He held them open.

"And sexy as hell."

He hooked his fingers under the elastic of my panties and slowly drew them down my legs.

"And I've been thinking of fucking your cunt with my tongue and making you come on my face for months."

I choked at his dirty words, then shrieked out loud as Cameron dived between my legs and sucked my clit into his mouth.

My limbs went limp as I fell back against the bed. His lips and tongue and mouth on the most sensitive part of me was a full frontal assault. I felt like a ship lost at sea, waves of pleasure hitting from every side. I moaned and squirmed and I grasped at his hair, pulling him closer.

"Oh my god," I whimpered.

I trembled and shook and gasped for air as the pleasure sent me higher and higher, through the clouds and into the stratosphere.

Two fingers pushed inside me and I saw stars, a burst of light and color crossed my vision. I called out Cameron's name with a strangled breath, then words were impossible as I tumbled over the edge.

Shocks of pleasure sang through me. My entire body tensed up, then went limp as I sank into the mattress.

I blacked out.

When I finally peeled my eyes open, I found Cameron lying on his side, staring at me. He cracked a smile and placed a kiss on my lips. I fumbled for him, my arms weak, but still strong enough to cling to him. I buried my head in his chest and tangled our legs together.

The rough scratch of his jeans against my bare legs was unbearable. I was still throbbing inside, something in me longing to be filled.

I tugged at his button and zipper. "Off. Now."

"So demanding." He stroked a hand through my hair, tilting my head up to meet his eyes. "We don't have to. This was enough."

"No, it wasn't." I was aching and pulsing. I needed him inside me. "I'm not scared anymore. I want you."

I popped the button and pulled down the zipper. That stiff length nearly fell into my hands. I reached inside and pulled him out.

My eyes went wide as I took in his size. I swallowed hard, starting to get second thoughts.

But the velvety smooth skin under my hands made my inner walls clench down with need. I stroked up and down experimentally. Cameron groaned. He kicked off his jeans and boxers in a hurry. He turned over and reached into the bedside table, opening the drawer and pulling out a square foil packet.

"I know I didn't put those there," I said.

"With the kind of parties I throw, I make sure each room is fully stocked."

He rolled over and pinned me beneath him. I spread my legs to make room for him. I could feel the tip just at my entrance, blunt and unyielding. I held my breath, my eyes squeezing shut without thinking.

"Hey." Cameron stroked my hair with soft fingers. I opened my eyes to meet dark blue. His pupils were blown wide open with need. "You still sure?"

Even in this position, even with us so close, he still took the time to ask.

My heart thumped madly in my chest. My eyes threatened to tear up. I pulled him down into a desperate kiss, tongues battling, hot and wet.

"I'm sure," I breathed into his mouth. "Fuck me."

He groaned and tightened his grip in my hair. "Say that again."

I flushed, but complied. "Fuck me, Cameron."

"You're going to be the death of me, Angel."

Our eyes locked as he slid himself inside me. He went just as slowly as he had with his fingers. Slow enough to drive me crazy.

I was thankful for it. I struggled to accommodate his size, panting in short gasps. I wriggled and shook as my insides fluttered around him.

When our hips finally met, I let out a breath. I'd taken him all. I'd been wondering whether I could or not.

This was it. I was no longer a virgin.

And Cameron was my first.

The thought sent my heart soaring. I was so high on the feeling I didn't even realize Cameron had stopped moving.

His face was lined with something almost like pain, eyes narrowed and dark. His body was tense, trembling with the effort to keep still.

I shifted my hips, pulling him closer.

"You can move," I told him.

With a low grunt, he pulled out and pushed back in. More sparks of pleasure shot through me, even better than when he'd had his fingers inside me. The stretch of him, the burn of it, was at once pleasurable and painful and the combination made my head spin.

Cameron returned to kissing me, devouring my mouth. He thrust his tongue between my lips with the same pace he thrust his hips, mimicking the motion.

I rocked my hips in time with his. The two of us moved together in a fluid rhythm, coming together then moving apart, over and over again, the pleasure building between us.

"So fucking sweet," he murmured into my mouth. "Angel, you have no idea what you're doing to me."

Our speed increased as we both began to reach our peak. I could sense he was close when his length pulsed and hardened even further inside me.

Cameron pressed his thumb down on my clit and rubbed in circles. It was enough to send me over the edge again.

He wrapped his arms around my waist and drew me closer, slamming his hips into mine. With a final thrust, Cameron cursed and went tense, muscles straining.

I clawed my nails into his upper arms, digging into the skin as we fell into the abyss together, clutching each other tight.

After long moments, when the pleasure finally began to subside, I let myself go limp and eased down into the mattress. Cameron fell on top of me. He kept his full weight from crushing me, holding himself up with his forearms.

We lay there together, catching our breath as we trembled.

My insides felt sore and achy. I reveled in the feeling, knowing that it was Cameron who had made me feel that way. I ran my hands up and down his bare back, now slick with sweat.

He eventually pushed himself off me. We lay side by side, our limbs still tangled.

I pressed my cheek to his and snuggled down into his embrace. Both of us closed our eyes and sank into the mattress.

As much as I wished we could have just fallen asleep then and there, the party still raged around us. Loud voices and booming music and the sound of things crashing to the floor interrupted what should have been a quiet moment of tenderness.

"We better get dressed," Cameron murmured into my hair.

"Why?" I tried to snuggle down further into his arms.

"Don't want to leave the party guests unattended for too long. Who knows what kind of shit they'll get up to."

With a sigh, I sat up to gather my clothes. I winced. The ache between my legs was less pleasurable and more painful.

"Are you okay?" Cameron asked immediately, concern on his face. "Did I hurt you?"

"I'm fine. Just a bit sore."

I swung my legs off the bed and gathered my skirt and shirt. My panties had been flung halfway across the room.

Cameron hugged me from behind, his naked chest to my bare back. "I'm sorry."

I turned in his arms and returned the hug. "I'm not sorry at all."

The door of my bedroom slammed open, the doorknob embedding

itself in the wall, again. Another laughing couple stumbled in. They stopped when they saw us, just like the last time.

"Ohmigod!" the girl yelped.

I flinched and scrambled for the sheets.

Cameron had no shame. He stood up, fully naked, and waved them out. "You mind?"

"Sorry, Cam," the guy said. He threw Cameron a sly grin and a thumbs up, nodding to me. The couple left, forgetting to close the door behind them.

"And this is why we should get dressed," Cameron said.

I hurried to pull on my clothes before anyone could peek inside and see me naked.

A terrible thought occurred to me. "Do you think they recognized me?"

Cameron tilted his head toward me as he buttoned his jeans. "Why?"

"What if they say something?"

"About what?"

"About me. And you. Together." Nerves threatened to overtake my common sense. "What if they tell everyone they saw us together? What if everyone finds out?"

Cameron stilled. "You... don't want people to find out about us?" he asked slowly.

"You do?" I asked, surprised. "I thought you were terrified Noah would find out."

"It's one thing for Noah to think I'm perving on his little sister. This is different. I'm not just playing around."

My heart melted in my chest. The worry still wouldn't dissipate though.

"I don't know if Noah will see it that way," I said doubtfully. "He's still going to be really upset."

"You let me deal with Noah."

"I don't think you understand—"

"No, you don't understand." Cameron took me in his arms. "I don't care what your brother thinks. We're together now. I'll do anything to keep you."

Ever since that night at the concert, Cameron had been the one running away, terrified of my brother's reaction. I'd been the one who balked at Noah's restrictions, the one who wanted to live my life out from under my brother's thumb.

But now that Cameron and I were together, I had something to lose. I knew Noah wouldn't react well to this news. I didn't want Noah and Cameron to fight. I didn't want Noah to make me choose between them. And I didn't want Noah to force Cameron to leave the band.

Cameron had been right. This thing between us was probably not going to end well.

"I don't think we should tell anyone," I said.

The hurt on Cameron's face was evident.

"Yet," I hastened to add. "Not until I can figure out a way to tell Noah and not have him freak out."

Cameron reluctantly agreed.

"I'm going back out to supervise the party," he said after his shirt was back on. "Come with me?"

"I should probably try to do a bit more studying and then get some sleep." I fidgeted with the hem of my shirt. "How long do you think you'll be up?"

"My parties usually go 'til dawn."

"Oh." I had been hoping Cameron and I could fall asleep together. After what we'd just done, the idea of going to bed alone felt unbearable.

"I can shut the party down early." He stepped closed to me and pressed a kiss on my lips. "Will you give me an hour to empty out the place? Then we can go to bed together."

My heart went light with relief. "I'd love that. I want to fall asleep in your arms." I flushed when I realized how sappy I'd sounded.

"Fuck, you're so cute." Cameron kissed me again, desperate and heated, turning me into a writhing ball of need. He began to get hard again, his length pressing into my stomach.

We broke the kiss and panted into each other's mouths.

"You're fucking amazing, Angel." Cameron's voice was hoarse.

"Did anyone ever tell you that you swear a lot?" I teased.

He tensed, his eyes turning pained. I didn't know what I'd said wrong, but I sensed a shift in the mood.

"I like it when you swear," I continued, trying to repair whatever harm I'd caused. "It shows you're passionate."

Cameron relaxed. "You don't think it makes me sound uncivilized?"

"No. Especially when you call me Angel right after. I like that part."

"Then I'll call you Angel as often as possible."

Cameron pressed another quick kiss to my lips before leaving to round up the party guests and kick them out.

I sat back down on my bed. I wanted to bask in the moment. My first time, with Cameron. So many thoughts and emotions swirling around inside me.

But my mind had turned to only one thing.

What had I said that had bothered him so much?

CHAPTER TWENTY

"**W**hy do we never sleep in your room?" I asked. "You always come to mine."

We were outside on the patio, enjoying the sun. Cameron's poolside lounge chairs were as comfortable as the leather armchairs in his movie theater room. Plush and soft, perfect for sunbathing.

Cameron laughed.

"You know that bachelor reputation of mine?" he said. "If you saw my bedroom you'd lose all respect for me."

"Who says I respect you now?" I teased.

"Fucking ow." He faked a blow to his chest, pressing a hand over his heart. "This is the thanks I get? I put you up in my own home, I let you eat my food, I give you multiple orgasms. What more can a man do?"

"A man can clean his room like an adult."

"Says the girl with dirty laundry piled in the corner and soda cans stockpiled on her nightstand."

"I never said I wasn't a hypocrite."

Cameron poked me in the side. I didn't flinch.

"You're the ticklish one, not me," I told him.

Cameron turned the poke into a caress. My insides fluttered.

I'd worn my skimpiest swimsuit. Not that it was all that skimpy. Really, it was just a normal bikini. Cameron enjoyed it though. He especially enjoyed exploring my sun tan lines whenever he got me naked.

Which was often.

"You don't have any tattoos," he noted.

I shuddered. "Ick. Needles. No thanks. I'll leave that to you rock stars."

"Not even in any secret places?" he teased.

"You've thoroughly examined all my secret places."

"Speaking of, you need more lotion?" He reached out with grabby fingers.

"You just want an excuse to put your hands on me."

"I don't need an excuse for that."

In one swift motion Cameron picked me up, hefting me over his shoulder like a sack of flour.

"What are you doing?" I shrieked.

"It's hot. You should cool off before you get sunstroke."

He walked us to the edge of the pool.

"Oh no," I said in a warning tone. "Don't you dare."

"I'm just looking out for my girlfriend's wellbeing."

I stopped breathing.

That was the first time Cameron called me his girlfriend.

Maybe it was juvenile, but I had been hoping to have the *relationship status* talk sometime soon. I'd never had that talk before. I hadn't known how to bring it up.

"Lily?" Cameron prompted. "You alive in there?"

"Yeah," I choked out, fighting back tears. I'd never been this emotional in my life. Not like the way I'd been since moving into Cameron's. I thumped him in the back. "Put me down."

"Anything you say, Angel."

"No, wait—!" I protested.

He jumped into the pool with me still in his arms.

We landed with a splash. The cold water was a shock to my system, especially after basking in the warm sun. I kicked off the bottom of the pool and burst to the surface with a gasp.

"I hate you," I sputtered, my eyes squeezed shut. I didn't like that sting of chlorine in my eyes. It always turned my face red and blotchy.

Cameron was still under the water. He swam towards me and grabbed my legs. I kicked out. He used me to climb up, clinging to me the entire time.

He surfaced, hair plastered to his face, covering his eyes and cheeks.

"You look like a mop," I told him.

He slicked his hair back with a grin. "There's that grumpy face. You've been so smiley and happy lately. I missed that patented pissed off Hart look."

"I hate you," I repeated, now that he was out of the water and could hear me.

"What was that?" he said, putting a hand to his ear. "You love me and adore me and want to have my babies?"

I whirled around, water splashing everywhere, not wanting him to see my stunned expression.

Love and *girlfriend* and *babies*.

All those words spoken so close together sent my heart thumping madly.

I hadn't even begun to think about that kind of thing.

My heart squeezed in my chest, feeling light and airy. A small smile spread across my face unbidden.

Was that where Cameron's mind was already going? Was he thinking that long term already?

Then reality sunk in. Of course he wasn't thinking things like that. He'd just been joking.

Disappointment filled my chest, but also a sort of relief. I was only nineteen. I shouldn't have been thinking those sort of thoughts. Not yet.

But there was something about this man that made me want to throw all caution to the wind and jump in head first.

Cameron wrapped his arms around me from behind, pulling me back against him. Our legs brushed as we treaded water.

"Of course, if I really wanted to piss you off, I'd do this."

Cameron ducked under the water. He grabbed my ankles. I thought he would pull me under.

Instead, he tickled my feet.

I yelped and squirmed and kicked. My foot made contact with something soft yet firm.

Cameron exploded to the surface.

"Fuck," he cursed, a hand to his face, but still laughing. "I think you broke my nose."

"It's your own fault," I grumbled.

He rubbed his nose gingerly. I pushed his hand aside, prodding at his nose.

"Ow," he complained.

"You're fine. It's not broken." I poked his nose one more time for good measure. He winced. "How'd you know my feet were ticklish? I'm not ticklish anywhere else."

"It was an experiment. You always flinch when I go near your feet."

"Maybe I should do my own experiment. See how many other places you're ticklish."

"Ceasefire," he said hastily, throwing his hands up in surrender. A sly smile crossed his face. "Besides, there are more interesting ways to experiment with your body."

I swam closer to him. "Like what?"

He grabbed me by the waist and tugged until we were pressed together. "How about I show you?"

He pressed his mouth to mine, giving me a wet kiss. I smelled and tasted the mixture of chlorine and suntan lotion and something that was uniquely Cameron. Warm and fresh, like sunshine.

I returned the kiss, brushing our tongues together in a hot slide. We'd done this many times already, but each kiss still sent shivers through my spine. Still sent heat soaring straight between my thighs. The touch of his lips and tongue against mine did something to my insides, made me instantly wet and needy for him.

I would have been embarrassed at my overreaction to a simple kiss if Cameron hadn't reacted the same. He was already pressed against my thigh, growing stiff.

I heard a rustling of the bushes. My heart stopped. I pulled away quickly, looking for the source of the noise.

No one else lived here. Cameron hadn't invited anyone over. It was supposed to just be the two of us.

I began to shake.

Who was here? Were they supposed to be here?

My lungs seized up, fear spiking through me. I couldn't breathe. The anxiety made me shiver and quake.

The bushes began to move.

Someone was coming.

I took quick gasps of air, unable to breathe through the panic. My arms and legs thrashed as I fought to tread water. I couldn't make my limbs work properly. I began to sink.

"Shit, are you okay?"

Cameron's voice was like a bright light in the darkness. I grasped on to it, using it like a lifeline to pull myself out of my panic.

He swam up beside me and caught me, keeping me from dipping under the water.

I clutched at his arms. My trembling fingers dug into his skin.

"Just take slow breaths." Cameron stroked the back of my head, sifting his hands through the long, wet strands of hair. "Slow breaths, okay?"

I nodded shakily and tried to do as he said.

"Can you tell me what's wrong?"

"Th-there's someone here," I stuttered out through a tight throat, clinging to him.

The concern on Cameron's face was touching, but it wasn't enough to ease the panic taking hold inside me.

"It's probably just the gardener. Yo, Jerry, come on out," Cameron called.

An older gentleman wearing a sunhat and carrying a pair of hedge clippers appeared between the bushes.

"Yes Mr. Thorne?" the man asked with a cheery tone.

I let out a choked sigh of relief. My racing heart slowed down somewhat. The panic began to subside. My lungs let out a whoosh of air. I began to take slow breaths in and out.

After a few moments, mortification set in.

I couldn't believe I'd let myself get that worked up again. Of course it was just the gardener. It could have even been one of the housekeepers, or Cameron's parents showing up again, or any number of people.

My mind had immediately gone to a break in.

Anger and self-loathing fought for dominance inside me. I hated myself for always overreacting. First that false alarm when I'd hid in the bathroom, and now this.

Was I going to be living in fear forever?

Cameron waved the gardener off. He gathered me close, wrapping his arms around me.

"You alright?" he asked, a concerned expression on his face.

I nodded silently, still shivering from the aftermath of my panic attack.

"Were you scared?"

"It's so stupid," I mumbled. My lungs still burned. I'd almost drowned. "I'm acting like..."

Cameron took my face in his hands.

"Something really scary happened to you. It's okay to still be affected by it."

I didn't meet his eyes, ashamed. "It was ages ago. I should be fine by now."

"It's okay if you're not. Maybe..." He looked hesitant. "Maybe you should see someone about it?"

"Maybe." I didn't think my fears were that bad. Were they? Surely not bad enough I needed to see a therapist. I just got a little scared sometimes. That was all.

A small voice in my head snorted. No big deal, I'd just *almost drowned* is all.

Cameron pressed a gentle peck on my lips, nothing like the passionate kiss I'd interrupted.

"You can always come to me if you're scared or afraid. I want you to know that."

"Thank you."

But even as I said the words, I hated the idea.

All along I'd chafed at Noah's rules. I'd wanted to be on my own, to live my own life.

But maybe my brother had been right. What if I'd been by myself? What if Cameron hadn't been here to save me from freaking out? I might have drowned. Just like I might have passed out from my panic attack that night in the bathroom.

I hated the idea of being so weak. I didn't want to rely on anyone else this way.

But I clearly didn't have these panic attacks under control.

Maybe Noah was right.

I wasn't ready to be on my own.

I was still just a scared little girl inside.

CHAPTER TWENTY-ONE

I had almost forgotten about the plans for dinner, until Cameron reminded me, a nervous expression on his face. I wondered why he was so worried. It was just dinner.

It seemed like months since I'd first met Cameron parents. So much had happened since. Cameron and I had confessed our feelings. We'd had sex for the first time. And second time. And many, many more times after that.

When the evening finally arrived and we walked into the restaurant, I immediately felt self-conscious. Everyone was dressed up in suits or at the very least business casual, along with a handful of cocktail dresses and luxurious evening wear. I wasn't one to splurge when it was technically my brother's money. Even the nicest dress I owned had only cost around thirty dollars.

Cameron wore black skinny jeans with chains hanging from the belt and a tight black t-shirt. His wild, bright red hair stood out in stark contrast to the restrained hairstyles of the other restaurant patrons.

At least he wasn't wearing his usual thick eyeliner.

Cameron's parents waited for us in the foyer. They greeted us with hugs and handshakes, dressed in their perfectly tailored business attire.

The hostess didn't blink an eye at our mismatched group, but it seemed to me everyone stopped in the middle of eating to stare as she led us to a table.

I ducked my head as I hurried to sit, avoiding their gazes. When we were seated I snuck a glance at Cameron, expecting him to feel as out of place as I did.

Instead, his expression was blasé, relaxing into his chair, legs spread out as if he hadn't a care in the world. I supposed someone as self assured as Cameron, a rich and famous rock star, wouldn't care if snooty people looked down on him.

Cameron's parents were perfectly pleasant, despite my initial doubts. His dad wasn't too chatty, but his mom was good at small talk. She peppered me with me questions about school, my art, and my experience in France.

I didn't bring up boarding school. It would only lead to questions about why I'd attended high school somewhere so far away. That was an issue I definitely didn't want to get into with Cameron's parents.

"Nice place," Cameron said after our waitress came to take our drink orders and hand out menus.

Normally I would have thought he was making fun, in his usual obnoxious way, but he sounded genuinely impressed.

"The Masons took us here," Sharon explained. "I fell in love with the salmon. You should try it."

"Sure, sounds great," Cameron said earnestly.

This whole exchange was odd. I side-eyed him.

"Although usually I'm more of a burgers and pizza kind of guy," Cameron quipped.

His parents chuckled politely.

I thought it might have only been me who noticed his relieved grin as they laughed.

The four of us were quiet as we perused the selections. I decided to go with the salmon myself, partly because it did sound good, and partly because I wanted to...

I mused to myself for a moment. What exactly was I trying to do? Make Cameron's mom happy? Make her like me? I didn't know why I cared. I barely knew them.

But there was something about the way Sharon kept throwing pleased, almost ecstatic glances my way. It was disconcerting. I looked to Cameron every once in a while, trying to gauge his mood.

He kept looking between his parents with an almost nervous, wavering smile. Like he was trying hard to keep up the polite conversation. Trying hard to impress them.

"I haven't asked yet," Grant said. "How have things been with you? Music industry treating you well?"

"We're just getting ready to release the new album." Cameron gave his father an eager look. "I think this one's gonna be even bigger than the last. We've been doing so much promo shi—"

He cut himself off as his dad gave him a warning look.

"I mean, we've been doing a lot of promo stuff," he continued weakly.

Grant nodded distantly, as if not really hearing the words. "Good, good. It's important to have a good team behind you."

"You said you had something to talk to me about?" Cameron asked, forcibly changing the conversation.

Sharon cleared her throat and placed both clasped hands on the table.

"As you know, I've been a member of quite a few boards for a few non-profits."

"Right. Save the whales and all that."

"I'm not sure how much attention you've been paying to local politics recently—"

"The answer would be none," he joked.

"I've been approached by some interested parties about running for office," she said matter of factly.

Cameron's brows furrowed. "Like city council or something?"

"No. For mayor."

Cameron's eyes grew wide. "Holy fuck."

"Language," Grant warned.

Cameron slumped back in his seat. "Sorry."

I'd never seen Cameron look so abashed. He never listened to anyone, and he certainly never seemed to care whether his foul-mouth would offend someone.

Cameron was trying so hard to act... well, *good*. Well behaved and well mannered. I had no idea he even cared about that. Cameron was the type to do whatever he felt like and say fuck it to anyone who complained.

"I guess I should say congratulations, Mom." He still looked taken aback. "This is a pretty big deal."

Sharon looked at her husband. He nodded. She turned to Cameron.

"We need to talk about what this means for us. For our family. For you."

Cameron froze. He slowly glanced between his parents.

"Right." He stretched out in his seat, running a hand through his hair in a fake-casual motion. "I get it." He forced a grin. "Same deal as always?"

"We'll obviously need to work through the details, but I don't think you'll have a problem with business as usual?" His mother seemed oblivious to the strained tone in Cameron's voice.

"It's cool." He gave her a wavering smile. "I know the drill."

"Wonderful," Sharon said blithely.

I was befuddled at the exchange taking place in front of me. There were undercurrents to this conversation that I was clearly not privy to. The corners of Cameron's lip threatened to twitch downward into a frown as he tried to keep the pleasant smile plastered on his face. His parents didn't notice the struggle.

I was contemplating what to say when the waitress arrived with our food.

"Congratulations," I told Sharon as we made small talk over the food. "This must be very exciting for you."

She flashed me a bright smile. "It is exciting. There are lots of challenges to consider, of course. I'm still not sure what's going to happen, but the next few months are certainly going to be interesting."

"More like years, if you go through with it," Cameron murmured low enough so only I could hear.

For all that he had tried to seem happy for his mom, the words only came out sounding oddly sad.

When the waitress came and placed the bill on the table, Grant reached for it. Cameron snatched it up before he could take it.

"I've got this."

"Cam, honey," Sharon started.

"I'm a big boy," he threw out with a bright smile. It was almost too bright. "You don't need to take care of me."

Grant tilted his head at Cameron, a curious frown on his face. The motion reminded me of all the times Cameron had given me the same expression. As if he wanted to say something, but was thinking better of it.

I could sense a standoff about to happen.

"Why don't we split it?" I jumped in.

"That's a fine idea," Grant said with a nod to me.

I reached into my messenger bag to get out my wallet. Cameron pushed it away and shook his head.

"I've got yours."

I began to protest.

"You want to know my net worth?" he interrupted with a crooked grin.

"Fine," I gave in. "Pizza's on me next time."

We shared a quick smile.

"Lily, I would love to take you out sometime soon," Sharon said as we left the table. "A girls-only day, you and me. What do you say?"

That desperation was back again.

"Sure," I said hesitantly, flicking a glance to Cameron. I wondered if I should have asked him if it was okay first. He seemed oddly chagrinned.

"Wonderful!" The delight in Sharon's voice was impossible to mistake. "Let's exchange numbers and I'll give you a call."

It was weird entering my phone number into Cameron's mom's phone, like we were new besties.

We'd taken a taxi to the restaurant, so Cameron's parents drove us back to the mansion. His mom and I kept up the small talk, me discussing my classes, and her talking about the various charities she had worked with.

After dropping us off, Cameron's dad gave me a warm handshake. His mom gave me another tight squeeze. Her flowery perfume filled my nostrils again. This time, I held onto her a few moments too long. She didn't seem to mind. She just gave me a kind smile as they climbed into the car and drove away.

"Fuck."

That was all Cameron said as soon as they were out of sight.

"Is something wrong?" I asked.

He exhaled loudly. "No. It's fine."

He mouth was pressed in a firm line, no trace of the bright smile he'd worn in front of his parents.

"You seemed happy for your mom back there," I said hesitantly. "Are you not?"

"It's just the same as always."

"What do you mean?"

"Nothing. I'm gonna go workout."

He left before I could say anything else, leaving me to wonder.

Exactly what kind of relationship did Cameron have with his parents?

CHAPTER TWENTY-TWO

Cameron didn't sleep in my bed that evening. He'd made his excuses, saying he had to be out late, working in the recording studio, and didn't want to wake me when he got in.

It had been a long, lonely night.

I had intended to track him down the next day after my classes. I wanted to talk about that dinner. There had been something odd about the entire evening. Something off with Cameron's behavior around his parents.

Sharon and Grant were certainly different from how I'd imagined them. They weren't terrible monsters at all. They seemed to genuinely love their son. And Cameron clearly loved them.

He also clearly lived for their approval.

I wondered why that was. Nothing in their words or actions had led me to believe they disapproved of Cameron. He had probably been quite the wild child growing up, but whatever antics he had gotten up to hadn't created a strained relationship.

Except for that odd tension when Sharon talked about getting into politics.

She said they would need to discuss what that would mean for their family.

When I stepped into the mansion foyer, backpack loaded with heavy-as-brick textbooks, my ears were immediately assaulted with the deep, bone-shaking tones of a bass guitar.

I followed the noise up the stairs and down a hallway to a closed door. I hesitated before knocking. I didn't know which room was Cameron's bedroom, but I knew it was on the second floor. I still hadn't been in it yet.

"Cameron?" I called through the door hesitantly.

No answer.

The music was loud enough that Cameron wouldn't have been able to hear me call through the door. The music was also loud enough that I couldn't imagine being able to get any studying done while Cameron kept it up.

I had been meaning to speak with him anyway. I might as well use the excuse that his music was bothering me. Otherwise, I'd have to admit that I was worried about him. Worried about whether or not he was okay.

I was sure the last thing Cameron wanted was for me to worry about him.

I forced myself to overcome my hesitation and decided to enter the room anyway. I pushed the door open a crack.

It was Cameron's bedroom. Or, there was a bed at the far end of the room. But that was the only piece of furniture that lead me to believe Cameron might sleep in there.

Instead, the place looked like it could have been a music store. A very disorganized music store.

Half a dozen guitars in their stands and two drum sets were scattered throughout the room. A small piano was situated in the corner across from his bed. Music sheets were scattered across every surface. Amps were stacked on top of one another with wires crisscrossing the floor.

The place was a mess. No wonder Cameron didn't want me to see it.

Cameron stood in the middle of the room, facing away from me. He held his bass guitar in both hands, wailing away at the strings. Although bass was part of the rhythm section, it sounded like Cameron was shredding. I didn't even know that was possible.

I'd rarely heard bass guitar solos before, but this one was impressive. Even with his back turned, the speed with which his fingers flew across the strings left me breathless.

Cameron was breathless as well, his vigorous playing having taken its toll. His chest was heaving, his shoulders tense, his hair slightly damp with sweat. I wondered how long he'd been playing. It might have been for hours.

I waited until he was done, not wanting to interrupt. When the pounding beat subsided I knocked softly on the door jam.

Cameron turned to me with an inquisitive look.

His skin was pale, with dark bruises under his eyes. His eyes were glassy and almost unfocused. When he pushed away the strands of hair that stuck to his cheeks, his hands trembled. It looked like he hadn't slept in days.

"Sorry." His voice was dull and full of exhaustion. "Was the noise bothering you?"

That was going to be my excuse, but now that I got a good look at Cameron, I thought better of it.

"Are you okay?" I asked instead.

"Why wouldn't I be?" he replied. He sounded as if speaking was a monumental effort.

"How long have you been playing?" I asked.

"I dunno. What time is it?"

"Past dinner time."

"Oh." He looked down at the bass guitar in his hands. His fingers clenched around the fret board. "All day, I guess."

"You look tired. Why don't we go get something to eat?" I offered.

"Not hungry."

"Not even for pineapple pizza?"

He moved to put the bass guitar back on its stand.

"Did you need something?" he asked, ignoring my pizza comment.

I paused, contemplating. I didn't want to pry, but Cameron was upset. I decided to take the roundabout way.

"Your mom asked if I wanted to do a spa day with her."

Cameron visibly flinched. There it was. I knew his mood had something to do with his parents.

"I told her I would have to check my schedule. I didn't want to agree without asking you first."

"Why? It's not like you need my permission."

My fingers twisted in the hem of my shirt. "I just met your mom. Isn't it weird for her to want to hang out with a perfect stranger?"

"You're not a stranger. You're my—" Cameron lifted his fingers in air quotes, "—lady friend."

I stilled. "She knows we're...?"

I supposed that explained why she wanted to get to know me.

"She's overjoyed, no doubt." Cameron lifted his eyes to the ceiling and exhaled a deep breath. "After all, you're perfect."

I frowned, confused. "Perfect?"

"Respectable," he clarified.

I nearly laughed. "I'm an orphan who grew up in foster care. I don't have a job because I'm mooching off my brother. I'm taking a college degree that will leave me almost no real employable skills."

"You're a polite, educated, driven young woman. Not to mention beautiful and classy as hell."

Classy? I'd never thought of myself that way. I always considered myself the artsy dreamer type.

"I suppose growing up in a fancy boarding school with snobby mean girls will do that to a person."

"I'm surprised she hasn't dragged us to the altar already."

I flushed. My heart jumped in my chest at those words. "Is that really what she's thinking?"

"I dunno. Maybe. I just know that with this whole politics thing, it's going to get complicated."

His expression grew downcast again.

"You sounded happy for your mom at dinner," I said.

"I am." He paused. "Or, I know that I should be happy for her. But things are going to go back to the way they were before."

"Before?" I jumped on the last word, hoping to finally get some understanding. "What were things like before?"

"Shitty," Cameron said bluntly. He turned away from me and flopped down on the edge of the bed. He leaned forward and rested his elbows on his knees. "Whatever. It's fine. You don't want to hear my sob story."

I sat down on the bed next to him, leaving some space between us, not wanting to crowd him.

"You told me your parents moved out when you were sixteen. That they were always traveling for business. When they first showed up, you mentioned that you didn't talk to them much."

Cameron looked at me in surprise. "You remember all that?"

"I've been piecing things together," I admitted. "I'd begun to think your parents were these horribly distant, cold, parental figures. But I met them and now... I don't know what to think."

"They're not terrible," Cameron said. "I love my parents."

"I sense a *but* in there somewhere."

He let out a deep breath, tilting his head back and closing his eyes.

"My parents wished they'd never had me."

CHAPTER TWENTY-THREE

I almost thought I'd heard wrong. How could Cameron think his parents didn't want him?

"They never approved of me," he continued, ignoring my shock. "I was an embarrassment."

"I'm sure they don't think of you that way," I protested.

"They do."

Cameron's eyes were flat and dull. He wasn't upset. He spoke as if he were reciting facts.

"You already know half the story. My father was in business. All high powered and shit. My mother was involved in all these well known charities. They were invited to fancy events full of powerful people. And they in turn invited those powerful people to our home."

"What's wrong with that?"

"I was never allowed to show my face," he said bluntly. "I had to stay in my room. They didn't want me having dinner with their important guests." He let out a rueful laugh. "Didn't want me to embarrass them."

My heart clenched in my chest. "I'm sure that's not true."

"I don't think people even know they have a son," he said quietly. "My mom would get honored with some society award and they'd tell me not to attend the event. When interviewers asked my dad about his family, he never once mention having kids."

I scooted closer until my thighs pressed against his. I took his hand in mine not saying anything, just listening.

"I can't blame them," he said with a rueful laugh. "I was a wild child, with my crazy hair colors, always dressing in black like some emo-goth kid, skipping class to play in shitty bands with my friends. I was never going to be the clean cut, Ivy League prep school son they always wanted. I was a disappointment."

"I can't believe that." I squeezed his hand. "I saw the way you were around your parents. You're a wonderful son."

"I thought things had been getting better. Dad's retired. Mom cut back on her charity work. Fewer fancy events and parties and ceremonies. They actually didn't mind being seen with me in public every once in a while."

"I'm sure it's all a misunderstanding. They took us both out to dinner."

"When my mom said we needed to talk about what this all meant for our family, that's what she was talking about. She's going to be in the public eye. People are going to want to know all about her." He let out a derisive snort and lowered his head to his chest, looking down at his lap. "We need to go back to pretending I don't exist."

I took his chin in my hands and guided his head up until we were face to face. The pain I saw in those deep blue eyes made my heart ache.

"I saw the way your parents look at you. I can't believe they're ashamed of you. They love you. "

"They love their careers more." Cameron placed on hand over mine. "That's why they like you so much. They probably think you're going to be a good influence on me. Maybe they think you can make me respectable."

"There's nothing wrong with the way you are now."

"They think there is. That's why I'm going back to being their dirty little secret." He gave me a sad smile. "They've never been to one of my shows. Not when I played in shitty garage bands, and not when we hit it big. I don't think they've ever actually seen me play bass guitar."

I swallowed past the lump in my throat. I knew what it felt like to be rejected by a parent. After my mom took off, I always wondered what I'd done wrong to make her leave.

"Whatever. It's fine. I'm used to it."

Cameron heaved himself off the bed and paced over to his bass guitar, running his fingers over the strings.

"I think it's about time I threw another house party," he said out of nowhere. "It's been a while." His turned to me with a slightly wicked grin and rubbed his hands together. "I've got just the game to play, too. It'll be fucking awesome."

"Cameron..." I began hesitantly.

"I've got to go start planning. Getting the guest list in order. There's a couple guys who trashed the place last time. I need to keep them out."

I knew it was just a deflection. But if Cameron didn't want to talk about his parents any more, I wouldn't make him.

I just couldn't believe the people I'd met a few days ago could be the same people who had kept their son a secret. Was Cameron really an embarrassment to them? Had they really not told their friends and colleagues they had a son? And was that why they've moved out when they did? So they could continue living their lives as if their son didn't exist?

I couldn't imagine how lonely of a life that must have been for him growing up. I'd always had my big brother by my side.

It seemed that Cameron had no one.

"Normally I don't mind a little mess but these guys totally destroyed the bathroom on this floor," he continued. "Pipes busted and everything. No more parties for them. They're banned for life."

I came up behind Cameron and wrapped my arms around his waist, squeezing. He stopped talking.

I laid my cheek on his strong back. "I'm sorry."

He placed his hands over mine, lacing our fingers. "Or maybe we can throw a party of our own." His voice turned sly as he swung me around to face him. "A private party. Just the two of us."

I raised an eyebrow. Another deflection. I didn't call him on it. "And would we also play games at this private party?"

He smirked. "I can think of a hundred different games I'd like to play with you."

My heartbeat sped up at the wicked glint in his eyes. "Tell me one."

"Go Fish."

"That's a kid's game."

He gave me that familiar carnal grin. "Not the way I play it."

"Why am I not surprised you managed to take a game for five year olds and turn it dirty."

Cameron cupped my ass, caressing and kneading. "Angel, there's no shortage of innocent things I've made dirty."

"And I suppose I'm one of them?"

"Not yet." He lowered his head and murmured against my lips. "I'm not even close to being done corrupting you."

My cheeks flushed, arousal already coursing through me. "I think you've been doing a pretty good job of it so far."

He chuckled darkly. "I haven't even broken out the toys yet."

Toys? My heart hammered against my ribcage. "I thought you were joking about that."

"Not in the slightest."

"Dare I even ask what kind of toys?"

Cameron made a deep, almost purring sound in his chest. "It's so much better if I show you."

My inner muscles clenched at the heat in his voice.

He caressed my ass one last time before giving it a light spank. Heat pooled between my thighs at the slight sting.

"Why don't you wait here?" he suggested. "I just need to collect a few things."

There was an evil glint in his eyes.

I couldn't help remembering the talk about kinks I'd had with him. I hadn't been able to think of anything dirtier than handcuffs and spanking.

If this was what it took to get his mind off his parents, I was more than willing to go along with it.

I shivered, wondering just what exactly he had planned for me.

CHAPTER TWENTY-FOUR

Cameron went into a large walk in closet adjacent to his bedroom.

I sat on the edge of his bed, waiting. Nervous anticipation flowed through my veins. My ears were straining to listen for the sound of Cameron rummaging around.

It felt like I'd been waiting forever. My fingers clenched and unclenched in the bedsheets. Was making me wait part of his plan?

Finally, I heard him stop rummaging. My heart pounded wildly in my chest. When he walked out of the closest, I was greeted with his wicked grin.

I looked to see what he was carrying, wanting to know what *toys* he'd collected. He held a heavy canvas bag, completely opaque, preventing me from guessing.

He noticed my stare and chuckled darkly. "You'll find out what I have in store for you soon enough." His eyes turned heated. "Lie back on the bed."

My toes curled at that demanding tone. I scooted to the headboard and lay down. I propped myself up on my elbows so I could see what he was doing.

Cameron tossed the bag on the bed and followed it. He knelt above me, body looming over mine.

"Are you going to do everything I say, Angel?"

I nodded silently.

"Good girl."

I moaned as he placed sucking kisses on my neck. His hands skimmed over my sides and stomach, caressing my skin. He lifted up my shirt and tossed it over my head. He deftly unsnapped my bra. It fell to the bed, leaving me topless.

"If I ask what you're going to do, would you tell me?" I asked, my voice wavering.

"I'm going to make you come more times than you've ever come in your life."

"You sure that's possible?" My heartbeat raced. "You've already set the bar pretty high."

He flashed me a carnal smirk, not saying anything. He dug into the bag and pulled out something long and black. I recognized the item. Thick straps with buckles on one end. Bondage restraints.

I inhaled sharply.

Cameron looked concerned. "We don't have to use them if you don't want to."

A small part of me was reminded of the break in. Of when they tied me up.

But as I examined that memory, I realized it didn't affect me as much as I thought it might. This was completely different. I trusted Cameron.

"I want to," I told him.

He examined me closely. He nodded.

"Put your arms over your head."

I did so. The demanding tone sent a fresh flood of heat between my legs. I was already getting wet. I pressed my thighs together.

"I didn't know you were into BDSM," I said, trying to keep my voice steady.

"I'm not, really." He took each wrist in his hands and gently looped them through the straps. "This is just to keep you from squirming away."

I swallowed hard as he fastened each strap to the headboard. My arms were now tied above my head. I tugged experimentally. The restraints were solid. I wouldn't be able to get out of it if I tried.

That was as exhilarating as it was terrifying. Cameron could do whatever he wanted to me now. The thought nearly had me whimpering.

"And why would I want to get away?" I asked.

"You'll see." His eyes flashed with wicked amusement. "If you really want to me to stop, say red."

I frowned, confused. "Red?"

"Like stoplights. Red for stop. Yellow for slow down. Green for go." Cameron placed a soft kiss on my lips. "Let me know where you're at, okay? Don't feel bad if you need to say red."

"Why can't I just say stop?"

"Because pretty soon you're going to be shouting out a lot of things, Angel. I need to be sure you really mean them."

Despite my arousal, I couldn't help but feel slightly nervous. This was all so new to me. Was I ready for this, whatever *this* was?

Cameron must have sensed my nerves.

"I told you, I'm not into BDSM. None of that sado-masochism stuff. This is all for you."

"Why won't you tell me what you're going to do to me?"

"It's much more fun if you experience it yourself first." Cameron pulled something else out of the bag. A black blindfold. "I'm going to put this over your eyes, okay?"

I hesitated before nodding.

The blindfold was soft and silky against my eyes. It blocked out all light.

"Is this the part where you torture me with ice cubes or feathers or something?"

"Nothing so cliché." Cameron almost sounded offended.

He shuffled down to the edge of the bed, between my legs. He ran his hands up my calves, then up between my thighs. He followed his fingers with a trail of kisses.

The touch of his lips against my sensitive skin had me reeling. My inner muscles throbbed. He'd barely done anything and my panties were almost soaked. My body always responded so readily to him.

Cameron spread my legs open and pushed my skirt up to my waist. I held my breath as he moved closer. I felt the hot air of his breath wash over me as he exhaled.

He pulled down my panties, tossing them away. He licked a line between the valley of my legs, sucking at my clit. I moaned along with him.

"Fuck Angel, you always taste so fucking good."

Maybe this was what Cameron had planned. Tying me up and eating me out until I was satiated and exhausted.

Then I heard him rummage around in the bag again. He pulled something out. I felt something hard and cool press against my core.

"You ready, Angel?" he teased.

Before I could respond, my world exploded in a symphony of sensation. I gasped sharply, my every nerve ending on fire, pleasure surging through me. It centered between my legs and rushed outwards, down my legs and up my arms, to the very tips of my fingers and toes.

"Oh fuck fuck fuck!" I shrieked, the words sounding strangled. I thrashed back and forth on the bed, hips bucking and rolling.

The sensations were so intense, half pleasure, half pain. I didn't know if I was trying to get away or move closer. A distant part of my mind thought Cameron had been right to tie me down. I might have flailed myself off the bed otherwise.

For long moments I had no idea what was causing the sensation, only knowing that it was mind blowing as hell. I'd never felt anything this intensely before.

I can't say I got used to the sensation, but after several minutes I was finally able to think through the haze of pleasure. A light buzzing sound floated to my ears, and I registered the slight vibrations against my clit and lower lips.

"Is— that—" I gasped.

When Cameron spoke, I could hear the smirk in his voice. "Magic Hitachi Wand."

The buzzing shot up in volume. I let out a choked breath. Cameron must have turned up the intensity. The vibrations got stronger. I was sent higher and higher as new waves of pleasure crashed through me. I hit my peak, orgasming with a high-pitched moan.

But unlike other times, when Cameron's touch abated after my orgasm, he didn't stop. He kept the vibrator pressed against my clit, rubbing in small circles.

"Cameron— I can't—" My fingers and toes flexed unconsciously, as if reaching for something just out of my grasp.

"Say the word and I'll stop."

Red.

The heat inside me was nearly scorching. I opened my mouth to say it, but another spark of pleasure hit me. I groaned as I came again, falling apart into pieces, every part of assaulted with sensations.

I panted and gasped as I recovered. I was almost starting to get accustomed to the vibrations when they increased again. Pleasure slammed through me like a wrecking ball.

"Fuck," I choked out as I fell over the edge again. My eyes rolled back into my head as I nearly passed out.

On and on it continued. It was almost too much, the pleasure on the brink of turning into pain. I cursed and flailed and cried out. I came so many times I lost count. I'm sure that was Cameron's intention.

My lungs were burning. I was out of breath. My muscles ached. And yet still, the pleasure soared through me. One more spike of heat struck me to my core and I gasped out.

"Red!"

The buzzing immediately stopped. I collapsed back on the bed, limbs limp, energy spent. I was covered in sweat, body slick and palms clammy.

I panted heavily through a hoarse throat. I didn't know what words I'd been screaming, but I'd been doing it loudly.

Cameron's warm body came to rest at my side. He carefully unbuckled the straps and lifted my wrists free. He pressed soft kisses to each one. He pulled the blindfold off. I blinked blearily at the too-bright lights.

"So how many was that?" Cameron teased. He ran his hands up and down my sides. It sent shivers running through my body. Every inch of me was over-sensitized.

"Lost... count..." I murmured through heaving breaths.

I was soaking wet, my thighs sticky and slick. I was sure I'd made a mess of the bedsheets. I couldn't bring myself to care.

Cameron gave me a long, slow kiss. I returned it wearily. His hip molded against mine. I felt his hardness through the rough scratch of his jeans.

I shifted to press against him, cupping him through the thick material.

He shook his head and pushed my hand away.

"You don't want to...?" I trailed off.

"This was all for you," he murmured against my lips.

"Thank you," I said.

"No need to thank me. Getting to watch you squirm and writhe on the bed, blissed out in pleasure? It was beyond hot."

As we snuggled together, me catching my breath and Cameron caressing every inch of my skin, I began to formulate my own naughty plan.

Cameron wasn't the only one who could play games.

CHAPTER TWENTY-FIVE

"It was crazy hard trying to coordinate everyone's schedules," Jen told me over the phone one night. She had finally set a date for my welcome home party.

"Who's everyone?"

I had assumed it would be Jen, my brother's band, and me. I didn't know anyone else. I was friendly enough with my classmates, but I wouldn't have called them friends.

Cameron was the closest thing to a friend I had.

"That's sad," Jen said when I told her as much. "You need to get to know more people. That's why I've invited everyone."

"Again, I have to ask, who is everyone?"

"The guys, obviously, and Ian's girlfriend and her sister. And my friends and their boyfriends. And those boyfriend's friends, and their girlfriends. And my one friend's boyfriend's childhood friend and maybe some of her friends. That's all."

"Just how many people are going to be at this party?"

"Enough to have an awesome time."

I could hear her grin through the phone. It was almost enough to make me nervous. Was this going to get as wild as Cameron's parties? Still, I was excited and couldn't wait.

On the evening of the party, Cameron called us a taxi.

"So we can get wasted and not worry about driving home," he said.

"I've never been wasted in my life," I reminded him.

"No time like the present." He gave me a saucy wink.

"Can we talk about—" I hesitated to bring it up, but I had to make sure Cameron and I were on the same page, "—about how we're going to act at the party?"

His brow furrowed. "What do you mean?"

"When we're together," I clarified.

"Oh." His lips turned down into a frown. "You mean you want to make sure we only act like friends and not a couple. Right?"

I hated hearing that note of hurt in his voice. But no one knew about the two of us yet. And it had to stay that way. At least for now.

"I'm sorry," I said honestly. "It's not like I want to keep us a secret or anything."

"Except that's exactly what you want to do." The corners of his mouth twitched, threatened to curve down. He gave me a rueful smile instead. "I get it. No worries."

"I just don't want Noah—"

"I said it's cool," he interrupted. Cameron wrapped an arm around my waist and tugged me to his side. "It'll be our little secret for now."

I wanted to feel relief, but my heart sank instead. Those were the same words Cameron used when he talked about his parents. About how they didn't want anyone to know about him.

But this was a completely different situation. I wasn't embarrassed of Cameron. This was for his own good. Until I could figure out a way to tell Noah about us... until I could figure out a way to make sure Noah didn't freak out...

I mused on that thought on the drive to the party. Cameron held my hand in the backseat of the taxi, brushing his thumb against the back of my hand. That small touch was a comfort. Maybe Cameron really wasn't upset.

I hoped.

When we arrived at the venue, I saw Jen had rented out the intimate back room of a tiny venue just for the group of us. It would have fit fifty comfortably. As it was, about half that number jumped out to surprise me with streamers, banners, and whistleblowers the moment I walked in.

"Welcome home!" the group cheered.

"You're only supposed to jump out when it's a surprise party," I said with a laugh.

"But it's more fun this way." Cameron smirked at my side, keeping a few feet between us. He must have known what they had planned.

With the floor covered with confetti and streamers, Noah and Jen immediately pulled me into a dual hug.

"Thank you for putting this whole thing together," I told her.

"I'm sorry it took this long," Jen said. "But, well..." she gestured to the crowd behind her. "As you can see, lots of schedules to work around."

"Let me guess," I said, taking in the greater than normal amount of black leather, black mesh, black eyeliner, and black nail polish. "They're all in rock bands?"

"Not *all* of them," Jen stressed. "Half are significant others or friends."

I took a head count, trying to see if I recognized anyone. One guy with blond waves falling over his forehead and talking very loudly looked vaguely familiar, but the rest were all unknowns to me.

"I want to see August and the twins," I said. "It's been way too long." I hadn't seen them when I scanned the room.

"Over there." Jen pointed behind me.

I turned to find the three of them coming out of a side door. The twins held a chocolate cake with a lit sparkler between their hands. August held a dark purple gift bag, complete with tissue paper and bow.

"Welcome home, Lily." August's low tones were as familiar as the soft look in his ice blue eyes.

"You better eat this now or I'm going to eat it for you." One of the twins lifted the cake to his face and mimed taking a huge bite.

August placed the bag in my hands. "I hope you like it."

I gingerly pushed away the tissue paper to uncover the gift.

Inside was a picture frame with a photo of all of us, taken backstage at the very last concert I'd been to before moving away.

The guys all looked so much younger, their youthful energy apparent even through the camera's lens. They were softer and boyish, with punk and emo haircuts. I was young, too, and much shorter. I hadn't hit my growth spurt yet.

August's hand was on my shoulder. Noah had me tugged against his side. Damon and Ian were both making faces behind my back. Cameron was giving me bunny ears.

My heart melted a little, both at the memory and at the gesture.

"You guys..." Tears sprang to the back of my eyes.

"Aw, is little Lily Hart getting sappy on us?" the other twin teased. "What happened to our bad ass troublemaker?"

"I was never a troublemaker," I retorted with a teary laugh. "That was all you two."

"Two?" Cameron sounded affronted. "Am I not included?"

"Troublemaker is too light a word for what you got up to," August said, amused.

"Remember that time Cam jumped on an amp in the middle of the show and knocked it off the stage and nearly killed a fan?" One of the twins smacked Cameron in the stomach.

"Remember that time Damon was a dick?" Cameron grinned, smacking him back.

I was a bit startled Cameron had called one of the twins by their first name. Normally Damon and Ian went by the portmanteau *Damian*. Last time I'd seen them, the twins loved to plays tricks on people and pretend they were the same person.

Before I had time to ask what had changed, a young woman came up behind the other twin and took his hands in hers. She was the same girl I'd seen at Cameron's party.

"It's lovely to meet you, Lily." She was pretty, with long dark hair, slightly messed up as it fell down her back. Her big brown eyes were earnest as they met mine. "I'm Hope, Ian's girlfriend."

Ian pulled her close to his side and pressed a kiss to the side of her forehead. She smiled up at him, a sappy look on her face.

"Get a fucking room," Damon mumbled under his breath. Ian ignored him.

Ah. This was the same tension we'd seen at the party. Was that why Ian and Damon were no longer playing up the twin thing? I supposed it would be hard to continue tricking people if one of them always had his girlfriend by his side.

"The DJ is here," Hope told Jen. "He wants to know where to set up."

"I'll show him," Damon said, stalking off.

The group of us followed him with our eyes silently.

"He still doesn't like me." Hope's wide brown eyes turned sad like a kicked puppy.

"He'll get over it," Cameron said. He turned to me with a mad grin. "Let's get this party started, shall we?"

"We've got some food and drinks catered, and the DJ should start playing soon," Jen said.

With those words, a pounding beat began vibrating the walls. Wait staff brought out platters of pub food, nachos and fries and onion rings, along with the all important alcohol.

Noah and Jen took me by the arms and led me around the room, making introductions. Cameron gave me a small smile and wandered off, leaving me to my brother and his girlfriend. I mourned the loss of him at my side, but it would have been too suspicious if we spent the entire party glued to each other's hips.

Jen eagerly introduced me to her friends, a cute girl with a shy smile and a total knock-out with an aristocratic air about her.

Aristocratic, until she began speaking a mile a minute.

"It's so good to meet you, Lily! I've been a fan of your brother's band for years and everyone always wondered where you'd gone." The girl chatted on, oblivious to Noah's dark look. "It's so cool that you're back after all this time, you must be so happy to be with your brother again."

The quiet girl clapped a hand over her friend's mouth. "Natalie means welcome home."

"Thank you," I replied, nonplussed.

"Natalie and Ivy were my roommates before they moved in with their boyfriends," Jen explained. "They're both dating members of Feral Silence. Those guys are here, too."

More rock stars. It seemed I would live my life surrounded by a never-ending parade of them.

"I've heard some of their stuff. I thought they were your rival band?" I asked my brother.

"That's what the media calls it," Jen said. "They're all good friends, though."

"Tell that to August," Noah snorted. "He's still pissed Kell stole his album concept."

Sure enough, when I searched the room for August, he was frowning in the direction of the loud wavy-haired blond guy. It was the most negative expression I'd ever seen on August's face. He was normally so cool and unflappable.

"Just keep them away from each other and it'll be fine," Jen said.

"Or," Cameron came up behind Noah and threw his arms around

his neck, "We pit them both against each other in a death match and see who wins."

Noah jabbed his elbow into Cameron's side. Cameron held on with a grin. Noah looked to the heavens, as if praying for patience.

"Have you made the rounds yet?" Cameron asked. "I'm putting together a game of—"

"Don't you dare say Strip Go Fish," Noah warned. "It's bad enough when Jen takes part. No way is Lily playing, too."

"There really is a Strip Go Fish?" I blurted out. "I thought you were just joking about that."

"Why were you telling my sister about your sick games?" Noah asked.

I froze, panic hitting me. I didn't want Noah knowing about the kind of things Cameron and I talked about. I didn't even want Noah to know Cameron and I talked at all. The less Noah knew about how close Cameron and I were, the better.

But Cameron didn't seem to care.

"I can talk to Lily about whatever the hell I want," Cameron said, a stubborn expression crossing his face.

"I asked Cameron about what other kinds of games he plays at his parties," I said in a rush. "Like that scavenger hunt game. I was curious." I forcibly turned my attention to the man who I was pretending was not my boyfriend. "What game have you planned this time?"

Cameron eyed me, no doubt sensing my rising panic. "Kell wants to play a drinking game."

Jen's eyes lit up. "Is it *Never Have I Ever*? I've heard a lot about Feral Silence drinking games. I'm in."

"Count me out," Noah said. "I'll just watch and make sure the rest of you don't end up in a ditch somewhere by the end of the night."

Jen gave Noah a soft smile and squeezed his hand. If it hadn't been my own brother, I would have said he almost blushed.

"You in, Lily?" Cameron asked.

"How do you play?" I asked.

"We go around the circle saying something we've never done," Cameron explained. "If you have, you take a shot."

Take a shot. I'd never even been drunk before. And now I was supposed to do multiple shots in one sitting.

A small jolt of excitement went through me. If I was ever going to start drinking, at an intimate party full of family and friends was the place to do it.

"I don't know if I want you playing that game," Noah said.

I punched him lightly in the shoulder. "Remember that conversation we had? About overprotectiveness and letting me run my own life?"

"I just don't want you dying of alcohol poisoning."

"Is that likely, in a game of *Never Have I Ever?*"

"Depends," Cameron said with a grin. "If you've lived an exciting life, you'll get tanked."

"I'll probably stay stone cold sober, then."

"We'll be sure to get a few drinks into you by the end of the night," Cameron promised. "It's no fair if you don't get to drink at your own party."

"No getting my sister drunk," Noah warned.

"Don't worry," Cameron said. "I'm mostly in this to team up with August against Kell." He took my hand and tugged me along to a table near the back.

Jen and Noah followed. Noah took a seat and pulled Jen into his lap.

"Am I supposed to play the whole game this way?" she teased.

He tugged her closer and whispered in her ear. She blushed a thousand shades of red, but stayed perched on his knees.

August was already at the table, along with the blond, Kell I assumed, and a pretty girl with almond-shaped eyes. We almost looked similar, if her auburn hair showing black at the roots was any indication.

"Guys, this is Lily, Noah's sister," Jen introduced. "Lily, this is Emily."

Emily gave me a bright smile from across the table. "Nice to meet you."

"And this is—"

"I need no introduction," Kell declared. He stood from the table, hopping up on the bench-style seat. He thrust his chest out proudly. "I'm sure this lovely young lady already knows who I am."

"Emily's boyfriend?" I guessed playfully.

He threw his head back with a wince. "Fuck, she wounds me. I've been wounded, Emily. I don't think my ego can take this."

"Your ego's taken worse and yet, still it rages on." The girl yanked on his shirt, pulling him back down into his seat. "Sorry about this one," she told me. "He's had a few too many red bull and vodkas."

"Shit, that's the last thing he needs," Cameron said. "He's a miniature tornado to begin with. Don't get him high on caffeine."

"It's not the caffeine he needs to worry about." August's eyes were daggers, skewering Kell. It was odd, seeing such an expression on the drummer's face. He must have been really upset. I'd never seen August lose his cool at anyone.

The lead singer of Feral Silence returned the look with an evil smirk. "You still think you can drink me under the table?" he taunted.

"You're going to be hurting tomorrow, if I have anything to say about it."

"Oh really? Which one of us has the reputation for being a cheap drunk?"

"August might be in trouble," I said. "I've heard Kell Pierce can hold his liquor."

The blond turned from August to me in the blink of an eye. He hopped up on his seat again, a giddy expression on his face.

"You do know who I am!" Kell looked down at his girlfriend from his stance on top of the bench. "I told you everyone knows who I am. I'm a household name."

"Sit," Emily said with the grace and patience of a saint.

Kell obeyed and sat back down, looking more than pleased with himself.

"Is this it?" Emily asked, glancing around the table. "Only seven people?"

"Six," Noah said. "I'm not playing."

Kell made a face. "You're never any fun, Hart."

My brother smirked and ran a hand up Jen's thigh. She squeaked. "I get up to more fun than you can imagine, Pierce."

A sly grin crossed the blond's face. "Join the game and we'll see."

"Let's get started," Jen interrupted before Noah could retort, or feel her up any further.

Emily pulled a pen from her purse and put it in the middle of the table before spinning it. The tip landed on Jen.

"Looks like Jen goes first," she said. "We'll go clockwise from her."

Jen played with the shot glass in her hand, looking thoughtful. She nodded to herself and spoke with a satisfied expression.

"Never have I ever had sex in the backseat of a car."

Kell, Emily, and August all took drinks.

Cameron looked to Noah in surprise. "You and Jen never...?"

"Long legs," Noah grunted.

"Where there's a will, there's a way." Cameron grinned.

I shifted uncomfortably, not liking to think about either my brother or Cameron's sex lives.

Kell jumped in, although he was sitting almost across from Jen.

"Never have I ever had sex in the backseat of a *police* car." He grinned and knocked back a shot.

Emily elbowed him, her face red. "Wait your turn." She took her own flustered sip.

I frowned. "Can you drink on your own turn?"

"When you're Kell, it's practically the point of the game," Cameron said.

"And are all the questions supposed to be about sex?"

"They don't have to be," Kell replied with a mad grin. "But where's the fun in that?"

"It's your turn August," Jen said.

"Never have I ever been a complete dickface and stolen another artist's album concept."

August's voice was cool and deadpan, but his laser stare was enough to burn a hole straight through Kell's chest.

The blond threw his hands up in surrender.

"Blame Jayce. He's the one who wanted to go all artsy and meaningful and shit. I would have been perfectly happy singing about biting the heads off bats for another album or two."

"Is that really what you sing about?" I asked.

"No." Cameron smirked. "This guy likes to think he's a hardcore metalhead, but deep down inside he's just some soft-core indie hipster."

Kell squawked. "I object to that statement!"

"I've heard your solo work." August looked his nose down at Kell. "Acoustic indie shit."

"Only some of it," he complained.

"Oh no," Emily groaned. "Are we getting into the *who's-more-hard-rock* argument again?"

I spoke up. "From what I've heard, both bands sound kind of the same."

The entire table went silent for a moment, before chaos broke out.

"You take that back!" Kell pointed an accusing finger at me.

"My work is leagues beyond what this one is capable of." August tried to sound unruffled, but I could see his eyebrow twitching.

"We're never going to hear the end of this," Jen moaned.

"It's Lily's turn!" Cameron declared loudly. He pounded his glass on the table, shaking it. "Shut up and let her go."

The grumbling quieted down, although Kell still had a disgruntled look on his face.

I thought quickly, trying to come up with something fast while their attention was diverted.

"Never have I ever marathoned The Hunger Games trilogy in one sitting," I said.

It was a guess, but it paid off.

"Technically there's four movies, if you want to be accurate." Cameron gave me a wink as he took a drink. He was the only one to do so. "My turn." He rubbed his hands together gleefully. "Never have I ever gone swimming in my underwear."

The entire table moaned, myself included, as we drank.

"You live in that house," Jen pointed out. "Of course you're always going to have a swimsuit ready."

Cameron arched a brow. "The point of the game is to make the others drink. I'm just following the rules."

"When did you swim in your underwear?" Noah asked me, his expression dangerous.

I fought back a wince. "Um. It was a really hot day and I hadn't gone shopping yet and I wanted a dip. It wasn't like I did it at a party or anything. I was alone."

I flickered my gaze to Cameron nervously. I'd been alone, except for him.

Noah's frown eased somewhat.

Out of the corner of my eyes, I caught Jen staring at me.

"It's Emily's turn," I said hurriedly.

"Never have I ever been tied up during sex." Emily said matter of factly.

I flinched.

"What! You're kidding me." Cameron looked to Kell with an exaggerated expression of shock. He didn't seem to realize the predicament I was in.

Kell shrugged. "Some of us are into the bondage thing, some of us aren't."

Cameron clapped him on the shoulder. "Kell, my man, you are missing out."

I sat frozen in my seat, eyes wide and locked on Cameron.

I was supposed to drink.

I sure as hell wasn't going to drink in front of my brother.

Jen was still staring at me. She followed my gaze to Cameron. She looked back to me, taking in my terrified expression.

A look of realization dawned on her face. She could tell, couldn't she?

She knew I'd been caught off guard.

Oh god.

I was in a world of trouble.

CHAPTER TWENTY-SIX

Cameron and Kell were debating the various merits of bondage when Jen interrupted, telling them it was her turn.

She was still eyeing me, giving me that considering look. She didn't say anything, except to take her next turn.

"Never have I ever signed a girl's boobs after a concert."

All three guys took a shot.

"No fair ganging up on the rock stars," Kell complained. "Of course we've all done the same things."

August spoke up for his turn. As far as I could recall, he'd only had three shots, but his eyes were already beginning to glaze over.

"Never have I ever whined about the unfairness of playing by the rules for a game of *Never Have I Ever*."

Kell made a face at the drummer and took another shot. "You still trying to get me drunk, Summers? If I didn't know better, I'd say you were planning on taking advantage of me."

"No one gets to take advantage of you but me." Emily ran a hand up and down Kell's chest and kissed him on the cheek. Kell tilted his chin up smugly.

It was my turn again. I decided to use Jen's strategy.

"Never have I ever taken my shirt off on stage."

"Picking on us rock stars is too easy," Cameron said. "We should have planned this better." A wicked smirk crossed his face. "Never have I ever had sex with a dude."

I inhaled a sharp breath. I could feel the blood draining from my face. My heartbeat raced.

What the hell did Cameron think he was doing? Was he *trying* to get me into trouble? Even if I lied and didn't drink, surely everyone would notice my reactions.

"Does it count if it's a threesome where the swords don't cross?" Kell asked with a grin.

"If it means you have to take a drink, then yes," Cameron said matter-of-factly.

Kell downed his shot with a wink at Emily. She flushed and took a drink.

As Jen took her own drink, she side-eyed me.

I stood abruptly, scraping my chair against the floor with a screech. "I need to use the restroom."

With quick steps, I hurried to leave the table. I avoided everyone's eyes, hoping to god no one thought anything of my fast getaway.

The restroom was a single stall. I stared at my flushed cheeks in the mirror, grateful for the privacy.

I hadn't taken a shot, I reminded myself. I'd been able to escape before they were any the wiser.

The swirling ball of panic in my gut began to subside.

It was replaced with a kind of disbelief.

Was Cameron crazy? Why in the world had he brought up having sex, of all things, when it was his turn?

I supposed it made sense, considering everyone else seemed to rely heavily on the subject. Still. He should have thought it through.

I also probably should have realized what a game of *Never Have I Ever* would entail, especially when it was being played by rock stars.

I splashed cold water on my face to cool my flushed cheeks. I would go back to the table and bow out. I would just make some excuse.

As I left the washroom, a shadow loomed over me. I jumped, heart in my throat.

"Shit, sorry."

Cameron came into the light. I let out a lungful of air.

"I keep on forgetting," he said, chagrinned. "I shouldn't sneak up on you."

"Forget about scaring me." I felt my brow furrow in a fit of pique. I fought to smooth it. I wasn't angry at Cameron. Not really. I just wished he'd think before he spoke. "Why did you say that thing about sleeping with guys?"

He looked confused. "What?"

"You really wanted me to confess to my brother that I've had sex?" I whispered harshly.

He still looked befuddled. "Does he think you haven't?"

"I'm sure the thought has never crossed his mind. And I don't want it to."

"Is that why you ran off?"

"I certainly wasn't going to announce it to the table."

Cameron gave me a sly smile. "Noah's going to find out eventually. Why not at party full of witnesses so he can't murder me?"

"You were so scared about him finding out you flirted with me. Now you want to announce it to the room?"

"I told you. I didn't want Noah to think I was just playing with you. But I'm not playing. This is for real. We can't keep our relationship a secret forever."

"No, but—"

But I wasn't ready for Noah to know about us. Not yet. Not until I figured out a way to tell him that wouldn't make him freak out.

"I need more time," I said weakly.

Cameron stared at me. He nodded curtly. "Right. I get it." He pushed his bangs out of his face, revealing both deep blue eyes. The downcast look in them made my chest ache.

"I just don't want Noah flipping out. I need to figure out a way to ease him into the idea of his baby sister dating, especially since..." I trailed off.

Cameron's mouth twisted. "Especially since it's someone like me, you mean?"

"That's not what I meant."

"You know, I really thought—" he cut himself off with a dark, rueful laugh. "Never mind. I don't know why I expected things to be any different."

"I know what you're thinking," I said. "It's not like I'm ashamed of you, or that I want to keep this a secret. It's not like with your parents."

"Of course. I know that." Cameron avoided my eyes. "You don't have to play the game anymore. I'll tell the others you weren't feeling well. Blame it on the alcohol."

"I'll tell him," I promised. Standing on my tiptoes to bring us face to face, I laid a hand on his chest. "Just... not yet. Okay?"

Cameron stared at me intently, examining me. He nodded once. "Okay." The beginnings of a sly grin crossed his face. "If I'm not allowed to molest you in public yet, we better head home soon." He slid his hands from my shoulders, to the small of my back, and then lower. He cupped both cheeks. "Your ass looks amazing in that dress."

"Quit it." I batted his hand away, glancing around nervously. We were in an empty hallway, with only two doors leading to the restrooms. Still, someone could wander in at any time. "We need to at least stick around for a few more hours. I can't leave my own party too early."

He leaned in and placed his lips next to my ear. "Not even if I promise to lick your cunt until you're screaming?"

I flushed. "You've already done that."

"Don't tell me it's not worth a second go around."

Heat pooled between my legs. I honestly debated for a moment how suspicious it would look if Cameron and I disappeared together.

"Just another hour or two," I said. "Then we can leave."

Cameron faked a considering pose. "I suppose I can live with that." He gave my ass one last pat before stepping away. "I better go make sure August hasn't hit the floor yet. Poor bastard really can't hold his drink."

I waited until Cameron had sauntered off, then counted to one hundred. I didn't need for people to see the two of us leaving the restroom area together.

But Cameron was right.

Sooner or later, Noah was going to find out.

CHAPTER TWENTY-SEVEN

I spent another hour and a half mingling, drinking, and eating. The people Jen and Noah introduced me to were more than nice, but there were too many to keep track of. They ended up turning into a whirlwind of names and faces. Jen's friend Natalie was memorable because she tended to speak as if words were at a premium and she had to use every syllable as fast as possible.

"I'll arrange some lunch dates with only a few people at a time," Jen promised me. "It'll be easier to get to know everyone in smaller groups."

I thanked her, feeling relieved. It was a bit overwhelming, partying with so many people who seemed to already know everything about me, when I knew so little about them.

Cameron kept his distance. He seemed to be having a good time hanging out with his friends, though. He actually seemed happy around these people, in a more genuine way than I'd ever seen at his parties. With this crowd, he seemed at ease in a way he never did with the hangers-on he surrounded himself with at his house parties.

Although he was busy having fun, laughing and drinking and telling jokes, it didn't keep him from throwing quick, wicked smirks my way. The heat in his eyes was enough to make me flush. When he looked me up and down, lingering on my legs and chest, I knew exactly what he was thinking.

And I couldn't help but think the same things.

We were only five minutes away from the two hour mark when Cameron came up to me, interrupting a conversation I'd been having with a girl named Cerise. It turned out she was a rock star too, the lead singer in her own band Cherry Lips. Between her name and the dyed, dark cherry red hair cascading down her back, she really had a theme going.

"Just the woman I was looking for." Cameron grinned as he slung an arm around my shoulders.

I stiffened at first, then relaxed. It wasn't too intimate a touch. In fact, it was the exact same gesture I'd seen Cameron give my brother a handful of times. Cameron really was the handsy type.

"Hope I'm not interrupting you two lovely ladies?" Cameron asked.

"Would you care if you were?" Cerise retorted.

"Nope," Cameron said cheerfully.

"I was just asking Cerise what it's like being a girl in the rock music industry," I said.

"You thinking of starting up your own riot girl band?" Cameron teased, poking me in the cheek.

I swatted his hand away, brows furrowing. "I'm afraid Noah got all the musical talent in the family."

"You'd make a bad ass rocker chick," Cerise noted with a smile. "Your pissed off, don't-fuck-with-me look is on point."

"It's that patented Hart scowl," Cameron said with a laugh. "I can't get enough of it."

I fought to smooth my displeased expression. Noah was grumpy enough for the both of us. I didn't need to add to it.

"It's about that time for me to get going," Cameron told us. He tilted his head toward me, giving me a secret smile. "I'm calling a taxi to take me back to the mansion. You want to hitch a ride?"

"You live together?" Cerise asked, her interest piqued.

"It's like a roommate thing," I hurried to explain. "Just until school starts and I move into the dorms." I let out a nervous laugh. "Noah wanted me to live with him, but after walking in on him and Jen having sex one too many times, I decided I needed my own space."

"A billion square foot mansion certainly counts as space," Cerise agreed.

"I am getting a bit tired," I lied. "I think I'll head home with you."

Cameron kept his arm around me as I went about the room saying my goodbyes. It made me slightly nervous, to be touching each other so publicly, but I tried to reason with myself. Cameron acted like this with everyone.

I spotted Noah and Jen as we made our way to the exit. Noah turned his head to us. Instinctively, I ducked out from Cameron's arm.

I saw Cameron's lips twitch downward out of the corner of my eyes, but I didn't have time to say anything. Noah and Jen were already approaching.

"You leaving now?" Noah asked. "Are you feeling okay? Had too much to drink?"

"No, I'm fine. Cameron's heading home so I figured we could share the taxi."

Jen stared at me. No, she was staring at both me and Cameron, flicking her eyes between the two of us.

I knew she was already suspicious. We had to get out of there before Cameron forgot himself and did or said something to confirm those suspicions.

"Thank you for throwing the party," I said. "It was awesome meeting your friends, they're really great. Hopefully we can all get together again soon."

Jen nodded slowly. "Everyone loves you," she told me. Her eyes were fixed on Cameron.

I quickly moved to give Noah a hug goodbye.

"You make sure Lily gets home okay," Noah told Cameron over my shoulder. "No crazy detours."

Cameron smirked. "Don't worry, I'll keep her safe. It won't be like last time I took a taxi home."

I eyed the two of them. "Do I even want to know what happened last time?"

"No," they both said at the same time.

Cameron and I left the party and got into the waiting vehicle. The moment the doors were closed he pulled me into his lap.

"It was torture, watching you in that tight little dress all evening and knowing I couldn't touch you." Cameron placed a sucking kiss on my collarbone. "I might just have to keep you up all night before I'm satisfied."

He ran his hands up and down my exposed thighs. Tingles began to form between my legs.

"We're in a taxi," I scolded him, but my words came out breathless.

His thumbs brushed the soft inner skin. "You sure you want to wait until we get home?"

I seriously considered it for a moment.

I pushed away from him, taking my own seat. "It won't take long to get there."

Cameron let out a fake sigh. "I suppose I can be patient." A wicked gleam appeared in his eyes. "But that just means I'll have to keep you up even later." He placed his lips near my ear. "I'm going to fill up that sweet cunt of yours and make you come on my cock for hours."

I crossed my legs, pressing my thighs together, trying to relieve the ache pulsing inside me.

The ride was mercifully short. Cameron pushed a handful of bills into the driver's hand and pulled me out of the taxi. His tongue was in my mouth before the driver had even squealed away.

I clung to him, the press of his lips making me as dizzy and breathless as they had the first time we'd kissed.

We stumbled through the front door. Cameron kicked it closed. He pressed me up against the wall. His hand cradled the back of my head, protecting it. I tilted my chin up, taking more of his kisses. His tongue played with mine. Desire surged through me. I breathed in sharply. The taste and smell of him, something warm and fresh and uniquely *Cameron,* made my head spin.

We kissed with a fierce passion. One hand pressed on the small of my back, urging me closer. The other gripped the back of my neck, tugging me forward to crash our lips together again and again.

I made a soft noise of disappointment when Cameron pulled away. He trailed his lips from my mouth, down my chin, to my neck. He licked a slow line up my throat. Shivers coursed through me. He nipped at my collarbone. I gasped. His one hand moved from my back to my thigh. He dragged my skirt up to my waist, revealing my panties. His hard length pressed against his front zipper, jeans and thin cotton the only thing separating us. I rubbed myself against him shamelessly, wanting more. Wanting everything.

Cameron groaned as I squirmed, his length turning even harder. His grip on my hair tightened as it twitched.

I could feel him against me, the heat of that stiff cock burning me even through layers of fabric. My mind went hazy with desire. I felt a sudden urge to feel him on my lips, to taste him on my tongue.

I squirmed out of his hold and lowered myself to the floor, until I was on my knees in front of him. I peeked up through my lashes. His stare scorched me from the inside. Cameron cupped the back of my head, fingers sifting through the long strands.

"You sure?" he asked. The words were rough with need.

I nodded.

His eyes darkened, pupils blown wide. "I've wanted that sweet mouth of yours wrapped around my cock for months."

My breathing went shallow. My face flushed red hot, those words nearly undoing me. I slowly popped open the button and pulled down the zipper. His cock fell into my hands, warm and thick, and weeping a single drop at the tip.

I darted out my tongue with a small lick.

Cameron groaned.

I placed my lips on the head and gave it a light kiss.

He twisted his fingers in my long strands.

I opened my mouth and slowly slid down his shaft, enjoying the taste and texture of him on my tongue.

Cameron cursed and bucked his hips. I choked a little and pulled back.

"Shit, sorry," Cameron breathed.

"It's okay," I said hoarsely.

But I didn't let it deter me for long. I dived back down, taking him further into my mouth.

I didn't really know what I was doing. I just thought about what might make Cameron feel good.

I licked at the underside with my tongue as I pulled away. I sucked at the head, pressing my lips together in a tight circle. I bobbed my head forward and began the process all over again.

Before long Cameron was tugging at my hair urgently. "Fuck, Lily—"

I pulled back with a pop, letting his cock leave my mouth entirely. He cursed, panting heavily, close to the edge.

I took him in my hands again. I placed another sucking kiss on the tip. I licked around the crown. I took him back in my mouth.

I waited until his thigh muscles were straining, until his cock began to twitch.

I pulled back again.

"Shit!" Cameron groaned. "You're killing me."

A sly smile crossed my lips.

I tongued a slow line up his cock, from the base of his shaft to the head. I sucked lightly on the tip, just putting enough pressure to make him moan. I took him down again. This time I tried to go as far as I could. My throat muscles fluttered as I suppressed a cough. I didn't want to ruin this.

Cameron groaned as I fought to relax, trying not to gag. I waited, breathing shallowly. I kept his cock in my mouth until his thighs were trembling.

I swallowed.

"Fuck!" His hand slammed against the wall keeping him from falling forward.

I let out a pleased hum, causing another moan to escape his mouth.

I decided to have mercy on him. I slid my mouth up and down his shaft in a steady rhythm, using my lips to tease at the head on every withdrawal.

Before too long, his cock filled out in my mouth, becoming even thicker.

"If you don't stop, I'm going to come on those pretty pink lips," Cameron warned with a short, panted breath.

My only response was to suck harder.

Moments later his cock pulsed, warm fluid hitting the back of my throat. I fought to swallow it down before I drowned.

Cameron slowly pulled out, still hard, still pulsing, coating my tongue. He took himself in his hand and popped free of my mouth. He let the head rest on my bottom lip. He continued pulsing, painting my lips with sticky wetness.

His eyes were transfixed on my mouth. I slowly brushed my tongue along my bottom lip, catching a taste of his tip along with it. I licked at the head, catching every drop. I kept my eyes trained on him the entire time.

He grunted and finally pulled away, too sensitive to continue. He tucked himself back in his jeans. He pulled me up from my knees, planting his mouth on mine in a heated kiss. He didn't seem to mind that he was tasting himself on my lips.

"You fucking tease," he murmured into my lips. "You like playing games?"

"Not as much you do," I replied with a playful smile.

"This isn't the kind of game I'd want us to play at my house parties."

I shuddered at the thought. "I'm not into exhibitionism, sorry."

"No?" he grinned mischievously. "Sometimes the thrill of getting caught is worth it."

"Not when you're Noah Hart's little sister."

The smile slid off Cameron's face. I knew exactly what he was thinking.

"I'll tell him soon," I promised. "I want everyone to know about us, too."

Cameron examined me closely. "I know you're worried about how he'll react. Fuck, I'm worried too. But whatever happens, we'll work through it."

I buried my face in Cameron's chest and breathed in deeply.

I wished I could be as optimistic as him.

But I knew my brother.

Telling Noah wasn't going to be easy.

CHAPTER TWENTY-EIGHT

S ummer was almost over. That meant my classes were almost over. It was a relief, in one way, because my brain was beginning to feel fried from all the coursework and readings and papers. I was looking forward to a first semester filled with art, not essays.

I also couldn't help but feel a little sad.

My living situation was going to change soon. I was only supposed to be staying at Cameron's until I moved into the dorms. Once school started, I wouldn't have a reason to stay in the mansion with him.

Cameron hadn't broached the subject yet. For all I knew, he couldn't wait to get his bachelor pad back. We were a couple, yes, but moving in together so soon was rushing things, wasn't it?

I supposed that, since we'd already been living together, it wouldn't really be that odd. But still. Cameron hadn't said anything about me staying past the end of summer.

Not to mention, how in the world would I explain to Noah why I was staying at Cameron's without him getting suspicious?

Because I still hadn't been able to figure out a way to tell Noah about me and Cameron.

I could tell him when we were alone together, just the two of us. Noah wouldn't be able to punch my new boyfriend in the face if Cameron wasn't there.

Cameron and I could present a united front and tell him together. Convince him that we were serious about each other, and that this wasn't just Cameron playing around. Of course, we risked Noah flipping out and beating the shit out of Cameron then and there.

I could tell Noah ahead of time that I had some news to share. Let him brace himself of the worst before I spilled and hope that whatever he thought up wasn't as bad as what I was going to tell him.

I could always just spring it on him, matter-of-fact. Pretend like it was no big deal and hope he didn't overreact.

I had to snort to myself. Hoping Noah wouldn't overreact was a futile wish. I knew he wouldn't take my relationship with Cameron lightly.

I was thinking through my options as I drove back to the mansion from campus one afternoon. I was so absorbed in thought, I didn't notice the front door until I'd already parked and left the car.

When I saw the front door, wide open on its hinges, my heart immediately ran into overdrive.

Why was the door wide open?

I always closed and locked it behind me.

Cameron did as well.

Was somebody inside?

I broke out in a cold sweat. The hairs on the back of my neck tingled with warning.

Had somebody broken in?

With my heart in my throat I inched away, plastering myself to the exterior of my car. Shivers wracked my body, my fingers cold and trembling.

I tried to calm myself down. Tried to reason with myself.

Maybe Cameron had ordered pizza, and the delivery guy was still in the foyer.

But there wasn't a delivery car in the long driveway.

Maybe the housekeepers were in a rush and had forgotten to close the door behind them.

But Cameron said the housekeepers only came on Wednesdays, and it was Friday.

The anxiety was clouding my mind. I couldn't talk myself out of it. My breath came in short pants. My legs wavered. I hit the pavement, landing on my butt. I scooted back against the car as far as I could, as if the vehicle could protect me.

I heard myself struggling to breathe, wheezing as I sucked in air. My vision was beginning to go fuzzy around the edges.

A sudden thought occurred to me, briefly piercing the clouds. I could jump back in the car and lock the doors. No one would be able to get to me, then.

With shaky hands I fumbled for my purse. I clutched the keys in my hands. The feel of the cool metal calmed me somewhat.

I had a plan. I could get out of this.

My heart still jackhammered in my chest from adrenaline, but the tightness in my chest loosened some.

There wasn't anything to fear.

I closed my eyes and I took a long, slow breath. I counted to ten. I let it out. My mind began to clear. Some of the panic began to subside.

I was finally able to breathe in shallow breaths. My racing heartbeat began to slow. I wiped my clammy hands on my skirt.

The gravel of the pavement was digging into my skin. The slight pain reminded me that I'd fallen to the ground in my panic.

Squeezing my eyes shut, I pressed my palms to my face, feeling the hot flush of embarrassment.

I chided myself for having gotten so worked up. An open front door shouldn't have sent me into a panic like that.

Strong arms wrapped around me, tugging me to a warm, firm chest.

"Fuck, Lily, are you okay?"

I opened my eyes, finding myself pressed against Cameron, my head under his chin, my legs tucked under his.

"Did something scare you?" he asked, sounding worried.

"No. I'm fine," I said through a shaky breath. "I just—"

I hated having to explain that an open front door had sent me into a panic.

But I was a bit proud of myself, too. I'd fought through the panic. I'd made a plan.

The first time, Cameron had found me hiding in the bathroom, about to pass out.

The second time, I'd almost drowned in the pool.

But this time, I was able to calm myself down. I was able to get the fear under control.

Maybe I wasn't as helpless as I'd begun to think I was. Maybe I could learn to work through the fear and anxiety.

Cameron still had his arms wrapped around me.

"I'm fine," I repeated. "You can let me go."

Cameron pulled back a few inches, still keeping his arms around me. He examined me closely as he crouched in front of me.

"You're really pale," he noted. "And your hands are clammy." He gave me a concerned look. "Are you sure you don't want to see someone about this?"

"I had a bit of a scare," I admitted. "But I'm okay."

Cameron looked doubtful. "You can tell me if you're not."

"I know. But I managed to calm myself down this time. I think I'm getting better at handling it."

My heart lifted a little as I said the words. I really did feel better. My breathing was steady, my heart no longer pounding.

Cameron pulled me to my feet. He brushed the dirt from the pavement off my skirt. I thought he might take the opportunity to cop a feel, but he didn't. He just looked at me carefully.

"I want you to feel safe," he said.

"I do, most of the time."

"Remember what I said before? You can always come to me when you're scared or afraid. I'll always be here."

That was true only as long as I lived at Cameron's. Once I moved out...

A dozen different emotions ran through me at the thought. Excitement at finally being free. A still lingering worry that I might not be able to handle being on my own. Sadness at leaving Cameron.

He must have seen the bevy of expressions cross my face.

"What are you thinking?" he asked.

I spoke the next words quietly, fearing his reaction.

"What happens when I move out?"

CHAPTER TWENTY-NINE

C ameron looked taken aback.

"Why would you move out?"

"To live in the dorms," I reminded him. "This is only supposed to be temporary."

"It was only temporary as long as you were just Noah's sister." Cameron gave me a soft, teasing smile. "Did you think I was going to kick you out?"

"No, but... don't you want your place back to yourself?"

Cameron laughed. "I have eighteen bedrooms, remember? If I wanted space, I'd find it." He tugged me against his side. "You can't get rid of me that easily. You're mine."

I threw myself at him, clinging to him.

"I love you," I blurted out desperately.

Cameron stilled under my arms. My heart thumped rapidly. With my head buried in his shoulder, I couldn't see his expression.

All the anxiety I'd felt before returned full force. A different kind of anxiety this time. Why had I said that out loud? I hadn't meant to say it. I shouldn't have said it.

He squeezed me tight. One hand cupped the back of my head, pressing us cheek to cheek. His lips touched my ear.

"I love you, too," he replied softly.

The fireworks I'd felt when he first kissed me were nothing compared to the explosion that went off when he said those words.

I love you.

I hadn't meant to say them first. Hadn't meant to say them at all.

But Cameron returned my feelings.

Cameron said he loved me.

But even before the words had been spoken out loud, Cameron had showed me he loved me. With every thoughtful gesture, with every kind word, he had proven himself.

A few stray tears fell down my cheeks. He clutched me to his chest.

"I hope those are tears of happiness," he teased.

I laughed and sniffled at the same time.

"I love you," he repeated. "I don't want you to go. I want you to stay here." He pulled back, looking uncertain. "If you want to, I mean."

"I do want to." My heart felt light and airy. Cameron loved me. Cameron had officially asked me to move in with him. A small giddy laugh threatened to bubble up inside me.

"I have something I want to show you," Cameron said. His expression was a combination of nerves and excitement. "I hope you don't mind."

"Mind what?"

"Cam, honey?"

A voice called out from the front door.

"Shit, sorry." Cameron cringed. "My parents are here. They said they've got some important stuff to tell me. I got distracted when I heard your car come up, but you didn't come into the house." Cameron gave me a crooked smile. "They want to talk about my mom's whole mayor thing with me."

"That's a good sign, right? They probably want you involved somehow."

"Yeah, maybe. It would be cool if I could help out somehow." There was a hopeful note in his voice. "You should come, too. You're a part of my life now. Anything that affects me will affect you."

"What about that thing you wanted to show me?"

"It can wait."

Cameron took my hand and led me into the mansion, keeping a tight grip the entire time.

Sharon and Grant were waiting in one of the living rooms. They looked overjoyed to see me again. Sharon stood from the sofa and gave me a warm hug in greeting.

"So good to see you again, Lily." Sharon took note of mine and Cameron's clasped hands. She gave Cameron a knowing smile. "I'm glad to see you're still here."

"Lily and I are together," he told them, beaming proudly.

The ecstatic look on their faces made me flush.

"We're so happy for you, dear. And I hope you'll be happy for me," she added.

"Is it official, then?" Cameron asked.

"It is." She straightened her shoulders. Her expression was one of slight nerves underneath a steely sort of resolve. "I've put my name in to run for mayor."

Cameron and I gave his mother a round of congratulations.

"Your father and I are going to be working very hard with my campaign stuff over the next few months," Sharon said. "Unfortunately, that means that we'll be very busy for the foreseeable future."

Cameron nodded. "I get it. No more impromptu dinners."

"There will also be quite a few events to attend, fundraising and such. That's not to mention when we actually start campaigning and doing town hall meetings and debates."

"We've got a fundraising dinner coming up next week," Grant said. "Just for close friends and family."

Cameron brightened.

"You won't be there, of course," Grant continued blithely.

Cameron stilled. The look on his face nearly shattered my heart. He clenched his fist, his eyes going flat, his expression blank.

"But Lily is more than welcome to come," Sharon added, oblivious. She turned to me with a smile. "I'll text you the details, sweetie. Just let me know if you're free."

I was too shocked to answer.

I had thought Cameron was just mistaken when he told me his parents didn't want him anywhere near their colleagues. When he told me Sharon and Grant were ashamed of him and kept him from the public eye.

But they had disinvited him from a family event right in front of me.

His parents talked through a few more details about his mother's campaign. I listened with half an ear. My attention was on Cameron.

He nodded and agreed and chuckled at all the right times, but that emotionless look was still on his face.

Only I caught the pain behind that blank gaze.

Immediately after his parents left, the strained smile left Cameron's face. It was replaced with a twist of his lips. His dark blue eyes turned almost obsidian.

"I'm gonna go work out."

I grabbed for his hand before he could storm off. "Cameron, I'm sorry."

He cast his eyes down to the floor. "I should have known it was coming."

"You should talk to them about it."

"What difference would it make? They clearly don't want me anywhere near this whole political campaign thing." Cameron gave a sort of half-hearted shrug. "I get it. I'm not exactly wholesome-family material."

But the hurt on his expression was heartbreaking. I threw my arms around him, squeezing tight.

"It's wrong of them to treat you this way."

"I've dealt with this my whole life. It's nothing new."

"Still. You don't deserve being treated like that. You're a wonderful son. And a wonderful boyfriend. And a wonderful person in general."

He wrapped his arms around me. He buried his face in my hair. "You're the only one who thinks so."

"No, I'm not. Everyone loves you."

He let out a sick laugh. "Even Noah? That's why you won't tell him about us, right? He thinks the worst of me."

I shook my head. "It has less to do with you, and more to do with me. I don't think he'd take my dating anyone very well."

"I'm just so fucking sick of being everyone's dirty little secret."

I pulled away to meet his eyes. "I'll tell him."

Cameron stilled. "About us?"

"Yes. The next time I see Noah, I'll tell him about us."

The relieved look on Cameron's face eased my worries. Maybe I couldn't make what his parents did feel any better, but I could do this for him.

Then that relieved smile turned into something darker. Something heated.

"If you're going to tell your brother, I guess that means I can do this."

He leaned down and nipped on my neck. I gasped. He placed his lips on my skin and sucked.

I pushed him away. "No hickies!"

"You're no fun."

"At least not anywhere people can see," I conceded.

His eyes held an evil glint. Cameron bit down on my bottom lip.

I gasped, then moaned. He licked a healing path along that lip, tongue seeking entrance to my mouth.

I parted my lips, allowing his tongue to play with mine. The moment I tasted him, a wave of need crashed into me. Any reservations I had flew out of my head. His scent filled my nostrils, warm and sunny and so very *Cameron*.

I tangled my hands in his hair, pulling him closer. I threw myself at him so fast, our knees and hips bumped together awkwardly. We almost lost our balance. Cameron caught me by the waist. He slowly lowered us onto a nearby sofa, settling me onto his lap. We never broke our kiss as we nipped and licked and crushed our mouths together.

His hands wandered under my shirt. The roughness of his calloused fingers burned deliciously into my soft skin. They skimmed a line down my back to deftly unsnap my bra. They continued tracing a path to my front. His thumb brushed my nipples under thin cotton fabric. He tweaked one, then the other. A jolt of electricity shot through me at each light pinch.

His lips left mine to trail kisses down my neck to my collarbone. I took the moment to peel my shirt off and toss it to the floor, along with my bra. With a hand on my shoulder blades, he leaned me backwards, angling my chest until his lips found my nipples. He latched onto one, a heated suction that shocked me to my core. I tugged on his hair, urging him closer.

As his mouth teased at my breasts, his hands searched beneath my skirt. He ran a path up and down my inner thighs, stopping just before he hit the apex, teasing me. Liquid heat pooled in my center. My inner walls clamped down on nothing, already wet and aching and needing his touch.

I was a shaking, panting mess when he lifted his head. I whined and wriggled at the loss of his lips on my breasts.

"You've got the most fucking beautiful tits," he mumbled against my skin. The cool air of his breath made my nipples tighten even further.

Cameron met my eyes. His fingertips found the elastic of my now damp panties. My breath hitched. Slowly, he hooked his fingers underneath and tugged down. I shifted, helping him draw them down my legs.

I settled back down on his lap, naked except for the skirt pushed to my waist. He was still dressed, still in his t-shirt and jeans. My core pressed against the stiff length still trapped in the thick fabric. I palmed him through the rough material. He stifled a groan. I pulled down the zipper and took him out. He was burning in my hand, silken smooth over a heavy, solid weight.

I brushed my thumb over the weeping tip. He twitched.

My inner walls were throbbing, the emptiness inside me turning into an almost painful ache. I needed to be filled, and I needed to be filled by this man alone. I rolled my hips and said the words that I knew were his undoing.

"Fuck me, Cameron."

His gaze went dark. He gripped my hair in his hand, fisting the strands. He tugged my head back and crushed his lips to mine.

"The things you do to me, Angel..." he murmured into my mouth.

Cameron made a move to reach into his jeans pocket. I knew what he was going for.

"Wait." I put a hand on his wrist.

He paused with a questioning noise.

"I want to feel you," I told him, cheeks burning.

His eyes blazed with heat, understanding my meaning. "You sure?

'Cause I would fucking kill to come inside you. But—"

"I'm on the pill," I reassured. "I mean, as long as you..." I trailed off.

"I'm clean." He ran a soothing hand up and down my hip. The touch sent shivers through my spine. "I made an appointment to get checked right after our first time."

"Then I'm sure. I want to feel you inside me, skin to skin."

I angled him towards my entrance, nestling the tip between my folds.

He cursed, falling forward until his forehead touched mine. "You're so fucking wet."

"It's all for you."

"I don't think I can go slow."

"I don't want you to."

He narrowed his eyes at me. "You want it hard and fast, Angel?"

"God, yes," I breathed.

He nudged my thighs wider. The tip brush my clit. I almost came instantaneously from that touch alone.

With a thrust of his hips, he drove himself into me. My wet walls stretched around him. I let out a choked cry. He captured it with his mouth.

He held himself there, letting me get used to his size. My insides fluttered around him. That sweet ache began building again. I arched my back, trying to take more of him.

Despite his words, he moved slowly at first, with smooth deep strokes. A universe of sensations gathered between my legs. I locked my legs around his hips and writhed shamelessly, urging him to go faster.

Cameron gripped my hips in his hands and lifted me up, until the head had nearly left me. He snapped his hips at the same time as he pushed me down, impaling me on his cock. Then he did it again, and again. I cried out, a continuous series of gasps and moans. He didn't try to quiet me. The look of utter concentration on his face, the trembling of his muscles, told me he was fighting for control.

"More," I urged breathlessly.

His eyes glinted darkly. He lifted me up and shoved me back down again. I moaned. He picked up the rhythm, grinding into me before pulling out and slamming in. My mind was sent reeling. The dig of his fingers in my thighs was going to leave bruises. I relished the thought. I wanted evidence of his passion, of his need for me.

He drove his cock deeper and deeper inside me. I felt it swell even further. The hardening length rammed into me, hitting me in just the right spot. I let out a choked breath as a powerful orgasm rose within me.

Cameron crushed his mouth to mine and pressed a thumb into my clit. He ignited an inferno inside me, fanning the flames higher and higher. I clung to his shoulders and lost myself in him. Those skillful lips and tongue and fingers and cock unraveled me from the inside out.

My mind was still soaring through the clouds when I heard him grunt and felt him pulse inside me. He spent himself into me, twitching and throbbing. His thighs were straining, his jaw clenched.

The pleasure slowly abated. I found myself collapsed against his chest, panting heavily. His arms were wrapped around my waist. His face was buried in my hair. We leaned into each other, catching our breaths.

After long moments, my hips began to ache. I shifted uncomfortably.

"Did I hurt you?" Cameron immediately asked.

"No." I was slightly achy, but in that wonderful, amazing, life-altering way. "This is just an awkward position to be in for too long."

Cameron reached for a box of tissues on the closest end table. He helped me clean up as I gingerly lifted myself from his lap.

When we were clothed, Cameron pulled me in for another kiss. He traced a line down my cleavage, to my breasts.

"See? No visible hickies," he said.

"I'm astounded at your restraint." I traced the lines of his chest through his t-shirt. We hadn't even stripped down completely in our haste.

"What was that thing you wanted to show me?"

"How about I show you tonight? We're doing a small concert. I can show you, and then we can tell Noah."

Clearly that was still weighing on him.

"We'll have the rest of the band around us." Cameron smirked. "He can't kick my ass if we're supposed to go on stage right after."

I paused. I wasn't so sure about that. Tonight was so soon. I'd been hoping to have more time.

I nodded slowly. "We'll tell him tonight before the concert."

Cameron placed a soft kiss on my mouth. "No more secrets. We'll tell him we're dating and that we're going to be living together."

"Right," I said hesitantly. "No more secrets."

CHAPTER THIRTY

The club venue Darkest Days was playing at looked only slightly bigger than the club Jen had booked for my welcome home party.

"It's a special VIP event to help promote the new album," Cameron explained. "Exclusive tickets were only sold to super fans. Management wanted to keep it low key for now, since the album still isn't released. We're going to be playing a few new songs."

"Aren't you worried people will take video and leak it?"

"That's the whole point. We want to hype people up."

"So it's all sneaky marketing."

"That's how the game is played, Angel. I'm just happy it's not me who has to worry about all that shit. All I need to do is show up and play."

Cameron led me to the back entrance of the club, away from all the fans lining up.

"Don't want to cause a stampede by just walking in the front doors," he said.

We passed by a bouncer, who nodded to Cameron in greeting and opened the door for us. It was much easier getting into the concert with a rock star by my side.

The moment we entered the club, butterflies took wing in my stomach.

This was it. I was going to tell my brother about me and Cameron.

"Hey, you okay?"

Cameron gave me a squeeze with his arm around my waist. He must have sensed how nervous I was.

"I'm okay," I said through a tight throat. My breathing was speeding up. It wasn't like my usual panic attacks. It was nothing that bad.

But I was definitely feeling anxious over the thought of confronting Noah with the truth.

"However he reacts, we'll deal with it," Cameron reassured me. His thumb brushed the hollow of my hip. "We'll make him understand."

"Even if he tries to murder you in public?" I asked, only half joking.

Cameron frowned. "I'm not going to let him get in the way of us being together."

The possessive tone in his voice chased away some of the butter-flies, leaving only a gooey, sappy feeling in my chest. Cameron was determined to fight for us.

I wanted to be just as determined. I really did.

But the instant we stepped backstage and I saw my brother's tall form and dark messy hair, those butterflies returned full force, threatening to spew out of my mouth.

Noah began to turn.

"Here we go," Cameron murmured, tightening his hold on me.

I ducked out from under Cameron's arm in a panic.

Cameron turned to me, disbelief on his face.

I avoided his eyes, playing with the hem of my shirt.

Noah approached us, already dressed in his rock star best, leather pants and eyeliner included.

"Lily, Cameron. You guys came together?" he asked.

"We shared a taxi," I rushed to say. My heart pounded in my chest. "I was planning on coming to watch you guys anyway, so it just made sense to come together."

Noah nodded. "I should have thought to get you a staff pass earlier, sorry." He handed me a lanyard with a yellow card inside a plastic sleeve. I put it around my neck.

"It's cool," I said, my voice wavering. I was still avoiding Cameron's eyes. "So what time are you guys going on?"

"We've got about another half hour before show time. Sound crew's doing their last checks."

"Are the others here? August and the twins? It'd be cool to hang out with them again for a bit. It still feels like I've barely seen them."

I continued to babble nervously. Out of the corner of my eyes, I saw Cameron standing stock still. His eyes were dark. His face was blank.

My heart sank. I hadn't meant to dart away like that. It had just been instinct. I was so worried about Noah finding out. I thought I was ready, but now I wasn't as sure.

"Cameron, the guitar tech guys told me they needed to speak with you when you got here," Noah said.

Cameron nodded shortly. "Right. I'm off, then."

He stalked away without another look.

The panic in my chest that I'd felt when seeing Noah turned into a completely different type of panic.

I'd really hurt Cameron. I hated myself for it. I shouldn't have been so thoughtless, especially after the way his parents had treated him.

But the anxiety had taken over and I'd acted without meaning to.

I had to make this right.

I had to tell Noah.

"I've got something to tell you," I blurted out.

Noah was scanning the room, looking distracted. "What is it?"

"It's about me. And Cameron."

He nodded distantly, as if he were listening with half an ear. "Yeah, I really should thank him for letting you stay with him all summer." Noah's phone buzzed in his pocket. He pulled it out. "August says he needs to see me about changing the set list. Fucking perfectionist."

"Cameron and I—"

"Shit, he's really insistent this time." Noah's attention was still on his phone. "I'll see you after the show, okay?"

"But..."

"Go find Jen. She'll know the best place to stand to get a good view." Noah hugged me briefly. "Make sure to stay away from the pit. It can get crazy out there."

Noah walked off, thumbs texting away, not waiting for my response.

My chest deflated. My chance to tell Noah was gone. I'd have to wait until after.

Cameron would have to play through the entire show thinking I'd rejected him.

I was still cursing myself up and down, guilt and self loathing swirling inside me, when my own phone went off.

I checked it half-heartedly.

It was Cameron's mom.

She was texting me the details for the fundraising dinner.

That only set off another wave of shame coursing through me. I was as bad as Cameron's parents.

He'd spent years being ignored in public by his mom and dad. Of course going through the same thing with me would cause him pain. If it hadn't been for them putting him through years of this, maybe he wouldn't have been so upset at my hesitance.

My anger began to turn outward.

If it wasn't for them, Cameron wouldn't have been so upset over the idea of keeping our relationship a secret.

I rapidly typed a string of messages before I could talk myself out of it.

Why did you disinvite Cameron from the fundraising dinner?

Why did you invite me but not him?

Why is he not welcome at your events?

Didn't you think about how that would make him feel?

I didn't get a response for several long minutes. I began to feel a little embarrassed at having gone off on Sharon. It wasn't my place to question their decisions. To pick apart their family dynamic. Maybe I'd be disinvited, just like their son.

When my phone finally buzzed again, I looked at the screen reluctantly.

I frowned as I read the first few replies.

My mouth dropped open as I continued reading.

By the last message, understanding finally dawned on me.

I thought quickly. I thumbed a rapid series of texts, trying to explain everything as fast as I could. The concert would be over in a few hours. I didn't have much time.

When Cameron's mother gave me her last reply, my heart finally felt light with relief.

I'd hurt Cameron tonight with my actions.

Maybe with this I could start mending that wound.

CHAPTER THIRTY-ONE

Although I felt some measure of relief after having talked to Cameron's mom, my nerves got the best of me the moment I spotted Jen across the room.

I had a feeling Jen suspected something was going on between me and Cameron at my welcome home party. I hadn't wanted to stick around and have her find out for sure.

But now that I was ready to tell Noah, I supposed I didn't have much more to fear.

That didn't ease the slight feeling of trepidation rising inside me.

Jen's face brightened when she saw me. She waved me over with a smile and hugged me when I walked up.

"It's so good to see you again, Lily. You've been here all summer and it feels like we've barely hung out."

"I've been pretty busy with school," I said.

"All the work of three year long classes crammed into one summer must have been intense," Jen agreed. "Not to mention, it must have been non-stop fun living in Cameron's mansion."

"Yeah, all those crazy parties." I laughed nervously.

I wanted to tell her, but I didn't know how she would react. Jen probably wouldn't freak out like I was expecting Noah to, but what if she disapproved? I had been half-counting on Jen to keep Noah from flying off the handle when he found out. What if she agreed with him that Cameron and I together was a bad idea?

"It's not just the parties. You and Cameron seem to be pretty close." She got a slight twinkle in her eyes. "Have you been spending a lot of time together?"

I stammered, not knowing what to say. Jen definitely knew.

She laughed. "It's okay. I won't say anything."

I let out the breath I hadn't realized I'd been holding.

"Thanks," I said weakly.

She nudged me with her shoulder. "If you need help getting through Noah's thick skull, just let me know. I'm on your side. I've got an empty apartment you and Cameron can hide in. My friends and I all moved out, but the rent's paid up until the end of the year."

Jen thought we would need a place to hide.

"He's really going to flip, isn't he?" I asked mournfully.

"When does he ever not flip out when it comes to you?" Jen looked thoughtful for a moment. "But he might not. Noah's changed from the person he used to be when I first met him." She let out a small laugh. "Well, he's still pretty cranky, but he's definitely learned to tone it down."

"I'm just so worried what will happen if he finds out."

Jen raised an eyebrow. "If?"

"When," I corrected. "I'm planning on telling him tonight after the show."

"Just get it over with. Like ripping a bandage off a wound."

"What if he actually beats up Cameron?" I swallowed down the lump of fear in my gut. "What if Noah kicks him out of the band? Darkest Days means everything to him. It would kill Cameron if that happened."

"August wouldn't let him," Jen reassured me. "Noah might freak out a bit, but eventually I think he'll learn to accept it. As long as Cameron is serious about you." Jen eyed me. "He is serious, right?"

"Yes." I nodded fervently. "He's not playing with me. We're—" I paused, blushing. "We're in love."

Jen mimed a swoon. "You two are so cute together."

"You don't disapprove?"

"Why would I? Cameron, for all his faults, is a good guy underneath it all. We all just want him to be happy."

"I think I hurt his feelings earlier," I confessed quietly. "We were supposed to tell Noah before the show. I chickened out. But I'm okay with the idea of telling my brother, now."

"So you'll confront Noah after the concert's over?"

"Not right away. I have to do something else first."

The lights went down. The audience began cheering and hooting. The concert started with a clash of drums and guitar.

From my vantage point backstage and to the side, I could see all five members of the band. The twins, for all the tension between them, played the crowd together as easily as I remembered. They shredded back to back, and even switched guitars mid-song.

August's brow was furrowed, ice blue eyes concentrated solely on his drums, arms nearly a blur as he pounded away.

Noah's crooning voice emitted from the speakers. He strode from one side of the stage to the other, his dark eyes burning the audience to their very cores with his passionate singing.

Jen's full attention was on Noah, her expression slack-jawed with awe. Even after having been dating so long, she still seemed captivated by his performance. I supposed once a fangirl, always a fangirl.

But Cameron... something was off about his performance. He grinned and winked and teased the crowd as usual, but there was something in his expression. His full heart wasn't in it. His eyes were lined with pain.

And I knew I was the cause.

I just had to hope that what I had planned for after the concert helped heal some of that hurt.

The concert was almost over, the band playing their last song before the encore, when my phone buzzed again.

"I'll be right back," I yelled in Jen's ear.

She nodded, not taking her eyes off the stage.

I went to the back door, nodding to the bouncer. With the staff pass around my neck, I had free rein.

When I opened the door, I was greeted by the sight of Cameron's parents dressed in their conservative business attire. It was completely at odds with what everyone else backstage was wearing.

I waved them in.

"Thank you for coming on such short notice."

"It's no trouble at all, sweetie." Sharon spoke over the music into my ear as she pulled me into a hug. "I'm just so glad you said something."

"Do you two mind waiting here? I don't have staff passes for you, so you can't go any further."

"We don't mind at all," Sharon said.

I left them and headed back, hoping to catch Cameron as he left the stage after their last song.

I was in luck. Cameron was the first one out. His bright red hair glistened with drops of sweat. His damp t-shirt clung to every ab. His dark rimmed eyes were even smokier, his eyeliner having smudged from the heat of the stage lights. I swallowed hard as my heart sped up. Arousal threatened to flood my system.

Maybe I wasn't so different from Jen when it came to our attraction to rock stars.

I ran up to him as one of the assistants handed him a towel to dry off the sweat.

"Cameron!"

He looked my way. His mouth twisted.

"I'm sorry," I blurted out before he could say anything. "I didn't mean to pull away. I just panicked."

He stared at me. He nodded once.

"I get it. It's cool."

"No, it's not." I took his hand in mine and squeezed. "I'm really sorry I hurt you. I promise, I'm telling Noah tonight."

"I said it's cool," he repeated. His lips twisted in a sick smile. "I'm used to it."

I knew he was referring to his parents. My heart ached, but I knew everything would be better soon.

"I have something to show you. Come with me."

I tugged him along toward the back door, avoiding the controlled chaos of roadies and tech crew and assistants.

"We can't take off yet," Cameron said, worried. "I've still got to do the encore. We're just taking a break."

"This will only take a minute."

We turned the last corner. Cameron stopped, almost tripping in his surprise.

"Mom? Dad?" His voice was full of disbelief. "What are you doing here?"

His mother gave him a wavering smile. "We wanted to see you play one of your shows."

It was almost gut-wrenching, to see a hint of hope flicker across Cameron's face before it was replaced with a look of cynicism.

"How did you even know there was a show tonight?" he asked, brow furrowed.

"Lily invited us."

Cameron looked to me in confusion. "Why did you...?"

"I think you guys should talk." I faced his parents. "Tell Cameron why you've never come to one of his concerts before."

Sharon's expression turned hesitant. "Sweetie, we're not exactly the rock concert type." She gestured to herself and her husband, indicating their business suits. "Wouldn't it be embarrassing to have your boring old parents show up?" She gave him a small smile. "You certainly wouldn't be able to get up to your usual antics with mom watching over your shoulder."

Cameron looked utterly befuddled.

Grant continued. "Growing up, you were always off having fun with your friends, playing music, and getting into trouble. We knew the last thing you wanted was your mom and dad hanging around."

"I would have loved for you to come to one of my concerts," Cameron said. "I thought... you didn't care."

"Cam, honey, of course we care," his mother said, gently admonishing him. "We always knew you'd accomplish great things. We just wanted to stay out of your way and let you live your own life."

She took him in her arms. He stood stiffly, his own arms at his sides.

"We never meant to make you feel like you weren't welcome in our lives." Grant shifted awkwardly from foot to foot, looking uncomfortable, but powered on. "We never invited you to our business events because we knew you'd hate them. Hell, I hate them half the time. Boring and stuffy, full of snobs and suck-ups." He shook his head ruefully. "The last thing we wanted to do was subject you to those things."

Cameron's frozen stance softened. He slowly brought his arms up to return his mother's embrace.

"I always thought—" Cameron's voice cut off, not finishing the sentence.

"You were always such a free spirit," his mother said, smoothing his hair back, revealing both blue eyes. If she was taken aback by the heavy eyeliner, her expression didn't reveal it. "We never wanted to do anything to discourage that."

"I'm sorry if we hurt you, son." Grant clapped Cameron on the shoulder, giving his shoulder a squeeze. "You should know that we've always been proud of you."

Cameron swallowed hard. That hopeful look had returned.

"If you want to be involved in my run for mayor, you're more than welcome," Sharon told him.

"I dunno," Cameron said with a choked laugh. "My fans might not be the kind of people you're targeting for votes."

Sharon and Grant shared the laugh.

I breathed a sigh of relief. My chest felt a million times lighter. I had worried whether or not making Cameron confront his parents was the right thing to do.

When Sharon had texted me back, wondering why I'd ever thought she didn't want Cameron to be there, I'd been astonished. She and her husband honestly had no idea what their words and actions had done to their son over the years.

As soon as I told her, she insisted on talking to Cameron then and there. The fact that he was currently on stage at a concert made no difference. Sharon and Grant had left in the middle of a dinner to make their way to the venue.

Cameron's mom had said the only important thing was setting things right with their son.

CHAPTER THIRTY-TWO

Cameron and his parents were still reconciling when one of the twins came running, streaking down the hallway, out of breath.

"Yo, dickface, we're going on in thirty seconds!" The twin had a look of panic about him. "August's going to gut you if you don't get your ass on stage."

Cameron cringed and turned to his parents. "I'm sorry, I've got to go do the encore."

"Can... we watch?" Sharon asked hesitantly.

Cameron's face brightened, ecstatic. "Of course!"

With a rock star at our side, the bouncer easily let us breeze through.

"I'm sorry I sprung this on you," I whispered to Cameron just before he went on stage.

He stopped and looked at me. Sweat rolled down my back, half from the heat flowing off stage and half from nerves that Cameron was still upset with me.

He gave my hand a quick squeeze before grinning.

"I've got to go put on the best fucking rock show of my life." He winked. "Need to impress the 'rents."

Cameron ran onto the stage to a roar of cheers, joining the rest of Darkest Days.

"This is so interesting." Sharon glanced this way and that, taking in every detail as she clung to my side. "I've never been backstage at a concert before."

Grant looked around at the carefully controlled chaos of roadies and concert staff rushing around. He winced at the blasting music coming from the speakers.

"It's, ah... quite loud," he said, shouting over the noise.

"You get used to it," I shouted back.

Cameron did put on the best show of his life. He played to the audience, urging them to shout louder, jump higher. He strutted from one end of the stage to the other, leaning over the barrier to clap at his fans' hands. He laughed and grinned, dropping to his knees and hopping up on amps, a whirlwind of energy.

He didn't, however, take off his shirt. I had to assume that was for his parent's benefit.

When the concert was over, Cameron ran off stage first. His parents congratulated him with hugs and smiles.

"I'm sorry we can't stick around longer," Sharon said regretfully. "We left our guests in the middle of dinner quite rudely. We should probably get back."

Cameron nodded. "I'll let you know the next time we have a show. I'll get you special VIP tickets. It'll be awesome."

"We'd love that."

Before leaving, Sharon gave me a hug goodbye.

"Thank you so much, Lily," she whispered in my ear. "I want you to know you're a very welcome part of our family."

My heart swelled at those words. Family. For so long it had just been me and my brother.

It was a nice feeling, being part of a family.

Which reminded me. Noah. I had to tell him.

I looked around backstage, but didn't see him.

Cameron took my hand. "You need to come with me right now."

"Where are we going?" I asked.

His didn't answer, his gaze burning into me as he pulled me along. He led me through the busy backstage area and down a less crowded hallway.

He opened the door that read *artist lounge* on the door. He guided me inside the room with a hand on my back.

An empty room.

I flushed, my cheeks going red when I realized what this was.

Cameron closed the door behind us and locked it. My heart began thumping wildly in my chest at the sound the lock clicking.

"I—" I began to say.

He gave me a carnal grin and approached slowly, like he was a predator approaching its prey.

In all the times we'd had sex, it had never been anywhere other than in Cameron's mansion. In my bedroom, or on one of the sofas, or in the pool.

I'd never imagined doing it backstage at one of my brother's concerts.

Well. Maybe I'd imagined it once or twice. Or a few dozen times.

But I'd never thought it could actually happen. The last thing Cameron and I wanted was for us to get caught.

"Are you really sure—"

He cut me off with his mouth on mine. I let out a muffled squeak, heat pooling between my legs.

When he'd kissed the very air out of my lungs, he slowly pulled back an inch.

"Thank you," he murmured against my lips. "You were right when you said I should just talk to my parents. I guess I was afraid of having all my fears confirmed."

"I never meant to hurt you by pulling away in front of Noah," I said softly. "I just got scared." I met his eyes. "But I'm not scared anymore. I'm going to tell my brother right away."

"Not yet."

I frowned, confused. "You don't want to tell him?"

Cameron shook his head with a wicked smirk. "First, I need to bury my cock so deep inside that sweet cunt you'll be feeling me for days."

I flushed, my inner muscles clenching and throbbing.

"You want to do it... here?" I asked, nerves and excitement fighting for dominance.

"I can't wait until we get home." He dragged his hands up my inner thighs and under my skirt, his fingers burning a trail into my skin. "I need to get inside that sweet pussy and make you come on my cock."

My insides quivered, both at his touch and at his words.

"What if someone walks in?" I asked. It was a token protest. I was already leaning into him, our bodies mere inches apart.

"I locked the door."

"Isn't that suspicious?"

He smirked. "Who gives a fuck?"

"Better make sure your dad doesn't hear that language," I teased.

Cameron made a face. "Please don't bring up my parents at a time like this."

He pulled me into his arms and gave me a blistering kiss.

I heard the rattle of the doorknob.

My heart jumped.

"It's locked," Cameron whispered against my lips.

But it must have been a crappy lock because the door swung open anyway.

We froze.

In the hallway, just outside the door, stood Noah.

CHAPTER THIRTY-THREE

Noah looked confused for the briefest of seconds, as if he'd been expecting to see something else.

Moments later rage exploded across his face.

"You motherfucking—"

Cameron had no time to duck. Noah launched himself across the room and cold-clocked him in the jaw. Cameron's head snapped back.

I cried out in surprise.

Noah readied his fist to punch again. I threw myself at my brother, clinging to his arm, pulling him back.

"Noah, stop!"

Cameron had been sent reeling back from the force of the punch. He straightened and rubbed at his jaw gingerly.

"All those times you punched me in the side, you were really holding back, weren't you?" he said wryly.

"I'm going to fucking kill you," Noah hissed. He glared a burning hatred in Cameron's direction. I clung to him tighter, but he didn't move to throw another punch.

"Noah, listen to me," I said insistently. "Cameron and I—"

"You touch my sister, you die," Noah spat.

"It's not like that." I tried to use my best soothing voice. I placed myself in front of my brother, trying to block Cameron from view. Noah's brow furrowed, that patented pissed off Hart look out in full force.

Cameron hovered in the doorframe, looking uneasy. "Noah, it's not what it looks like."

Noah's expression turned murderous. His fists were balled and shaking with rage.

This was exactly what I'd been afraid of.

"Cameron, be quiet for a minute." I turned my attention back to my brother. "I know what you're thinking. But you need to listen to me."

I brought my hands to my brother's face and forced him to look at me. He reluctantly turned his gaze from Cameron to me.

I swallowed hard. I'd never been the recipient of Noah's glare like this. It was scary. No wonder Cameron had been so hesitant in the beginning. I powered on.

"Cameron and I are together." I kept my voice firm and calm. "We're dating. He's not using me, he's not tricking me into anything. We're a couple."

Noah's glare softened into a look of confusion.

"I know you want to protect me from the world, but you don't need to protect me from this. Cameron and I—"

I stopped and turned my eyes to my boyfriend. Noah followed my gaze.

"I love her," Cameron said softly, his eyes on me and me alone.

Noah let out a noise in the back of his throat, almost like disbelief.

"You think you can just lie to get my baby sister into bed—"

"It's not a lie," Cameron said sharply. It was his turn to frown. "I love Lily. I want to be with her."

The fury on Noah's face flickered. Uncertainty began to take its place. Noah looked to me, then back at Cameron.

Cameron continued speaking, having sensed that Noah was finally calming down.

"You can kick the shit out of me or kick me out of the band or whatever. But I'm not going to let you, or anything else, get in the way of me being with the woman I love."

Cameron pulled down the collar of his shirt, exposing his upper chest.

Tattooed on his skin was a lily. The same lily I'd been drawing for years.

"Cameron..." I was near speechless. I went over to him and traced the tattoo with a light touch. He placed his hand over mine.

"I want you to know how much you mean to me. I want your brother to know. You're it, Lily. You're the only one for me."

Tears sprang to my eyes.

"It's beautiful," I whispered. I stood on my tiptoes to place a soft kiss on his lips.

Noah growled, but didn't say anything. He continued glaring for a few more moments. Slowly, bit by bit, his stance softened. His balled fists relaxed at his sides. That burning hatred in his gaze eased somewhat.

My brother looked to me.

"You're serious about this?" he asked, his voice still low and dangerous.

I stood in front of my brother, hand in hand with Cameron. "I am."

"We're both serious," Cameron added.

His eyes snapped to Cameron.

"If you're just playing with her—" he warned in a growl.

"I'm not." Cameron's voice was final. "I love her."

"And I love Cameron," I said. I went to Noah and took his hands in mine, squeezing them tight. "I'm not a little girl anymore. I know what I want. And I want Cameron."

Noah squeezed back reflexively. "You know he goes through women like tissues?"

"Hey!" Cameron protested.

I flushed, half embarrassed, half upset. "Like you and the rest of your friends are any better? I've heard the stories, too, you know."

Noah had the decency to look chagrinned. He let out a long, slow breath through his nose. He lifted his eyes to the ceiling for a brief moment, the way he always seemed to do when mustering up the patience to deal with Cameron.

"Out of all the women in the world to fuck, you just had to pick my baby sister?"

"Noah!" I smacked him in the chest. He grunted.

"Lily's an amazing woman," Cameron said. His voice was stable and solid, not a hint of doubt. "She's talented and smart and kind and thoughtful." A small smirk crossed his lips. "Not to mention sexy as hell."

Noah growled and took a step forward. I held him back.

"Could you not?" I said with a groan, speaking to both of them.

"I'm serious," Cameron continued. "In the time that Lily and I lived together I fell for her. Completely. And I want to continue living with her." Cameron looked to me proudly. "Lily's going to stay with me when school starts."

"What?" Noah said flatly.

I cringed without meaning to. "Um. Actually..." I hedged, not knowing how to say it. I took a deep breath. "I decided I'm going to move out on my own."

Cameron and Noah both stared at me.

"No," my brother said, his stance unequivocal.

"What?" Cameron said, utterly shocked.

I babbled, knowing I had to try to explain before anyone got hurt.

"I feel like I've been living under someone's thumb my whole life. Foster care, and then living with my brother, and then being in boarding school. I never got to live life on my own. I feel like a sheltered bird in a cage."

Cameron's mouth dropped open, hurt flooding his expression. He began to speak.

I cut him off.

"I love you Cameron, and I want to be with you too, but on my own terms. As a fully fledged adult. I don't want to just move in with you by default because I have no other choice."

I turned to my brother.

"I'm so grateful for everything you've done for me. I know how hard it is for you to let go and watch me spread my wings. But I need to know what it's like to be by myself, even if it's only for a little while."

I stopped talking to take a breath.

The two of them continued staring at me, silent. I could see my words working through their respective heads.

I continued, trying to make them understand.

"Cameron, I'm not saying I want to leave you. That's not the case at all. You know how much I love you. And Noah, I'm not saying I don't want my big brother by my side. But I need this. I need this for me."

Slowly, ever so slowly, Noah nodded.

"Fine. I get it," he said eventually. "You need your freedom."

I let out a relieved sigh. "Yes. I need the freedom to make my own choices. To live life on my terms."

"Where will you stay?" Noah asked.

"Jen's old apartment. She and her roommates are all living with their boyfriends now, but they still have their lease until the new year."

Noah's eyebrow twitched. "You talked to Jen about this?"

"She figured it out on her own."

My brother looked put out, but didn't complain any further. I hoped he wasn't upset with Jen for not telling, but I knew Jen could hold her own against Noah Cranky-Pants Hart.

I turned to Cameron, hoping that he would take this well. His face was pained.

"You don't want to live with me?" he asked.

It seemed that was the one part he was stuck on.

I went to him and wrapped one arm around his shoulders. With my other hand, I traced his new tattoo through his shirt. Noah averted his gaze, looking uncomfortable at our display of affection.

"I do want to live with you. But I need to be on my own for a little while." I stood on my tiptoes to meet his gaze. "I don't want to just be the little sister crashing at your place. I want to be your girl-friend, your partner. I need some space before I can feel like I'm your equal. Can you understand that?"

"You are my equal," he said, confused.

"I don't always feel that way. I rely on you so much. Too much. You're always taking care of me. I need to feel like I can take care of myself, first."

The hurt in his eyes didn't completely go away, but Cameron nodded.

"Okay," he said quietly. He buried his face in my hair and clutched me to his chest.

"I'm not going anywhere," I explained. "We're still going to be dating. We'll still see each other all the time. I just need to have a place to call my own, at least for a little while."

Cameron pulled back, keeping his arms around me. He met my gaze, serious and intent.

"I suppose that just means one thing," he said solemnly.

"What's that?"

He gave me that familiar carnal grin, those dark blue eyes glinted with wicked mischief. "We'll have to have lots of sleepovers." He cupped my ass with both hands and squeezed.

I squeaked. Noah growled. Cameron laughed.

"At least have the decency to wait until I'm out of the room before you molest my sister." Rage threatened to take over Noah's expression again.

Cameron's face lit up, eyes sparkling. "So I have your permission to molest her?"

Noah snarled. "Don't push your fucking luck."

Cameron smirked. Noah scowled.

I let out a small laugh at the two of them.

With those familiar looks, Cameron's sly smirk and Noah's grumpy scowling, I knew we were going to be okay.

EPILOGUE

"**S**top picking at the turkey." I smacked Cameron's hand away as he darted under my arm for another piece of crispy skin.

"If I don't get the good stuff now, Damon's going to snag it all," Cameron complained.

"The both of you need to leave some for everyone else." I finished checking the internal temperature and put it back in the oven for another fifteen minutes.

Cameron rubbed at his stomach. "But I'm starving. This is like a real life Hunger Games. Why can't we eat now?"

"Because everyone isn't here yet," Jen said as she came into the kitchen. She carried an armful of fine china in her hands. She held out the heavy dishes to Cameron. "Here, make yourself useful."

Cameron took them easily. "Why aren't we just using paper plates?"

"Because we're not heathens," I said.

"Some of us aren't," Noah muttered as he came up behind Jen. He wrapped his arms around her waist and tugged her to his side. He whispered something in her ear. She blushed and melted into his arms.

I averted my gaze. It wasn't as bad as walking in on them having sex, but the quiet moments were almost more intimate. I supposed if my brother had learned to deal with mine and Cameron's displays of affection, I could deal with his.

We were all gathering for Christmas dinner at Cameron's place. It was a bit odd, being here again. I'd only been back a few times since I'd moved out. I'd wanted to make a clean break. Cameron mostly spent time at my apartment — which was in actuality Jen's apartment.

The lease was ending in the new year, and I still hadn't figured out where I was going to go next. I knew I could always move back into the mansion, but for some reason that thought made me oddly uncomfortable. Maybe it was knowing that the place would never truly be mine. Maybe it was that it only reminded me of all the panic attacks I'd had here.

Either way, I only had a few more weeks to decide what to do.

"August texted to say he's on his way," Noah told us.

Cameron perked up. "And then food?"

I laughed. "Yes, when August gets here we can have food."

My boyfriend fist pumped the air, forgetting he had dishes in his arms. They wobbled and almost came crashing to the ground. Jen and Noah steadied them at the last second.

"Why don't we go put these on the table?" Jen pushed half the plates into Noah's hands and ushered him into the dining room.

Cameron barely noticed, still overly excited about the prospect of food.

"You're acting like you hadn't eaten in years," I said.

"I've had no appetite since you moved out," Cameron said mournfully. "I'm wasting away."

"You're over at my place every day," I said with a laugh.

"It's not the same."

I nodded thoughtfully. "Things do seem different."

Cameron cocked his head. "Bad different?"

I smiled at him. "No. Good different. I finally feel like I'm my own person. I don't just feel like Noah's sister or your girlfriend. I feel... like Lily Hart. Moving out of the mansion was a good decision for me."

Cameron gave me a considering look. "You don't want to move back in, do you?"

I looked down at the counter, busying myself with wiping it down. "I just... don't think it's the best place for me to be. Not yet."

"Good."

I looked up at Cameron, confused. "Good?"

He nodded. "I'm selling it."

I blinked. "Selling... the mansion?"

"Yeah."

"Why?"

"Seemed like the thing to do," he said breezily.

I put down the towel I'd been cleaning with. "Cameron..."

His expression turned serious. "It's not just about you. I've been thinking about it for a long time. This place is pretty big for only one person. And you're right." He smirked. "It's pretty embarrassing for a grown man to still be living at home."

"Who says you're a grown man?" I replied automatically.

He raised an eyebrow and stalked towards me with a carnal grin. "Angel, you really need me to show you how much of a man I am? 'Cause I'll do it, right here and now."

He backed me up against the counter, hips pressed into mine. I flushed, but allowed it. If Noah walked in, let him growl. I'd seen worse with him and Jen.

"How will you throw all those raging house parties?" I asked.

"I guess I won't."

I faked a gasp of shock. "No more famous Cameron Thorne parties? How will we survive?"

"I only had those parties 'cause..." he shrugged, uncomfortable. "It got lonely, you know? Before I met the guys, it was just me alone in this huge house. Growing up, I was only able to throw them because my parents were gone. Because they didn't care what I did. And the crazier my parties got, the more I was reminded of that."

Not for the first time, my heart ached for Cameron.

He must have noticed my sad expression, because he shook his head and grinned.

"Don't get me wrong, I love a raging party as much as the next rock star. I'd just rather not have them in this mansion anymore."

"Where will you live? Are you going to get a new place?"

His expression turned oddly nervous. He pulled out his phone and swiped a few times.

"Take a look." He turned the screen to face me.

There was a series of photos of the interior of a house. It wasn't quite a mansion, but still big. It looked new and modern, but not in that sterile, austere way. Dark hardwood floors and black marbled countertops gave it a homey feel.

"I like it," I said approvingly.

Cameron looked relieved. "You do?"

"It looks cozy, in a weird *this house is five thousand square feet* kind of way."

"It's not that big," he laughed. He turned serious. "I'm glad you like it." Cameron put his phone back in his pocket. "Because I want to ask you something."

"You want me to help you decorate?"

"No." He took my hand and placed something in my palm, a cool, light weight. I looked down.

A key.

"I'd like you to move in with me. Officially. For real."

My heart swelled. I looked from Cameron to the key and back again.

"I want this to be our house," he said earnestly. "I want you to feel like you have a home."

Tears sprung to my eyes. I threw my arms around Cameron's neck. I fought back a rush of tears.

"Of course I'll move in with you."

Cameron let out a relieved breath. "Oh thank fuck."

I snorted a laugh. "Were you worried I'd say no?"

"A bit," he admitted.

"I love you," I said simply. "Of course I want to live with you. I just needed some time to myself first, that's all."

I reached into his pocket, fishing for his phone.

"You want to take me up on my offer to show you how much of a man I am?" he teased.

"I want to see my house again."

Cameron and I put our heads together, scrolling through the pictures. As he explained the details of each room, I ruminated on that thought.

My house. My home. A place to call my own.

I snuck a peek up at Cameron. His dark blue eyes were alight with happiness.

No, it wasn't my home.

It was our home. Mine and Cameron's.

Free of fears.

Free of secrets.

Free of loneliness.

I was no longer just Noah Hart's little sister. He was no longer just the playboy bassist of Darkest Days.

We were Cameron and Lily, two lovers ready to start our life together.

Next:

Darkest Days #4: Hard Rock Deceit

Featuring drummer of Darkest Days August Summers, *Hard Rock Deceit* is the fourth novel in the Darkest Days Rock Star Romance Series.

Want a sneak peek of August's story? Continue reading with an excerpt from *Hard Rock Deceit* >>>

HARD ROCK DECEIT EXCERPT

The room was near silent, soft whispers and hushed murmurs falling from each onlooker's lips. Compliments and accolades? Or critiques and snide comments? I could have wandered closer to hear the quiet conversations as the art gallery patrons perused my work. Staying back, I concealed myself behind a pillar, wringing my clammy hands.

I hoped to make it through without drawing attention to myself. My advisor and mentor told me to schmooze and mingle and network, using buzzwords that made me grimace. According to him, people only came to art gallery showings for unknown students on opening night to meet the artist themselves. So they could say, *I met her when* and impress their friends. So they could ask about the artist's inspirations and feelings and the meaning behind the work.

I only had to make it another thirty minutes. The art showing would end, the gallery would close, and I could make my escape.

My advisor turned his head and caught my eye. I cringed, butterflies wreaking havoc in my stomach. He motioned me to come forward. I shook my head no, trying to resist the urge to run away. He lifted his eyes heavenward, as if praying for patience, before returning to his conversation.

I'd have to find a better hiding spot. I'd escaped for now, but Professor Ashford wouldn't give up.

I avoided him as he did the rounds, shaking hands, pressing kisses to cheeks and chatting with friends old and new. Ashford was well connected in the art community. I was lucky to have him as an advisor and mentor.

If only he weren't so insistent on putting my face out there. He wanted me to pontificate about my work, to hold an audience, to let each patron inside my head, spilling all my inner thoughts and feelings about my art.

No. I much, *much,* preferred being behind the camera, not in front of it.

The place emptied, the stragglers heading to the door.

"Hiding again?"

Ashford shook his head ruefully as he meandered to the far side of the gallery where I'd taken up residence.

"Not hiding," I replied. "Just not bringing attention to myself."

"That's the point of these showings."

"I thought the art was the point."

"The artist and their art cannot be separated," he said. "Someday, you're going to need to talk about your work in public. People want to hear from the artist."

"Is it over now?" I asked. "Can we go?"

Ashford jerked his chin to the side, gesturing. "There's one person still here."

I followed Ashford's gaze.

A man with ice blue eyes and longish platinum hair stood off to the side. His hair was as light as mine was dark. He had an almost aristocratic air about him as he contemplated the black and white photograph on the wall. This man was beautiful.

"He seems familiar," I murmured.

"Perhaps you saw him at another gallery showing," Ashford said lightly. "He may be interested in buying. Do me a favor and speak to at least one person tonight, Cassie?"

Sweat dampened the back of my neck.

Speak with him? Speak with a person whose face was so perfectly sculpted it belonged on a runway? What would I even say?

"Ask him if he likes it," Ashford said, as if sensing my inner turmoil. He nudged me with his elbow. "Don't you want to network?"

I wanted to be back in my darkroom. I wanted to be behind a camera. The last thing I wanted was to talk to a stranger about my art.

But this man, so beautiful it made my heart ache, was staring at my photograph, intense and fixated.

I wanted to photograph him. I wanted to capture this moment.

I approached the man on light feet, almost tiptoeing. My veins thrummed with nervous energy. I rubbed at the seam of my shirt.

"Do you like it?" I asked tentatively as I came up beside him.

He nodded once, not turning to look at me. Staring at the photograph on the wall, his eyes were unfocused, as if looking through it, not at it. He wore black skinny jeans and a white shirt. Put a stereo-typical French beret on him and he would have looked like a carica-ture of the stereotypical artiste.

I was at a loss, not knowing what else to say. I didn't want to tell him it was mine. It always felt odd asking a stranger what they felt about my art when I was right there in front of them. How could I trust I'd get an honest opinion? Even if they didn't like it, most people would lie to spare my feelings.

And then the conversation usually turned towards questions about my *inspirations,* and my *thought process,* and the *meaning* behind my work.

I never understood why everyone always cared so much about those things. The art should speak for itself.

The silence between me and the strange man turned awkward.

"Why do you like it?" I asked.

"It's rousing."

Rousing? The black and white cityscape at night certainly wasn't dull, but rousing?

"Why do you think that?" I had to know.

"Do you want me to give a full art critique?" he asked. "I'd be more than happy to."

I almost said yes. I wanted to know what this man thought of my art. Something held me back. I had a feeling if I said yes, this man would tell me far more than I cared to know. About my art.

About myself.

"Do you like it?" he asked.

"Of course." I wouldn't have submitted it to my advisor if I didn't like it.

"Why do you like it?" he parroted my words.

Why did I like it? I didn't know how to articulate it in words. I didn't like that photo any more or any less than the other dozen pieces I'd submitted. My advisor chose which to display in the exhibit. Yes, there had been something about it that made me choose it from among hundreds of others, but... the words to explain why just wouldn't come.

Turning my focus to the photograph on the wall, I tried to look at it with new eyes. The contrast between dark corners of shadowy alleys and fuzzy, bright streetlights; the soft streaks of nighttime fog interrupted by clean, jutting lines of skyscrapers. I struggled to put my thoughts into words, although why I even wanted to tell this man anything was beyond me.

"I don't think it's rousing, really."

"No?" His eyes were still slightly glazed as he looked at the photo.

I hesitated before speaking.

"There's a stirring feeling to the image, yes. The electricity of a bustling city at night. But it's not hurried or rushed. The buildings look like they're being embraced by the fog. The streetlights are chasing away the dark corners."

"Maybe I'm wrong," he conceded. "Rousing might not be the best word."

"What else would you call it?"

He pinned me down with a stare. "Passionate."

I stared back wordlessly. That was a concept no one ever applied to my art, or myself. I'd been told the opposite. My art was stark. Bleak. Often harsh and cutting.

How did this man see something so different from everyone else?

Blue eyes gazed into mine. All fuzziness was gone, replaced by something sharp and knowing. I couldn't look away.

"The photo is full of passion. Full of desire." He gestured to the rest of my photos hanging on the gallery wall. "All these photos are like that."

Those words made my head spin.

Passion.

Desire.

Those were things I'd never experienced. I'd started to think I never would.

Ice-colored eyes stared at me, a considering look.

"It makes me wonder what the artist was feeling when they took them," he continued.

What had I been feeling? Under this man's gaze, I couldn't recall.

"Maybe they didn't feel anything," I said.

Or maybe they just couldn't express what they felt out loud, a small voice inside me said.

"All artists feel something when they create," he said. "That's why we do it."

"We?" I asked. "Are you an artist?"

"Of sorts." He turned back to the photo. "I think the passion was unintentional."

Of course it was unintentional. It was all cityscapes and street photography, not boudoir scenes. No one could say my photos were passionate.

But this man did.

"I might buy this one," he said. "I'll speak to the gallery owner."

The idea of my photos hanging on some stranger's wall always made me feel uncomfortable. Exposed. Even art showings were enough to cause unease. Still, if I wanted to make a living as a photographer, it was part of the job.

But the thought of my photo hanging on this unnerving man's wall wasn't discomforting. Instead, it stirred up something within me. Something that made my heart hammer in my chest.

The man left to speak to both the gallery owner and Ashford. My advisor eyed me. He'd been observing my conversation from afar. I hoped he hadn't heard what we'd spoken of.

Soon, the blue-eyed stranger made his way back.

"I'd like to make you an offer," he said. "Work for me."

I blinked at him, taken aback.

"As an event photographer," he continued. "It will be a short term contract. Only a few months."

This was completely out of the blue. But... a job was a job.

"What would I be doing?" I asked.

"I can't divulge that until you sign a Non-Disclosure Agreement." He nodded to the exit. "Come with me and we can talk about it."

I shot Ashford a panicked look. He smiled and waved me off. I had to assume my advisor wouldn't steer me wrong. Maybe he did know this stranger after all.

Following him outside, I found a shiny black limo waiting at the front door. A chauffeur in a suit jumped out of the driver's seat. He opened the back door for me with a slight tilt of his upper body, almost a bow.

I stumbled on my words as I thanked him, wondering if I should tip. Was that the kind of treatment I could expect if I took this job? Who exactly would I be working for?

With a moment of hesitation, I slipped inside and glanced around to get my bearings. The limo had cream colored leather seats, facing both the front and the back, with tinted windows. A partition separated the driver from the interior.

The stranger from the gallery slid in, taking a seat across from me.

"Is this a Fifty Shades thing?" I blurted out. "Where the billionaire kidnaps the young ingénue and takes her to his secret BDSM dungeon?"

He looked surprised for a moment before laughing and shaking his head, long blond strands falling over his cheeks.

"No," he chuckled. "Nothing like that. This is a real job offer." He pulled out a folder from between the seats and opened it, revealing a stack of papers. "If you sign this, I'll tell you everything."

"What is it?"

"The NDA. Non-Disclosure Agreement."

He handed me the papers and a pen. I took them from him carefully and flipped through the pages. The man waited patiently as I went over every line and paragraph. It seemed standard. I wasn't allowed to talk about my job or the people I worked with or else they would sue the pants off me.

"You sure you're not a billionaire?" I asked one more time.

"Not quite."

Not *quite*. How close to being a billionaire was *not quite*?

I didn't know what I was getting into, and this NDA didn't put me at ease.

The man sitting across from me stared intently, as if willing his eyes to peer into my soul.

"Why?" I asked. "Why me?"

"I've been following you for a while."

My heart thumped hard beneath my ribcage, the words turning vague nerves into fear. Did I have a stalker?

"Your work," he clarified. "I've been following your work for a while. There's a certain aspect in your photos I don't often see."

Passion. Desire. Was that what he meant?

He sensed my hesitation. When he spoke again, a shivery sensation took hold of me, sending my fingers and toes tingling.

"There's something in your art that calls to me," he said. "I don't know how or why, but you're able to express something in your work that not many people can. It's not always obvious, and it's not always overt. But it's there. I could use someone like you." He leaned forward in his seat. "And I think you could use someone like me."

"Like you?" I asked. That was sort of arrogant, wasn't it? "Why would I need someone like you?"

He quirked a small smile. "I have experience with this. Recognizing potential. Honing it. Polishing it. If we work together, I think we can take your art and transform it into something brilliant. If you're interested."

His gaze swept me up and down, a probing stare. My heartbeat quickened. The feeling in my chest was so unfamiliar I almost mistook it for nerves. But I wasn't nervous.

Nervous, I could understand. I could handle that. But my racing pulse, the way all air seemed to leave my lungs...

I'd known this man was beautiful, yes, but it had been an objective statement. An observation.

Now I was looking at him through new eyes, like I had with the photograph.

He thought my work was passionate. He thought I had the potential for brilliance.

How did he see something no one else did?

My heart squeezed tight, a fluttery feeling welling in my stomach. He flicked his eyes back to the folder of papers. I placed a hand on my belly, telling it to calm down. This was just anxiety. I was anxious about this job offer. That was all.

Fighting to gather my wits, I took deep breaths, calming myself. I pushed my ruffled hair back from my face, the ends just brushing my shoulders. I told myself this was the usual jitters I felt when discussing my art with potential buyers, or when receiving an art critique.

But that was a lie.

The trembling of my fingers, my racing pulse, the lightheadedness — none of it was simple nerves.

This feeling was foreign. It was terrifying. It was thrilling. I felt vaguely sick from the emotional whiplash.

Signing this thing meant I would work with him. I would work with the man who sent my heart pounding, who sent my stomach tumbling over on itself.

I would work with the man who looked at my photographs and saw something no one else had before.

I didn't like feeling so out of sorts, especially around a stranger. Especially around a stranger as intense as him. My world felt off balance.

But something inside me said I wouldn't regret this.

"Yes," I said. "I'm interested. I'd like your help."

Before I could question my actions, I scrawled my signature on the bottom of the page and handed it over.

"You'll be traveling across the country to work as an event photographer for a few months," he said without preamble.

"What event?"

He tapped his finger against the folder in a staccato rhythm. The look on his face was one of anticipation, eyes glinting. "Have you ever heard of Darkest Days?"

Everything clicked.

Platinum blond hair. Ice-blue eyes. Tall and straight-backed, with an almost regal expression.

Without all the leather, black mesh, torn ripped jeans and eyeliner, it wasn't immediately obvious. But I could see it now.

My heart went into overdrive.

This man was August Summers. Drummer, composer, producer, and reputed musical genius. The founding member of hit rock group Darkest Days.

This was a man who filled stadiums full of screaming fans, who turned every album he touched into gold.

I took a shallow breath, trying to suppress the rapid rise and fall of my chest. I couldn't make myself speak, afraid my voice would give away my mental state.

August examined me closely, his eyes narrowed, searching. I don't know what he saw, but he seemed satisfied.

"Darkest Days has a new album out," he continued. "We're going on tour to promote it. Your job will be to follow the band around for a few months taking photos."

My black rimmed glasses slid down my nose.

Going on tour. With a rock band. That wasn't something normal people did. Only people with connections, or people already established in the entertainment industry, got those jobs. It was unfathomable someone like me would get an offer like this.

"If you agree, you'll need to pack a suitcase tonight," he said. "We're leaving tomorrow."

Pack a suitcase. Leaving tomorrow. Not to mention, I'd just signed an NDA.

August watched me silently. I pushed my hair back, tucking it behind my ears. My mom always told me to get my hair out of my face.

This man saw passion in my art. He wanted to teach me.

"Okay. Yes." The words hung heavy in the air. "I'll do it."

The world went fuzzy for a moment.

What had I just done?

He nodded once, pleased. "A car will pick you up at your place tomorrow morning."

He opened the limo door, gesturing for me to step out first, then followed. I tried not to trip over myself. Ashford watched us through the gallery windows.

August stuck his hand out, offering me a handshake. "I'm sure it will be a pleasure to work with you, Cassie. You're a very talented woman."

I gingerly placed my hand in his.

Sparks shot through my body the moment our skin touched. His hand was warm and large, enveloping mine like a sensual embrace.

I stared at our joined hands for a moment too long. I tried to pull back with a start, not wanting to embarrass myself. He held on for a brief second, not letting go. My heart jumped as I met his eyes.

Maybe I should have felt excited at that touch. Maybe any other girl would have. And I did feel excited, a bit. But another part of me felt overwhelmed. Disorientated. I was out of my depths with this.

He let go. I pulled back my still tingling hand and hid it behind my back.

"You should think about it," August said as he slipped back into the limo.

I fought to make my voice work. "Think about what?"

August gave me one last look, his blue eyes sharp. "What you were feeling when you took that photograph."

ABOUT THE AUTHOR

Athena Wright is a USA Today Bestselling author of New Adult Romance. She has a fondness for rock stars and the girls who tame their wild hearts. Athena loves to write characters who are not always what they seem.

Find Athena online:

www.athenawright.com

athena@athenawright.com

81677896R00176

Made in the USA
Lexington, KY
19 February 2018